THE WATCHMAN

V. B. Tenery

THE WATCHMAN

COPYRIGHT 2014 by VIRGINIA TENERY

Contact Information: titleadmin@pelicanbookgroup.com

Scripture quotations, unless otherwise indicated are taken from the King James translation, public domain.

Cover Art by *Nicola Martinez*

Harbourlight Books, a division of Pelican Ventures, LLC
www.pelicanbookgroup.com PO Box 1738 *Aztec, NM * 87410

Harbourlight Books sail and mast logo is a trademark of Pelican Ventures, LLC

Publishing History
First Harbourlight Edition, 2014
Electronic Edition ISBN 978-1-61116-354-4
Paperback Edition ISBN 978-1-61116-373-5
Published in the United States of America

Dedication

To my daughter Holly. The love of my life.
And to my critique partners in Scribes 201 and
Scribes 222 in appreciation for your encouragement
and for keeping me straight.

1

"I have set watchmen on thy walls, O Jerusalem, which shall never hold their peace, day nor night. . ."
Isaiah 62

Hebron, Wyoming

What if you knew you could learn the deepest, darkest secrets of anyone you touched, but it would cost you emotionally? What if from your earliest childhood you could disappear in thirty-minute intervals and while invisible, you could move through solid objects with impunity? What if these anomalies came as natural as breathing—clothing and anything in pockets or hand disappeared—an unknown field that surrounded you erasing everything inside?

What would you do with such powers?

I'd settled that question long ago, but this afternoon, as I focused on the scene outside my car window, it occurred to me perhaps I needed to rethink my mission. I'd covered domestic abuse cases during my five years with the Hebron Police Department, and I'd put away a lot of bad people. Different scenario here. I was no longer a cop.

Ahead, a small boy stepped from a school bus into the upscale Crown Heights neighborhood. Dead leaves and powered snow swirled around his high-end sneakers as he shuffled along the sidewalk.

My foot hovered over the gas pedal. The image

disturbed me, and I almost drove away. His small shoulders slumped forward, and I was hooked. I had to know.

He stopped and turned around as if he might go back to the bus stop. He reversed and faced me again.

Confused? Lost?

Cute kid, maybe six years old. The designer logo on his backpack bounced with each step. Blond locks pressed against his brow under a blue baseball cap, reminding me of another little boy—minus the designer gear.

Decision made, I swung the SUV to the curb, snatched the cell phone from its holder, and texted my friend.

Got 2 bow out of dinner talk 2 u later.

I left the car and stepped to the sidewalk. With a glance both ways, I moved into the boy's path. Slow and easy. Not too close, not too fast. I didn't want to frighten him.

With my friendliest smile, I took a step closer. "Hey, son, can you tell me where to find Oak Street?"

He gazed up at me and shook his head. Eyes dull, as if he'd lived life and found it wanting.

I patted his shoulder. "Thanks, anyway."

He winced and jerked away as if I'd slapped him. I'd suspected abuse, but his pain caught me by surprise. In an instant his life opened up, film clips at the speed of light. Visuals of physical pain, overwhelming fear, helplessness, and a silent scream for help…*please, help me.* Emotions too heavy for a child to carry streamed through my consciousness. With proof of abuse came certainty. The violence at home was escalating.

Something frightening rose within me—rage

against the defenselessness of children and those who caused them pain. Abuse cases drew and repelled me at the same time, reviving memories I'd long ago buried.

I inhaled a resolute breath. When had I ever walked away from a troubled child? I couldn't save the world—just the small corner God gave me. A common man, given uncommon gifts—a watchman on the wall.

I scanned the area for traffic and pedestrians. When I turned back, the boy had quickened his pace through the gated entrance to his home.

Invisible, I wheeled and followed him.

Inside the house, a woman's voice called from the kitchen. "Cody, is that you?"

"Yes, Mom." The boy took the stairs two at a time to his room with me close behind.

"Get ready for dinner. Hurry, your father will be home any minute."

At the top of the second-floor landing, a spacious lounge area came into view.

Kid-friendly furniture, bookshelves, stereo components, and a wide-screen plasma television filled an area with scattered group seating. Four doors opened onto the landing. The boy's bedroom was the first one on the left at the top of the stairs.

Cody tossed his jacket and backpack on the bedpost, and darted into the bathroom. Hands shaking, he turned on the tap, splashed water on his face, and grabbed a towel from the rack. After a swipe at his cheeks, he bounded to the stairs. Halfway down, he stopped and then hurried back to the bathroom. He wiped down the sink with the damp towel and dropped it into the clothes hamper. With a quick glance, he scanned the room before heading back downstairs.

At the ground floor, the stairway emptied into the living room. The accoutrements of wealth spread out before me. More showroom than a home—decorative and spotless. The room held no smiling family photos, books, or personal touches, no warmth. Even the Christmas tree with its silver and glass ornaments seemed cold and sterile. Not my taste, but what did a former Marine know about interior design?

On the right, a formal dining room opened into a kitchen exuding homey smells of spices and yeast.

Cody took a seat in the bay window, drew up his legs, and wrapped thin arms around his knees. His gaze followed his mother as she put finishing touches on the evening meal.

The woman examined each piece of china with care and then replaced the dish on the placemat. She picked up the silverware and polished each piece with a towel. Her frantic actions told a story. A lump formed in my throat. I knew the drill by heart. Perfection was an elusive goal she could never attain.

From the back entrance, a car hummed into the garage.

With quick, deft movements, she placed Beef Wellington, browned to perfection, on the table. She must have spent half the day preparing this meal.

A door slammed. "Rachel," a male voice called.

"We're in the kitchen, Harry." Her mouth formed a thin, strained smile.

Harry's linebacker form filled the doorway. Tough guy. He could beat up a woman and child.

He took the chair at the head of the table. Cody and his mother joined him, taking seats across from each other.

Rachel rose and filled Harry's wine glass as he cut the beef into precise, small bites, seemingly oblivious to the tremor in her hand.

The chimes of the analog wall clock sent a reminder my time limit had run out. I could leave or let the family find an intruder observing their evening meal.

I left with reservations.

Cody should be OK for a short time. His father would look for a reason to justify his cruelty, a reason to convince Cody the abuse was his own fault. Tactics used by abusive parents everywhere.

Back in my car, I drove to the front gate and forced my attention to the job. Cody needed a champion, and like it or not, I'd been tagged his designated knight.

Half an hour later, again invisible, I re-entered the kitchen. The meal had ended, and Harry sipped coffee from an engraved demitasse cup.

I braced for the explosion, and it didn't take long.

Cody removed the napkin from his lap, folded it, and laid it on the placemat. When he released the napkin, his hand hit the milk glass. The crystal tumbler spilled onto the tablecloth, bounced to the floor, and shattered, sending glass shards across the tile.

Harry's glare flashed at Cody. "You clumsy little fool. Look what you've done."

Rachel jumped to her feet, darted to the kitchen, and grabbed a handful of paper towels. "Don't yell at him. It was an accident. You make him nervous."

A vein popped out on Harry's left temple. "Proper table manners are important to his future, regardless of his *feelings*. Obviously, a lesson he'll never learn from his mother." Harry turned to Cody. "Go to your room. I'll be there in a minute."

Cody pushed back from the table and stumbled upstairs. I followed his dejected form back to his room.

Rachel's pleas echoed up the stairwell. "Leave him alone, Harry. He's just a little boy. Accidents happen."

A sharp slap sounded, followed by dead silence.

Doors slammed downstairs as though Harry searched for something. Heavy, deliberate steps ascended upward. Cody's eyes widened as his father drew nearer.

The knob turned, and Harry stood in the doorway, a leather belt clasped in his hand. He strode to Cody's window and closed the blinds.

Rachel slid into the room. She skirted around Harry and stood between Cody and his father.

Cody screamed. "No, Mom. He'll hurt you." He tried to get around her, but she held him back.

"Get out of the way, Rachel." Harry bit out each word.

Rachel's chin went up, and her shoulders squared. "I'm not moving an inch. Not now—not ever."

My hands shook so badly I had to squeeze them into fists to keep from decking Harry. Breaking his jaw would ease the chaos in my gut and let him feel the pain he'd dealt Rachel and Cody. Inwardly, I railed against my limitations, but common sense prevailed. I couldn't just materialize in Cody's room without serious repercussions.

I had to leave again, but this wasn't the end. I was coming back for Cody and Rachel.

Outside the gate, once more flesh and blood, I punched 9-1-1 on my cell. "I want to report a disturbance at 1220 Cedar Hills Drive. I hear a child screaming." I gave my name and waited.

The authorities wouldn't take long, but that didn't

stop me from pacing. Crown Heights' four-man police department received few emergency calls. Vanity cops more than a law enforcement unit, but this wasn't the time to be picky.

In less than five minutes a patrol car passed. Brake lights came on, and the vehicle backed up and eased to the curb in front of the estate. Two officers emerged and marched to where I stood. They could have been brothers, both thin and athletic with neat dark hair and brown eyes.

"Officer Ryan," he said and thrust his thumb toward his colleague. "That's Officer Duncan. Did you report the disturbance?"

"That would be me. I'm Noah Adams."

"Did you witness an altercation of any kind?"

"No, only the child's screams. Sounded frantic. Perhaps someone should check it out."

Duncan strode to the gate and spoke into the intercom. "Police. Open the gate, please."

Ryan pulled a notebook from his jacket. He cocked an eyebrow. "Got some ID? You look familiar. You a cop?"

"Used to be. Five years on the HPD. Private investigator, now."

"You packing?"

"Goes with the job." I handed him my license and concealed weapon permit.

He examined them carefully and handed them back. "You don't live in the neighborhood?"

"No, just passing through."

"How did you come to be outside the home? You couldn't hear anyone scream driving by."

I looked the cop straight in the eye and lied. It didn't sit well, but I justified it—a kid's safety was on the line. "I pulled over to make a call on my cell phone. I don't like to drive through residential areas while I'm on the phone." That much was true.

Ryan pointed at me. "Wait here." He joined Duncan in the squad car. Someone buzzed them through the gate, and the cruiser inched up the drive.

Cody's mother waited in the doorway under the portico as the two cops walked up the steps. Voices drifted from the entrance, too low for me to understand.

Before long, an irate Harry stood at the door. He pointed in my direction and shouted something unintelligible, and probably unflattering.

Duncan motioned me inside.

Ryan took a step toward me as I reached the group. "You said you heard screams?"

"That's right." If the police didn't believe me, I could always confess an honest mistake. At least Harry would know someone knew his secret.

"You're a liar." The vein in Harry's temple popped out again. "No one here screamed." He glared at Ryan. "He's got the wrong house."

"I'm certain the sounds came from here. Where's your son?" In an instant, I realized my error. The screams could have been those of a daughter. I glanced at the group around me. No weird looks. I eased out the breath I'd been holding.

Harry's gaze turned hard. "What do you want with my son?"

Duncan turned and locked in on Harry. "Get your son, sir."

Harry disappeared and after a short wait, he appeared with Cody in tow.

"What's your name?" Ryan asked the boy in a soft

tone.

"C-Cody." He moved close to his mother.

"I'm Officer Ryan, and I'm here to make sure you're safe. You OK?"

Cody nodded.

"Has anyone hurt you?"

The boy shook his head, but his hands trembled, and he chewed at his lower lip.

I moved into his line of vision. "Cody, turn around and lift your shirt."

Cody blanched and backed closer to Rachel. Apparently he didn't recognize me from our earlier encounter. If so, he gave no indication.

Ryan turned a hard glare at me. "You're out of line, Adams. We'll handle this." He turned to the boy. "It's OK, Cody. No one will harm you. Lift your shirt."

Harry's confidence appeared to slip. A red flush started at his neck and spread over his face. He seemed to weigh the danger of refusal. "Do you know who I am? I'm Judge Harold London! You can't come into my home and undress my son. I'm calling my attorney." Harry swung around to face his wife. "Bring me the phone."

Rachel hesitated.

"Bring me the phone!"

The two cops looked at each other and then back at me. "You sure about this?" Ryan asked.

I couldn't back down now. "Sure as death and judgment."

Cody huddled against his mother. Right cheek red, her left arm held at an awkward angle, Rachel reached down, turned Cody around, and raised his shirt. Long black bruises stretched from the top of his shoulder to his waist. Two swollen red welts stood out among the older stripes on his back.

Echoes from my past reared their ugly head, but I pushed them away. This wasn't the time.

Suppressed anger mottled Harry's face. Hard dark eyes stared back at me. In that moment, I knew he wouldn't admit abusing Cody. Survival would supersede any sense of wrongdoing.

Duncan gave his partner a knowing nod and drew Rachel aside.

Ryan returned to the patrol car and came back with a camera and handed it to Duncan. He motioned Rachel and Cody to follow him indoors, presumably to photograph Cody's bruises.

Ten minutes later, Crown Height's finest led a cursing, handcuffed, Judge Harold London away, shoved him none too gently into the cruiser's backseat, and slammed the door.

Large snowflakes fell as the squad car moved down the driveway and onto the street. Arms clasped around her body against the cold, Rachel stood there, Cody at her side, and watched the cruiser until it disappeared from sight.

She looked down at her son. "Do you want something for pain?"

He shook his head. "No, Mom. I'm good. It doesn't hurt." He turned and disappeared through the entryway.

For the first time, I noticed Rachel London was a lovely woman. Tall, slim, with classic high cheekbones and large green eyes. Pale, bruised, and frightened, but strikingly beautiful.

I caught her gaze. "If you'd like, I'll take you and Cody to the hospital or to a shelter—somewhere your husband can't get to you."

She gave a short, sardonic laugh that wrinkled her mouth. "That would be useless. Harry knows the location of the Hebron shelter. We don't need a doctor; we need to get far away from here as fast as possible."

"Do you have any family?"

She stared at some point in the distance then turned to me. "No. I grew up in an orphanage in Cheyenne."

Typical abuse victim. A woman alone with no family. "I'm sorry."

Silence filled the space between us for a moment. She gave a dismissive shrug. "It was a long time ago. I'm over it." Her voice dropped to a husky tone and she looked up at me. "How did you know? Cody didn't scream."

"Are you sure? Perhaps you were too frightened to hear."

"Maybe." Uncertainty clouded her features. "Mr...I don't even know your name."

"It's Adams, Noah Adams. I'm a private investigator." I searched my jacket and handed her my card.

She studied it with blank eyes and slipped it into her pocket. A shiver ran through her body, her eyes wide. "We have to leave. Right away. Harry will never see the inside of a cell. My husband is a powerful man, Mr. Adams. A charter member of the good-old-boys network downtown. He'll be home within the hour, and he'll be raving mad. I don't even want to think what might happen." She shivered again. "We've left before. Wherever we go, he always finds us." Angry tears pooled in her eyes. "Harry said he would take Cody away from me if I tried to leave again. I'd go mad knowing Cody had to face his father alone." Her jaw clenched. "Harry London will be a dead man before I let him take Cody away from me." Desperation resonated in her stiff posture and jerky motions.

"Murder isn't the answer. Cody needs you with him, not in prison. There's a place I can take you, a place where your husband can't find you. You'll need to pack extra-warm clothing for the trip. It's colder in the valley."

Her eyes brightened. "Where?"

"A friend's ranch near Green River. I'll call and make sure it's all right." I reached for my cell-phone. "I won't let him hurt either of you again. I promise."

She stood motionless, not making eye contact.

The toll of clock chimes from the entryway spurred her into action. "Cody, we're leaving. Gather up any toys you want to bring. Hurry. Your father will be home soon."

He appeared at her side. "Where are we going?"

She gave him a gentle nudge toward the open doorway. "We'll talk about it later. Right now, we must hurry." Her gaze tracked him down the hallway, and then she followed him inside.

While they packed, I called my friend Emma Hand.

Rachel returned with two suitcases. She blinked rapidly, trying to convey her sense of despair. "I appreciate what you're doing. I...I have to trust someone. There's no place else for us to go. But if you let me down and Harry finds us—" She dropped her gaze and drew a long, shuddering breath. After a pause, she raised her head, and looked into my eyes. "It could cost us our lives."

2

Somewhere on Highway 80

City lights disappeared in the rearview mirror as we trekked west toward Green River. An exhausted Cody fell asleep in the backseat soon after we left Hebron. The glow of the dash lights reflected Rachel huddled close to the door, eyes glued to the blackness, white-knuckled hands clasped in her lap.

My mind focused on the small family. They had lived with pain for a long time. Thank God, Emma agreed to take them in.

Emma Hand's place sat two hundred miles from Hebron, off Highway 80, the interstate that ran across the lower half of Wyoming. A desolate, sometimes dangerous, drive this time of year. Relentless winds sheered across the highway, and violent snow gusts often shut down the road for hours.

God's hand guided us through the storm. Red taillights from the tanker in front of us cut a path through the darkness, a shield from the heavy storm.

The long day wore on me, and I began to depressurize from the adrenaline rush of the past hours. I glanced at my silent companion. "If you're in pain, there's aspirin in the glove box."

She tucked a strand of blonde hair behind her left ear. "I'm fine."

Wind danced flakes on the pavement before us like confetti at a Christmas parade. Through the flurries, I spotted a fast food restaurant sign at the next exit. "I need a caffeine fix. How about you?"

"I'll take a soda. I'm not much on coffee."

The drive-thru lane stood empty. I placed the order at the intercom, moved forward, and paid the pimple-faced kid at the first window. He handed me my change, and I inched to the second opening.

Rachel's troubled gaze searched my face. When she spoke, the timbre of her voice hardened. "The first time I left Harry, we went to the shelter. I thought we'd be safe there. Of course, as a judge, he knew where to find me. Harry produced a letter from my doctor saying I'd had a nervous breakdown, and he took us back home. I paid dearly for that little indiscretion."

"Why would your doctor lie? He could lose his medical license."

"Dr. Saunders is a personal friend of Harry's. I'm sure my husband applied a great deal of pressure. Anyway, after that I decided to try something new. The last time, Cody and I packed my car after Harry left for work. We headed for California. I'd stashed money for six months so I wouldn't leave a trail he could follow. Somehow, he knew we had left. Before we reached the state line, the police stopped me and brought us back. That's when I knew I'd have to kill Harry to get away."

While we waited for our drinks, I scanned her face in the dim lighting. Where did she find the courage to keep going with such odds against her? She'd kept herself and her son alive through sheer strength and bravery.

"I can only imagine how hopeless you must have felt."

She gave a short laugh. "Whoever you are, it's

difficult to imagine we could be worse off than we've been with Harry."

Her chest rose as she inhaled a deep breath. "You're my last hope. I don't know if you're a guardian angel or a serial killer—a stranger who showed up at my door. Yet here I am taking my son on a trip to God-only-knows where."

"I mean you no harm, Rachel. Though a serial killer would probably say that as well." I managed a half grin. "But killers rarely call the police, give them their license number, and home address before kidnapping victims. You and Cody were in trouble. I wanted to help. It's as uncomplicated as that. Emma Hand is a fine woman. You'll be safe there, and you can leave whenever you want."

She frowned and gave her head a slow shake. "I have an appalling record of making the wrong choices where men are concerned." She lifted her chin. "But this time, I'm leaving Harry for good, and I don't intend to become someone else's victim."

"Point taken. You're right to be wary of strangers."

Wind-driven snow speckled the windshield under the drive-through portico. "Do you have access to a bank account or other funds?"

Her eyes widened.

"You won't need money at the ranch, but you will need an attorney, and Cody should see a doctor. You'll have to prove ongoing abuse."

Her posture eased. "We have medical insurance, but Harry can trace us if we use it. I also have credit cards, but he'll cancel them before morning. He always cancels the cards when I leave."

"Half of everything he has belongs to you and Cody. But you'll have to file for a divorce to get it."

Her jaw set in an oddly vulnerable way. "Like I would ever do that. Stand alone against Harry in Hebron. He would have Dr. Saunders as a witness. It would be my word against two highly respected professionals. Taking him to court would be the mother of lost causes."

"I'd be there for you, and I know a good attorney. The sooner you take legal action against your husband, the sooner you'll be free of him."

The young woman at the window passed two cups out. I handed one to Rachel, took a sip from mine, and placed it in the console holder. "Do you guys have passports?"

"Why?" she asked.

"Just in case I need to move you into Canada."

She unsheathed the straw and punched it into her drink. "They're in a safe at home along with a large amount of cash. Harry brags there is more than a $100,000 dollars inside." She shook her head. "But I can't get my part of the money, or the passports. I don't have the combination."

Not surprising Harry denied her access. Money meant freedom, and abusers liked to keep their victims dependent.

"Does he open the safe often?"

She considered the question for a moment before she answered. "He opens it every Monday before he goes to work to pulls cash for the week. And probably other times I'm not aware of."

"Where's the safe?"

"In the library, behind an ugly modern painting." She lifted an eyebrow. "Don't tell me you crack safes in your spare time."

I shook my head and chuckled. "I can barely crack

an egg."

"Too bad. I was getting ready to hand you my house key."

"No promises, but there's a good chance I can help you get access to the passports and money when you need them."

She twisted the straw but didn't drink from it. "As hard as I've tried, I haven't been able to start a life for Cody away from his father. I'm a miserable failure as a mother. Cody has lived a nightmare every day of his life—thanks to me."

"How did you reach that conclusion?"

"I married his father, didn't I?"

"You can't change the past, Rachel. You can change what comes next. The blame for Cody's abuse lies squarely on Harry London's shoulders. Not yours. Just keep repeating your promise to never again be a victim."

༄༅

Hand Me Down Ranch

We reached the ranch just before midnight. The sheep farm lay in a valley surrounded by mountains and a few scattered pines. Next to a nearby barn stood a water tower and large corral, the landscape covered in snow. A low, rambling structure glowed in the distance like a beacon guiding us to a safe haven.

Emma must have heard the car pull in. The front door opened, and a welcoming smile wreathed her face. She swung the door wide for us to enter.

Cold wind nipped at my face and stung my eyes. With Cody in my arms, I hurried inside, making hasty introductions as we crossed the threshold.

Emma pointed down the hallway. "Take the boy to the third bedroom on the left."

Rachel followed me to the designated room and tucked Cody into bed. She pulled the covers up around his neck and smoothed damp, blond curls from his brow. I left her there, dashed back to the car, and brought their luggage inside to the entryway.

Emma gave me a hug when I entered the den. "I've made a bed for you. It's too late to drive back to the city tonight."

I nodded and hustled close to the fire, absorbing the warmth, letting it thaw the chill that numbed my feet and hands.

She turned to Rachel as she entered. "Your room is next to Cody. I lit the pellet stoves earlier. You should be cozy if you leave the doors open a little."

"We'll be fine." Rachel crossed the room to stand beside me in front of the crackling blaze, her hands outstretched to the heat.

"Can I get you folks some coffee or tea?" Emma asked. "It'll only take a minute to make."

Rachel looked utterly undone. The day's events showed, her mouth drawn tight, her posture strained. "Thanks, but none for me. If you don't mind, I'll go to bed." She started toward the hallway, and then turned back to Emma. "I'm not good at expressing my feelings, but I appreciate...what you're doing...for Cody and me. I hope I can repay you, somehow."

Emma crossed the room and gave Rachel a long hug. "You don't have to repay me, girl. I'm glad to help. There are blankets in the cedar chest at the foot of the bed if you get cold. Let me know if you need anything."

"Good night," Rachel said and headed down the

hallway.

I soaked up the heat for a few minutes and then picked up the bags and followed her. She'd moved Cody to her bed. Trust didn't come easy for her.

We met just inside the room. Her eyes misted as she touched my arm. "You're a good man, Noah. One of the very few I've met."

I console weepy women about as well as I tap dance. I squeezed her hand and withdrew it quickly. She flashed a weak smile and closed the door.

Her brief touch revealed more than I wanted to know about the tragedy of her life—the premature death of her parents, her troubled years with Harry, the ache of disillusionment, and the defensive wall she'd built to ward off pain. The enormity of it staggered me. I leaned against the wall for support and closed my eyes. Adrenalin bubbled in my chest and the horrors of abuse made me gasp for air like a loose vacuum cleaner hose.

After a moment, I inhaled a deep, calming breath, and rejoined Emma. "I'll take you up on that coffee unless you're too tired."

"You know me. I'm a night owl. I'd like some myself." She led the way into the kitchen.

The room was large and rustic with a sit-down island in the center. A working kitchen, with brick floors and knotted pine-cabinetry. The large window at the breakfast nook looked out over the distant hills and trees in the daytime. Dark now, reflecting moonlight on the pristine snow.

An attractive widow in her mid-fifties, Emma looked exactly like what she was, a sheep rancher with a big heart and kind face. Slim, with salt-and-pepper gray hair, she moved with easy grace while she fussed over the coffeepot.

I took a seat at the island and filled her in on the circumstances surrounding her guests. "I won't lie to you. This could be dangerous. Rachel's husband is a nasty piece of work. He won't stop until he gets his family back under his control. Feel free to back out of this deal anytime."

Minutes later, the coffeepot's red light came on, filling the kitchen with its fresh-brewed aroma. Emma poured two large mugs and placed one in front of me.

My stomach growled a reminder that I'd missed dinner. I nodded toward an apple pie on the counter. "If you'll cut me a piece of pie, you'll save a man in the throes of starvation."

A deep chuckle rumbled in her throat. "Deal. If you really think this London fella is dangerous, I'd best ask Bill to move into the guest house for a while."

Emma's son was ex-Army Ranger and pastor of a local church. He was also a friend. A good man to have on our side. And Rachel needed all the help she could get.

Emma cut a large wedge of pie, set it in front of me, and then topped-off my coffee. "I can make you a sandwich if you like."

I shook my head. "This will do just fine." I took a bite, and the buttery crust melted in my mouth, the apples sweet and tart. "Delicious. Thanks."

"You're welcome. Sure you don't want that sandwich?"

"I'm sure," I swallowed a mouthful. "Rachel's husband may try to have me followed, so I won't come back to the ranch unless it's necessary. He'll also have my home and office calls traced, so I'll pick up a throwaway and give you the number when I get back to town. Don't try to call me until I give you the new number." I wolfed down the last bite. "He'll also pull my phone records, and your number will be there. I'm hoping he won't realize its significance."

With a peck on her cheek, I said good night and went to my room.

Well after midnight, I stretched out on the feather mattress. The excitement of the past six hours faded as my body melded into the bed's softness. Folding my arms behind my head, I waited for sleep to conquer my overactive mind.

Rachel faced serious danger from her demented husband. The Hand Me Down would be difficult to find unless Harry somehow discovered my relationship with Emma. I had to face reality. With his unlimited funds and infinite resources, eventually Harry would find them if they remained in one place.

I couldn't afford complacency. With that unpleasant certainty, I fell asleep.

❧❦

Next morning, Bill Hand sat in the kitchen with a steaming cup to his lips. He placed the mug on the counter, stuck out his hand, and squeezed mine with an iron grip. Bill stood a little over six feet tall. All muscle. His steel-blue eyes twinkled. "You been out lookin' for trouble again, Noah?"

"Don't have to look. I'm a bona fide trouble magnet." I took a seat at the bar. "Sorry I've put Emma in such a precarious position. This situation with Rachel and Cody happened so fast, I couldn't think of any other place to take them."

I selected a cup from the countertop and poured

coffee from an insulated carafe. "A shelter was out of the question. Her husband's a judge and knew the location. I'll find a permanent place as soon as I can."

Emma bustled around the refrigerator and pulled out bacon and eggs. "Don't worry about that for now. That's why I asked Bill to stay for a while. This place is certainly big enough. Besides, it gets lonely out here. I'm glad to have the company."

A chorus of *good mornings* greeted Rachel and Cody when they eased into the kitchen. Cody clutched his mother's hand in a death-grip.

"Rachel, this is Bill Hand, Emma's son." I turned to Emma and Bill. "And the big guy holding Rachel's hand is Cody."

Rachel nodded a shy smile at Bill, placed Cody on a stool, and sat beside him.

Warm rays of sunlight filtered through the windows and bathed Rachel's face in a soft glow. The dark shadows under her emerald eyes had vanished overnight. The angry bruise on her cheek remained. She tugged at the sleeve of her sweater in an obvious attempt to cover the black marks on her wrist.

"Hi, Cody, I didn't get a chance to meet you last night." Emma ruffled Cody's hair. "You folks ready for breakfast?"

The boy gave Emma a wisp of a smile and shied away.

"Let me help. I make great pancakes," Rachel said. She moved to the counter beside Emma.

"You got yourself a job. I'll fix the eggs and bacon while you rustle up the pancakes." Emma pulled mix from the pantry and handed it to her houseguest.

Bill turned to Rachel. "Don't suppose you've had time to think about school for Cody?"

Rachel stopped stirring the batter and shook her head. "Not really. My only concern last night was getting away from Hebron. Christmas break starts next week. I'll have to make a decision soon. Enrolling him in public school would run up a flag his father would see."

"Just FYI, a number of women in my church homeschool their children," Bill said. "They use the church for things like science and social events. That lets the kids interact with each other. It works well for them."

Cody glanced at his mother. "Mom, could I do that?"

"We'll talk about it later. It's certainly an option." Rachel leveled her gaze at me. "I'm not sure how long we'll be here."

Emma flipped the sizzling bacon and glanced at Bill. "Why don't you and Noah take Cody to see the horses while we finish making breakfast?"

The boy's face brightened like someone lit a candle behind it. "Really?"

Bill smiled down at Cody. "Really. Come on. I'll give you a short tour before we feed you."

We struggled into our jackets and braced for the cold. Cody ran ahead to the corral.

Bill's smile disappeared, and he lowered his voice. "I didn't want to say anything in front of Mom, but if there's any hint that Rachel's husband will show up here, you'll have to move her and the boy. I can't let Mom's big heart put her in danger."

I couldn't fault him for his concern. "I hear you. At the first sign of trouble I'll find another safe house."

Snow crunched underfoot as we caught up with Cody at the paddock next to the stable. Our breaths hung in frosty clouds in the morning air.

Two colts played tag in the field, oblivious to the frigid conditions.

Cody's eyes danced with excitement. "What do they eat? Don't they get cold? Could I ride one? Please?"

"Whoa." Bill laughed and hefted the boy onto the corral fence "One question at a time, champ. They eat grass, oats, and hay. The weather doesn't bother them too much. God gives them a thick coat in the winter. We'll talk about riding later."

Bill whistled and the big roan came over to him. Bill reached in his pocket and pulled out a carrot. "Here, give this to him, and watch your fingers."

The morning chill added a red flush to Cody's cheeks, erasing the former pallor. The ranch could be good for him, a place to enjoy the animals while his mental and physical wounds mended.

Emma stepped out of the kitchen door. "Come on in, fellas. Breakfast is ready." The door banged shut with a loud crack when she re-entered the house.

Cody jumped, and in the next instant, his arms were around my waist, his face pressed against my side.

I looked away, numb as gall churned in my gut. The judge had done a number on this child. "It's OK, Cody." I placed my hand on his head. "The noise startled me, too."

Wind blew snow dust in behind us as we entered the kitchen. The smell of bacon and maple syrup left me feeling better, but not much.

Cody picked up Rachel's iPhone on the counter. He punched a few buttons, thumbs clicking away as he played a video game.

Food was on the table, and we sat down. After Bill said grace, Rachel smiled at her son. "Cody will love it here. He always wanted a pet, but Harry—" She paused. "Cody played with his friend Ethan's dog. Bullet stayed in our yard more than he stayed at home."

I looked at the phone next to the boy and the hair on my arms prickled. "Cody, did you call anyone this morning?"

He nodded and swallowed a bite of pancake. "I called Ethan to tell him I wouldn't be able to play today. He wanted to come over after school."

Stupid. I should have asked about cell phones last night.

Rachel's gaze held Cody's. "You used my phone? Did you tell him where you were?"

Cody shook his head. "I used your phone, but I don't know where we are."

Bill's gaze met mine.

Cody didn't have to know. If Harry traced Rachel's mobile calls, he could track them to the nearest cell tower, and right to Emma's front door.

3

Somewhere on Highway 80

Later that morning I hurried back to Hebron. Strong winds from Canada carried ominous gray clouds that portended heavy snowfall before the day ended.

I'd confiscated Rachel's cell phone before leaving the valley, in case it had the family map feature that told the location of family members at all times. My brain scrambled for a solution to overcome Cody's cell call. I needed to find a new safe house as soon as possible.

Halfway to Hebron, I pulled into a truck stop hoping a jolt of caffeine would spur some creative thinking. I stomped snow off my shoes, entered the café, and took a seat at the counter. The aroma of fried food and bacon made my decision. I ordered chicken fried steak with all the trimmings. The waitress filled a cup with coffee and gave my order to the cook at the back of the counter.

A stiff, cold wind blew a giant trucker into the entrance. He wore a Stetson and a heavy down-filled jacket. With long strides, he crossed the black-tiled floor to the counter and took the stool next to me.

The waitress placed a menu and a steaming cup in front of him. "How's it going, Howie?"

He took a long drag on the coffee. "Going good, Maybell. But it'll be better after you feed me." He handed the menu back.

"The usual?" she asked.

"Yep, and keep the caffeine coming."

"Where you headed?" I asked.

He shot a friendly glance my way. "San Francisco, and I can't wait to get out of this weather. It can get cold there, but nothing like this. I hate Wyoming in the winter, and it's always winter."

"I hear you. It's something you get used to but never learn to like."

I had a light-bulb moment. A long shot. I needed a minor miracle, but if I made this guy mad, he could sweep the floor with my broken body. "Howie, how would you like to do a favor for an abused woman and child, and make a little money on the side?"

His eyes narrowed, and then he arched an eyebrow. "You peddling something illegal, mister? I don't kill people."

I shook my head. This wasn't going well. "No, I'm a detective." I reached into my jacket pocket, took out a card, and handed it to him. "I work for a lady who has an abusive husband—a powerful man. Her son made a call on her cell phone that could help this man find them."

The skeptical expression never left his face and his clenched jaw made me nervous. "So where do I come in?"

I pulled Rachel's phone from my pocket. "I'd like you to take this and make as many calls as possible along your journey. When you get to California, toss the phone into the bay. I hope to throw her husband off the trail. Think you could help me?"

Howie removed his Stetson, replaced it, and furrowed his brow. "I guess I could do that. Can't see how it would be illegal." He pulled out his own phone, looked down at my card and punched numbers. My phone rang.

He grinned. "Just checking to make sure the card is legit. What are you driving?"

I pointed to my black Ford Explorer XLT parked out front.

Howie walked over to the window and wrote my license plate number on the back of my business card. He returned to his seat. "Let me see your driver's license."

When I gave it to him, he scanned it, listed the number, and handed back my ID.

He nodded. "Give me the phone."

I handed him a hundred dollar bill along with the phone. "You need a charger? I've got one in the car."

"Nope." He took the phone, but waved the money away. "Don't want the cash. No man worth his salt beats women and children."

I finished my meal and then slapped the trucker's shoulder as I left. "Thanks. And, Howie, if you ever decide to change careers, I could use a good man."

Howie would keep a GPS trace on Rachel's phone busy for quite a while.

God loves me.

❧❧

Hebron, Wyoming

At the Hebron exit, I took a right and drove under the bridge to the city's main drag. Hebron is not a pretty town except in winter. Carved out of the mountain in layers with evergreen trees scattered in patches across the landscape, it only shines when covered in a white blanket, and that happened often at an altitude of seven thousand feet.

After a stop at Walmart to pick up a throw away phone, I arrived at the office around one o'clock to check my mail and messages. The woman who runs the employment office across the hall stuck her head out.

"Morning, Mrs. Davis," I said.

She closed the door. No good morning. Still sore because I haven't hired a secretary from her. What Mrs. Davis didn't understand is that I would love to have a sexy blonde to answer my phone and greet clients. But a private detective was the only profession society deems lower than lawyers, and the pay wasn't as good.

Ergo, I couldn't afford to hire extra help. If business didn't pick up soon, I couldn't even afford the office space. I depended on the telephone and voicemail to keep in touch with clients. It might not be sexy, but it was cheap.

A burst of cold, tropical scented air filled my nostrils as I pushed open the office door and entered the empty reception area. My Hawaiian air-freshener still worked.

It felt like forty below as I flicked on the foyer lights and heat. I picked up the mail from the faded blue carpet under the letter slot. Mail in one hand, overcoat in the other, I shivered down the hallway past the bathroom on the left to my private cubbyhole. I placed the letters in the in-box and put the coat back on. With luck, the heat would overcome the chill before I froze to death.

The letter-opener sliced easily through the envelopes as Cody's call buzzed through my mind like a persistent bee, zeroing in for a sting. I grabbed my newly-purchased cell phone and called the ranch. While I waited for the call to connect, I put away the mail in the desk file. All bills.

Emma answered, and I asked to speak to Rachel. She picked up the extension. A click signaled Emma had disconnected.

I cleared my throat. "You haven't heard from Harry, have you?"

A slight tremor entered Rachel's voice. "No. I guess we dodged the bullet one more time. I've forbidden Cody to go near any of the house phones."

"How are things at the ranch? I'll find another safe house whenever you're ready." I wanted them to stay put, at least until we knew what her husband's next move would be.

"Emma and Bill are wonderful hosts, and Cody loves it here. He would hate to leave."

Cody and Bill's laughter rang in the background. Tense muscles in my neck relaxed, and I exhaled a long breath I didn't realize I'd been holding. Looked like the family had settled into The Hand Me Down's peaceful rhythm. Maybe they wouldn't be leaving anytime soon. If my luck held, the ploy with Howie and the cell phone would keep the judge far away from them.

My backup plan included asking a police detective friend, Amos Horne, to let me know if the judge asked for a trace on Rachel's cell calls. From my days on the Hebron police force, I knew tracing wouldn't take much time. Maybe an early warning from Amos would give me enough head start to move the family if needed.

After I finished the conversation with Rachel, I checked my call center and found a number of hang ups. Only one message recorded. Wealthy industrialist

Lincoln Webster Armstrong left his cell number. A call from Armstrong equaled a summons from the White House—not an everyday occurrence for a lowly P.I. A national mover-and-shaker, Armstrong headed Hebron's short celebrity A-list.

From the middle drawer, I retrieved a yellow legal pad and pen. The room had warmed enough my hand had stopped shaking. I punched Armstrong's number, and he picked up on the first ring. No pretense, no call screener. I could learn to like this guy.

"This is Noah Adams, sir, returning your call. How may I help you?"

"Thanks for getting back to me so promptly. Mayor Thornton suggested I contact you. He told me about your rescue of that child in Texas and assured me you were the best. I need the best." There was a slight pause. "I'd like you to look into the death of my wife."

A vote of confidence from Mayor Thornton surprised me. We had a history that didn't include being best buddies. "Thank you. That was kind of the mayor. The Texas thing was a lucky break, and please, call me Noah."

"Fine," he said. "But no false modesty, Noah. You insult my intelligence. I never take someone else's word on anything important. I did a comprehensive background check on you."

All right.

"Can you meet me at my home this afternoon at two o'clock? I'll fill you in on the details then." He gave me directions and ended the call.

After disconnecting, I scurried across the street to the *Hebron Herald* office to scan back issues on the Armstrong case. A small newspaper, it hadn't yet gone digital. The newspaper morgue was small, crowded with file cabinets and dusty back issues. But everything was well organized, and I soon found the back issues I needed.

The disappearance of Abigail Armstrong made national headlines for months when she vanished three years ago. Blood covered the interior of her abandoned car, but the police never found a body. Officially, she was still a missing person. Curious that Armstrong wanted me to investigate the case now.

After the prominent socialite vanished, *The Herald's* front page screamed:

WIFE OF TYCOON MISSING
ARMSTRONG A PERSON OF INTEREST IN WIFE'S DISAPPEARANCE

The last word on her turbulent life rested in a dusty cold-case file in the basement of the County Courthouse. It appeared Abigail's husband no longer accepted that as the final word on his missing wife.

Copies of pertinent articles in hand, I returned to the office and made a case file.

Skepticism was a by-product of my profession, and statistically speaking, the odds weighed against finding out what happened to Abigail Armstrong. Three years can be a lifetime in a missing person case. However, if I determined Armstrong hadn't been involved in his wife's disappearance, I would take the case. The idea of anyone getting away with murder, no matter how famous or how wealthy, stuck in my craw.

Lincoln Armstrong's Home
The Armstrong mansion sat on prime lakefront

property almost ten miles from the city. At a distance, it appeared half the size of the Biltmore Estate, the mansion that formerly belonged to the American Vanderbilt family, which was now a tourist attraction. Which made it a thousand times the size of my digs.

In this part of the country, only fashionable neighborhoods bothered with landscaping—and there were few fashionable neighborhoods. Most residents left their tiny plots of land barren. Why bother with a lawn covered in snow ten months of the year? Armstrong must have spent a small fortune on his. Terraced rock gardens led to the front door where hearty shrubbery and foliage struggled valiantly against layers of snow. Pushing aside the comparisons to my place, I rang the bell.

Armstrong opened the massive door, dressed in jeans, a long-sleeved sweater, denim jacket, and boots. I must have missed the casual-dress memo. A little insecure in my business suit and overcoat, I shook his hand.

My touch let me see the man perhaps better than he knew himself. I'd met few with his credentials. An honorable man with a strict code of ethics and living proof that wealth doesn't guarantee happiness.

Armstrong stepped outside, and the door made a soft click behind him. "Let's walk."

In silence, he led me to a pathway that meandered toward the lake through tall ponderosa pines and mountain cedars. As we walked, the lake played peek-a-boo through thick snow-laden limbs in the dense woods.

The spectacular shoreline came into view. The smooth surface showed only an occasional ripple as snow sludge washed ashore, the water so blue it looked unreal against the white backdrop. A light breeze tickled the tips of branches and left a whiff of cedar in the air. We reached a sheltered redwood bench close to the lake's edge. Armstrong dusted snow away with a gloved hand and motioned for me to sit.

He remained standing. "Abby and I came here often before her..." He paused. "It may sound irrational, but I feel her presence when I come here." He turned and gazed at the horizon for a moment.

I took the time to study him. Distinguished best described Lincoln Armstrong. Refined, not handsome. Neat gray hair covered a well-shaped head. His confident, direct gaze spelled power in capital letters.

"When we met, Abigail was this frail, ethereal beauty with lovely, haunted eyes. She brought out the knight-in-shining-armor in me. Before we married, Abby never spoke about the past, but I knew she'd lived a hard life. I wanted to protect her, to erase the shadows in her eyes. I succeeded for more than five years." He expelled a deep breath. "I let her down in the end. Someone got to her, and I wasn't there to protect her."

Perhaps if she had confided in Armstrong, he could have prevented the tragedy. "I doubt you could have done anything to stop it."

He shrugged. "For more than two years the authorities tried to pin her disappearance on me. By the time the police decided to look elsewhere, any trace evidence had long since vanished. Witnesses disappeared or their memories dimmed. Six months ago, after I realized the police had given up, I investigated Abby's past on my own."

"The authorities still have her listed as missing." I stated the obvious.

Armstrong shook his head. "If Abby was alive, she would have contacted me."

"You think someone from her past killed her?"

"That was my initial thought. It seemed the logical place to start. Now, I'm not sure." Armstrong tore his gaze from the view, punched his hands into his jacket pockets, and sat beside me. "My contact in California couldn't find anyone there who wished her harm. At that point, I realized I needed a professional investigator. That's when I decided to hire you."

He shifted his position on the seat, and his features tightened—a sea of sorrow in his gaze. "Abigail was married before we met. She had a son. At first, she wouldn't talk about that part of her life. Over time, I learned the ex-husband died in a riot while a prisoner at San Quentin and her five-year-old son was killed in an auto accident in San Francisco."

"I'll need copies of any reports you have. Who handled the California investigation for you?"

He waved a dismissive hand. "A friend in the San Francisco district attorney's office, for all the good it did. You're welcome to the report, but I doubt it will be of much help."

"Did you notice any change in your wife's behavior before she disappeared?"

He heaved a deep breath and nodded. "I covered all that with the police when she first went missing. Four days before Abby vanished, we went to a charity dinner at the country club. About an hour after we arrived, she asked me to take her home, said she had a headache. We left right away." Armstrong rose from the bench, paced a few steps, and then turned back. "The old haunted expression was back in her eyes. I asked what happened, but she wouldn't tell me. For the next four days, she took all meals in our bedroom. On the fourth day, she received a phone call and left home at noon. No one has seen her since."

"Did the police know who made the call?"

He shook his head. "It originated from an untraceable cell phone. The police never found out who placed it."

"Did you notice who she talked with at the country club that evening?"

"The usual club members. I've plumbed my memory for years trying to remember everything...but I never noticed any strange faces."

Banks of clouds moved in, and the temperature dropped. I had to concentrate to keep my teeth from chattering. "You gave this information to the authorities? They checked out the country club members and staff?"

Armstrong seemed oblivious to the sudden chill. "As far as I know. It's all in the report I obtained from the police." He grinned. "I had to pull some strings to get copies."

He stared at the lake again before shifting his gaze back to me. Deep creases ran across his brow, giving him a tired expression. When he spoke, it seemed almost a plea. "Find out what happened to my wife, Noah. She deserves a proper end to her life. I owe her that much. A final place to rest—here by the lake."

A surge of compassion ran through me. I'd never become immune to the unhappiness that came with my job. I got to my feet and clasped his hand. "I'll do all that's within my power to make that happen, sir."

He appeared to notice me for the first time. "You'll have to forgive me, Noah. I've kept you out in the cold too long. Come. Let's go back to the house. I'll give you those reports and some hot coffee, and we'll settle the financial arrangements."

Noah's Home, Hebron, Wyoming

The predawn nightmare returned and refused to loosen its grip. The images swirled and engulfed me in their depths. My heart squeezed with fright, foreshadowing events to come, and I couldn't breathe. The sequence varied, but the scenes never changed.

It's my tenth birthday and a bright Sunday afternoon. I ride home with my grandmother. I've spent the weekend with her. Warmth and happiness envelop me as we ease around the corner onto my street.

The day turns dark as the car pulls to the curb. I get out. Foreboding washes away the pleasure. A street lamp snaps on, shattering the blackness that suddenly settles over the neighborhood.

I trudge along the broken sidewalk toward the front door. My feet drag on the cement as I move forward. What lies beyond the entrance terrifies me. Each time I reach the door, it leaps farther away. Finally, I grab hold with a desperate grip and turn the knob.

On quiet feet, I ease inside.

Shouts and curses blast at me like noise from a boom box. Sounds become a physical force that drive me back into the entrance. My little brother sits wide-eyed, scrunched into the sofa's corner, his thumb in his mouth. I drop my overnight bag near the stairs and move toward the tirade that washes over me like waves before a hurricane.

Damp and breathless, I woke up hard. The familiar fear of the recurring nightmare—that didn't want to let go. After a few gulps of air, my sleep-fogged brain relaxed.

My heavy lids open, greeted by two pairs of hazel eyes just inches from my nose.

Bella and Brutus, two-year-old Saint Bernards, smiled at me. The pups didn't bark. They just grinned and stared. Staring can be incredibly effective.

I slipped into the warmth of a wool bathrobe and my gaze fell on a photograph of my father on the dresser. He wore his Air Force dress uniform, and his cap position according to regulations, over dark hair. Square jawed, his deep blue eyes that sparkled with life. I didn't remember him. His plane was shot down over a Vietnamese jungle when I was four. At six feet four, I'd inherited my height from him. My grandmother said I was his spittin' image, and her assessment was confirmed every time I looked in the mirror.

Half asleep, I stumbled downstairs and picked up the newspaper on the front stoop. Bella and Brutus plunged ahead into the kitchen where I tossed them a couple of fake-bacon treats. I filled a mug with hot, black liquid and thanked God once again for whoever invented the automatic coffeemaker.

Bella nosed my arm. I scratched her ear with one hand and unfolded the Sunday newspaper with the other. The dogs were family. Their presence kept me grounded.

Insistent door chimes ended doggie family time.

Craning my neck to the right, I checked the time on the microwave. 8:00 AM. That would be my neighbor, Ted Bennett. Coordinated Universal Time called Ted to verify their accuracy. I left my cup on the table and hurried to answer the summons.

I'd given Ted a key more than two years ago when he started walking the animals for me. Even so, whenever my car was in the drive, he always rang the bell.

At thirty, Ted was a little overweight with the mentality of an eager fourth grader. He lived across the street with his grandmother, Mabel Bennett.

The pups rushed past me to greet Ted—their second favorite human in the world. Ted dropped to his knees, relishing the affectionate slobber the dogs spread across his face. "Mornin', Noah. Can I walk the dogs now?"

"Sure, Ted. Come over after church, and we'll watch the game together."

In a flurry of white and brown fur, Ted leashed the animals and grinned at me. "I'll come back soon. I like to see the Cowboys play." Brutus strained to get through the door, Bella following in his paw prints.

Ted turned honest brown eyes toward me. "Grandma gets on my nerves a little, sometimes."

There was a story behind that, but I knew better than to ask. I clapped Ted on the back as he let the dogs pull him out the door.

While Ted was gone, I cleaned house. I checked in with Rachel to make sure things were still good, and the situation still under control. A Marine trained neatnik I caught up on my laundry and housework, and then dressed for church.

After the service ended, I came home and grilled burgers, made a big bowl of popcorn, and went next door to find Ted.

Mabel answered my knock, a smile in her blue

eyes. "Hi, neighbor."

"Hi, Mabel. Ted wanted to watch the game with me. Is he around? You're invited, too, if you want to hang out with a couple of jocks."

She laughed. "Thanks, but I have to go back to the restaurant."

"How did the court hearing go?"

She motioned me into the entryway. "We won. I'm now and forever officially Ted's legal guardian."

Mabel rescued Ted two years ago from the state mental institution where her son had placed him.

I pulled her into a hug. "Congratulations."

"Your grandmother wears combat boots" was a description that fit Mabel Bennett perfectly—her attitude—not her dress code. She had three passions in life. God, Ted, and her business, the Chateau Bennett, Hebron's only steak house. Mabel handled Ted like a fully functioning adult. And heaven help anyone who treated him otherwise in her presence.

She returned the hug with gusto. "Thanks. Wait a minute and I'll get Ted for you." She moved to the bottom of the stairs and called his name.

Soon, Ted hurried into the room in his weeble-wobble gait, and we strolled back to my place.

A navy blue sedan that caught my attention earlier in the morning still sat down the street. I'd never seen the car in the neighborhood before. Tinted windows hid the occupant from view.

I nodded at the car. "Did a new family move into the Clarkson place?"

Ted rooted his feet in the middle of the street and stared at the vehicle. He shook his head. "Nope. The Clarksons left to spend Christmas in Louisiana."

Ted knew almost everything about the neighbors.

They shared their lives with him as though he was the neighborhood mascot.

"Wait for me on the curb, Ted. I'm going to introduce myself."

"I'll come with you, Noah. I like to meet new people."

"No, Ted. Wait on the curb like I asked." I spoke sharper than I intended, but there was no way of knowing who or what the automobile contained.

Ted dropped his head and shuffled to the curb.

With Ted stationed a safe distance away, I walked toward the car. Six feet from the vehicle, the motor revved and the car whipped around me, too fast to get a good look at the driver. The car disappeared around the corner.

Real unfriendly for neighbors.

Big surprise, the license plate's surface was caked with a mixture of snow and mud, making the tag illegible.

"Why'd the car do that, Noah?"

I shrugged. "Maybe they were late for an appointment."

We entered the front door and I opened a couple of soft drinks. We took the burgers down to my man cave in the basement, and I gave two to the pups. Ted and I settled in to stuff ourselves and watch the game. Life didn't get any better.

At half time, I took Bella and Brutus outside for a stretch.

The blue sedan hadn't returned.

4

Harold London's Home

Early Monday morning, I drove to Crown Heights and parked a few blocks from the London home. I hurried through the gate in stealth mode, and into the library that lay just to the right off the living room. The ugly painting Rachel mentioned hung in prominence above a massive desk.

I scanned the room, and my gaze rested on the opposite wall. As expected, a man with Harry's conceit had a wall dedicated to his accomplishments. The trophy collection mirrored his sense of self, with a local Chamber of Commerce Man of the Year plaque in the center. Must have been a bad year for qualified candidates.

The awards didn't impress me. I had nothing but disgust for any man who used physical force on a woman and child.

I hadn't always used my God-given gifts altruistically. In my teens, I'd tormented a thug who bullied me—revealed his secrets—messed with his head. Power over others can be as addictive as drugs. Did revenge bring satisfaction? Far from it. Not even a shower could scrub away my self-disgust. That experience made me understand why the Lord said, "Vengeance is mine."

Harry London probably never had an emotion remotely close to remorse.

Twenty minutes after my arrival at the London home, Harry entered the library and crossed to the safe.

Rachel was right. He didn't go to jail, and he had shaved my time limit close.

Peering over Harry's shoulder I noted the spins and reverses his hands made on the dial, and then committed the data to memory. Before he jerked open the vault door, Harry wheeled around and stared directly at me. For one insecure moment, I panicked. Had I materialized? After a quick glance at the grandfather clock in the corner, only 6:27. I relaxed. Three minutes left.

Time is the enemy when I'm invisible.

Anxious to leave the premises, I scurried down the hallway. Passing through the den, I shot a quick look at the timepiece above the fireplace, 6:29 and counting. I had less than a minute.

So much for the accuracy of antique clocks.

From the library, I heard the safe door snap shut just as my reflection appeared in the plasma television screen on the wall. I scrambled into the kitchen and stepped into the walk-in pantry.

Harry's footsteps echoed on the tile floor moving toward me, they faltered, and then continued on, as if he looked for something or someone. With my back pressed against the wall in a gap at the end of a huge upright freezer, I sucked in my breath as Harry stalked into the food closet. I could kiss my P.I. license good-bye if he saw me. The profession frowned on breaking and entering.

Harry stood in the doorway for what seemed an eternity and then closed and locked the door. Locked the door? The man was seriously paranoid. The access had been unbolted when I entered. Why secure it now? Only a major control freak put a lock on a pantry, anyway. Probably made Rachel account for everything she used.

The ping of the security system told me Harry had set the alarm at the garage entrance. Within minutes, the car started, and the sounds faded into silence.

Harry's behavior unnerved me—too crafty and suspicious for my comfort. He could decide to return, and I didn't intend to wait another twenty-five minutes to become invisible again. I opened the pantry with a credit card and wiped away my prints.

As I left, I switched the sugar and salt. Juvenile? Yeah. But it felt good.

Aware I would break the Arrow Security circuit, I ran through the kitchen door. Outside, I checked the exterior for security cameras. None occupied the usual places. I scanned the street before opening the gate and took a less than casual stroll to my vehicle. I covered the two blocks, wrote the safe combination on a notepad and placed it in the console. The information would give Rachel access to the money and passports.

The imminent arrival of Crown Height's finest was a real possibility, so I started the engine and pulled away. A few blocks later a squad car passed, headed in the opposite direction. I groaned when the cruiser made a U-turn, switched on the strobe lights, and eased in behind me.

I swung to the curb and watched as the Irish twins, Ryan and Duncan, did the same. My luck had taken its usual turn. Out of Crown Heights' six-man police force, these two guys had drawn patrol duty in this section again.

Duncan sauntered over and pecked on the

window. I lowered the glass.

He leaned forward. "Hey, Adams, what brings you to this neighborhood? You live around here?" He already knew the answer. I'd given him my address Friday night.

My excuse was ready. "No. Can't afford it. My attorney lives one street over, Jacob Stein. You know Jake?"

Duncan ignored my question. "Isn't it a little early to call on your attorney?"

"Not for Jake. He retired last year, and he gets up with the birds. I'd ask you boys to come along, but he isn't fond of cops."

Duncan didn't smile. "The security system went off at Judge London's home a few minutes ago. You know anything about that?"

"Why should I?"

"No reason. It just seems strange. You call us Friday to report abuse at the judge's home, and when his security alarm goes off this morning, we find you a few blocks away."

"Life's full of coincidences. I'm just a guy on his way to breakfast. May I ask if someone has broken into the judge's home, why you're stopping me? Shouldn't you try to catch the burglars before they get away?"

Duncan's jaw tightened. "You telling me how to do my job?"

I shook my head. "Just a suggestion from a concerned taxpayer."

"You should know, *mister taxpayer*, Crown Heights has more than one unit on the streets. It might also interest you to know Judge London has cameras throughout his home." Duncan gave the top of my SUV a sharp slap and strolled back toward the patrol car. "Watch your step, Adams," he called over his shoulder. "The good judge doesn't like you even a little bit."

"That makes us even. I don't like him either."

If the judge's cameras caught any part of my reappearance, it would mean trouble in more ways than I wanted to consider.

❦

Jake Stein's Home

I eased my SUV back onto the street, and Ryan and Duncan moved in behind me. They stayed in my rearview mirror until I reached Jake's elegant address, and they watched as I picked up the intercom phone at the gate. When the portal swung open, they drove away.

I intended to visit Jake Stein soon, anyway, and this seemed a good time. However, I had embellished the truth a tad. Jake wasn't an early riser.

A former client introduced me to Jacob Stein six years ago at the athletic club. I played a couple of racquetball games with Jake. He hammered me like a jackhammer on the court that day. That's why he liked me. He becomes attached to people he can beat.

He was twice my age and half my size but most people never noticed Jake's stature. Intellectually, he was usually the biggest man in the room.

Imposing white columns greeted me as I drove up the circular drive and parked at the front door. Jake built the antebellum in the heart of one of the coldest places on the continent. The five-acre estate stood ankle deep in snow, stark and conspicuous with its southern architecture.

Jake opened the door wearing a silk bathrobe and cravat with a scowl on his handsome face. "Adams, do you know what time it is?"

"Yeah, it's time grumpy old men were out of bed. You're burning daylight, Stein."

He stepped back for me to enter. "Who's old and grumpy? I'm just a retired gentleman trying to enjoy his *retirement.*"

"Well, get up and enjoy it. I have a couple of clients for you."

"Do you know what the word *retired* means? I have a dictionary in the library; I'll look it up for you. You probably can't spell it. Is this another freebie case you found for me?"

"She doesn't have a dime, but her husband's loaded. What do you need with money? You're richer than Bill Gates."

"That's because all the cases I had before I retired weren't pro bono."

"Think of it this way, Jake. You'll be doing God's work."

He scowled. "God doesn't pay until you die, and I'm not ready to go."

"Stop complaining and fix me some breakfast while I tell you about my case."

"You drag me out of bed at seven in the morning, and you want breakfast, too?" He shook his head and moved toward the kitchen. "The day we met must have been my lucky day, Adams. I can't imagine what I did to God to deserve you." Jake really loved me. He just liked to complain.

A maid clad in gray rayon entered from the den. "Do you want me to make breakfast, Mr. Stein?"

He waved her off with a grin. "No, Ruby. I'll take

care of this freeloader myself."

He led me into a gourmet kitchen and pulled down a pan from over the island. While Jake whipped up omelets, I made toast and coffee and filled him in on Rachel and Cody. Jake's a great cook. He could make another fortune in the restaurant business.

I continued my story while we ate.

Jake gave a long low whistle. "If you take on Harry London, you'll take on a world of trouble. You know that, don't you? I heard about this at the club over the weekend. London didn't go to jail. He claimed his son fell out of his treehouse. The police chose to believe him rather than deal with it." Jake lifted a carafe from the table and refilled our cups. "London said his wife cooked up the stunt with a private eye to get the kid away from him. I should have known it was you. He'll be coming after you, big time."

"What can he do?"

"He can file kidnapping charges against you, for one. In any court system other than Hebron's, it wouldn't be so easy. You know the corruption downtown as well as I do. The best way to fight it is for your client to file for a divorce."

"What would happen to Cody during the divorce proceeding?"

"Courts almost always lean toward split-custody. I don't think I could get her full guardianship without proof of abuse. Has the kid seen a doctor?"

Rachel wouldn't leave Cody alone with his father for a minute, much less part time. I couldn't blame her. He might go into a rage and kill the kid.

"Rachel is taking Cody as soon as she can get an appointment. She'll never go for anything less than full custody."

Jake sipped the coffee, his brow wrinkled in a frown. "Then you'd better keep the family out of sight for a while. I don't want to know where you've hidden them. London might try to force me to tell where they are. Let me know when you get the X-rays and report from the physician. If they prove mistreatment, then I can take him on."

Jake folded his napkin and placed it beside his plate. "This thing could turn ugly very fast. You need to avoid the police; London will be gunning for you. My sources tell me he has some heavy connection with the less desirable elements up Chicago way. His rise to power was too fast to be honest."

Just what I needed. Harry London and the mob.

"You realize I haven't handled anything in the divorce and domestic violence field in years."

"Jake, I would trust you with anything. This family needs help, and you're the best man I know for the job."

"I'll do what I can." Jake sounded almost humble. He picked up a piece of toast and offered one to me. I shook my head. "You never said how you solved that Texas case so quickly. Want to enlighten me?"

A subject I preferred not to discuss, but I owed Jake the details. He financed the trip. My bank balance at the time hovered around five dollars.

"Some things are difficult to explain, but I'll try. The news covered the kids disappearing in the Dallas area, five in just over a year. The morning I borrowed the money from you, I'd watched the news and learned a little girl had just vanished. The reporter at the scene stood in front of the parents' home, lots of people milling around in the background."

Jake waved his hand in a rolling motion, anxious

for me to get on with the story.

"One guy in the crowd caught my attention. At first, I figured he just wanted to get his mug on the news, but he looked into the camera as most fifteen-minutes-of-fame jerks do. He seemed please with himself, rather than 'hey-look-I'm-on-TV.' It hit me that this might be the killer. Don't ask me how I knew...but I did, and if the police didn't catch him that day, he would kill that little girl.

"George flew me all the way to DFW, and I hopped a cab to police headquarters. You can imagine my reception. Like they needed an unknown private eye from Wyoming riding in to tell them their business."

Jake scowled at me. "And this perp took one look at your Honest-Joe face and spilled his guts."

I grinned and shrugged. "Pretty much." I sipped my coffee. Some of the details I couldn't confide to Jake.

One of the detectives gave me a friendly ear, and I convinced him to get the news tapes from all the disappearances. This wasn't anything new for police departments. They routinely check bystanders after a crime and, in fact, they still had the tapes. They'd already checked out my guy and cut him loose.

We viewed the tapes and the guy was visible in every crowd scene filmed after the children vanished. I asked them to bring him back in for questioning.

Police interviewers got nowhere with the perp, Willy Jackson. He stalled for two precious hours. Finally, I asked if they'd give me a shot at him, and they agreed to let me have thirty minutes. What did they have to lose? Their case was going nowhere.

My friendly detective let me into the interview

room.

Willy Jackson was a short man, about fifty pounds overweight with thinning brown hair.

"Hi Willy. I'm detective Noah Adams. You want something to drink? Coke, coffee, water?" I reached out and shook his hand. I almost gagged. It felt like sticking my hand in an open sewer, but it gave me all the details I needed.

"I'll take a water," he said.

I had to keep it together. A child's life depended on turning this creep. The problem, how to get the information to the cops watching me in the room next door without revealing how I knew.

I leaned forward in the chair, watching his eyes. "We know you took that little girl, Willy. People saw you. We even know the area where you took her. You can make it easy on yourself by giving us the address. Maybe keep you off death row."

He scoffed. "Sure you do. You don't know squat."

"Ah, but we do. You were careless, Willy. We know your history, what your father did to you. I understand, Willy. What you're doing...it isn't your fault."

He danced me around until my time was up, and I gave it one last shot. "Willy, have you ever considered that little girl feels exactly like you did after your father abused you? She's hurting, Willy. You can stop the pain."

His eyes filled with tears. He broke down and gave me the address.

The sad part was his father helped create the monster Willy became.

Naturally, the cops were curious about my knowledge of his past. I convinced them it was just lucky profiling.

What happened to those five children still haunted my dreams.

Solving that case brought me a lot of notoriety I didn't need any calls from hurting parents across the country whom I couldn't help. I didn't have all the answers. I wished to God I had.

Jake and I finished breakfast in silence. I pushed back my chair, slapped his shoulder, and went to the entryway. A fast scan of the street told me I could leave. Not a patrol car in sight.

Reaching for the doorknob, I shifted back to Jake. "Thanks for breakfast. By the way, you should know. Harry London may have pictures of me inside his home, taken this morning by his security cameras."

A deep groan from behind me reached my ears as the door clicked shut.

∂∞

Hole In-The-Wall Café, Hebron

I left Jake's place, called Amos Horne, and invited him to a late lunch. Since I stood him up on Friday, he accepted and said he'd meet me at one o'clock. We usually met at The Hole in the Wall, one of his favorite places. Appropriately named, the café looked like a dump, but a clean dump. I'd never figured out whether it was designed ambiance or just run down, but they served the best hamburgers in the free world.

In most situations, Amos would provide details on a case. I wanted to pick his brain about the disappearance of Abigail Armstrong. The department frowned on sharing police records with civilians, but Amos never worried about the rules.

I arrived early and took a seat by the window. Amos pulled his unmarked car in beside my SUV and untangled his big frame from behind the wheel. He glanced around, taking in everything at once and then sauntered into the entrance. A cop's habit. High cheekbones and an easy grace reflected his Cherokee heritage. Amos wore his ethnicity with pride. At thirty-five, and a twelve-year veteran of the HPD, he held the distinction of being the youngest detective in the department. But then, there were only two.

I'd learned to live with it but never enjoyed the freaky nature of my gifts. The sorrow, almost pain, to discover someone I admired and trusted could have feet of clay. This probably explained why I'd only found three real friends in my lifetime.

Jake and Amos were two of the three—not perfect, but good people. Public faces seldom reveal what goes on inside. Outward confidence can hide a mass of internal turmoil. With Jake and Amos, what you saw was what you got. Jake was complicated, precise, organized and crafty, where Amos tilted to the other extreme.

Amos had developed a paunch from lack of exercise and eating the wrong foods, but the diet hadn't affected his investigative skills. We partnered on the force after going through the police academy together. Our friendship remained strong, even though he never forgave me for deserting him to go into the P.I. racket.

Life as a rookie cop hadn't worked for me. A loner by nature, I had an aversion to getting trapped in a job with too many rules and too many bosses. Not to mention some of the cops made the crooks I hauled off to jail look like saints. So I bailed.

As my own boss, I could choose the people I worked with. The pay wasn't much better and the benefits lousy, but I slept well at night.

I joined Amos at the order line. We worked our way to the front and Marie, the clerk behind the cash register, greeted us with a bright smile on her pretty black face. "Hi, Amos, Noah. What'll it be today, the usual?" Marie had a photographic memory.

We nodded.

The usual for me consisted of a burger with everything, fries, and a large iced tea. The usual for Amos was a gastronomic nightmare. Two cheeseburgers with the works, which included jalapeno peppers, a double order of onion rings, and a super size soda.

Marie wrote our order and names on two brown paper bags. Later the cook would place the finished order in the paper sacks. Efficiency in action.

We sat in a shabby booth near the window while waiting for the food. Amos placed a thick manila folder on the table and shoved it across to me.

"What's this?"

He grinned. "I made a copy of the case book for you."

He pulled the envelope back, opened the flap, and fanned glossy photos before me. "Brought the crime scene shots. I'll have to take 'em back, but you can make copies at Walmart if you like."

I shook my head. "Thanks, I don't need copies, but I do appreciate getting a look at them. Hope you don't get in trouble over this."

Having the photos and investigation details was the next best thing to being at the crime scene.

"Not hardly. This case is as cold as a dead Alaskan

salmon."

The first photo of the car's interior caught my eye. Sometimes people try to fake their disappearance by leaving blood samples behind. Not so in this case—too much blood. It's hard to fake the splatter. All outward appearances indicated Abigail Armstrong died from wounds sustained in her car.

An expensive handbag and car keys lay on the floorboard. Obviously, robbery wasn't the motive.

"Where did they find the vehicle?"

Amos shifted his large frame and fingered the snapshots. "In a very rough neighborhood on the south side. Some kid was trying to remove the tires when the police spotted him. A crack house sat across the street, and a meth lab operated one block down. We've cleared the drugs from that area at least a dozen times. They come back like roaches."

We didn't have a problem with gangs in Hebron, or as far as I know, in most parts of Wyoming. My theory is it's just too cold to hang out on street corners. However, we do have a drug problem. Meth was a big deal here.

I looked over the case book copies. "Any reason to believe she might have been a user?"

"The blood stains had no trace of drugs. Since we didn't have a body, we couldn't be certain. None of the evidence pointed in that direction."

The pictures bothered me, so I turned them face down on the table. "Did anyone question her doctor? Most physicians suspect when a patient is an addict."

"The doctor said Abigail Armstrong wasn't the type to do narcotics. Much too level headed. Those were her words, not mine." He tapped the envelope. "It's all in here."

I handed the photos back to him and placed the file on the seat beside me. "Having access to your interviews will be a big help, save me a ton of time. Since she left home after getting a phone call, it's a sure bet she knew her assailant."

"You're probably right. Now all you have to do is find out which of the ten thousand people in town placed the call." He followed the comment with a smart-aleck grin.

"What's the theory in the department?"

"The popular guess—a stalker killed her. Abigail Armstrong was a looker. She must'a been forty but could have easily passed for thirty at the time she vanished. We checked Lincoln Armstrong inside and out, but we couldn't find a motive. We never found an affair on either side. If he did it, he's one smart *hombre*."

"He is that. Intelligent, I mean. Armstrong didn't kill his wife. Trust me on that."

"If you say so." He gave me a mock salute.

"Any evidence she was being stalked?"

"A couple of neighbors remembered a man parked in a car outside the Armstrong property several times the week she vanished. They couldn't agree on the model or even the color. We didn't have enough information to find the guy."

"Did you follow up on the country club angle?"

"Sure we did. It wasn't my case, but I helped Art, the detective who caught the assignment. We interviewed the staff and every guest there that night. Considering who she was, and the press frenzy, the mayor was on our backs. The people we talked to all agreed she seemed fine when she arrived, but her mood changed just before she left."

Marie called us to pick up our order, and we dropped the case while we ate.

"I hope my reward in Heaven will be a mountain of cheeseburgers just like this," Amos said and wiped his mouth with a paper napkin. "With a hill of banana pudding on the side."

I chuckled. "You're a man of simple needs, Amos Horne."

"Hey, guys. You plotting the downfall of the Republic?" A slender brunette laughed and slid into the booth beside me. The collar of her blue police uniform couldn't quite hide the ugly white scar that ran across her throat. Jessie Bolton and I were old friends. I'd been the officer on duty the night her husband tried to kill her.

"Nothing that easy, Jess. I'm trying to rescue an abused family."

"Anybody I know?" She took one of my fries and dragged it through Amos' ketchup.

I shoved the rest of the fries in front of her. "Do you know Rachel London?"

She dropped the food back on the tray and wiped her mouth with a napkin. "Yeah. I've met her, and I've met the judge. Ask me if I'm surprised. Mrs. London had the look of a whipped puppy."

"What are you doing these days," I asked. "Still patrolling the streets?"

She shook her head. "Mostly babysitting drunks in the county jail. It's worked out better for me. Regular hours and I get to spend more time with my two kids."

"Have you had lunch?" Amos asked. "Noah will spring for a burger if you want."

"Thanks, but I was on my way out when I saw you guys. Wanted to say hi since I haven't seen you in a while." She leaned in and kissed my cheek. "Take care, big guy."

The touch of her lips on my cheek told me all was not well with Jessie. Her husband would finish his prison sentence in ten months. And she knew he would be coming after her.

I watched her leave with more than a little concern. Jessie needed to get out of Hebron soon, without leaving a trail her husband could follow.

Amos tapped his finger on the Armstrong case book. "You gonna solve this, Noah, and make us look bad?"

"That's what I'll try to do. Not to make you look bad but to help a very sad man find out what happened to the woman he loved."

"That would be Armstrong."

"You never cease to amaze me with your perceptive grasp of the obvious."

"You have to remember, I'm just an underpaid detective, not a big-bucks P.I."

If only he knew how seldom a client like Armstrong came along. The lunch crowd began to trickle out to go do whatever they did. I leaned back in the booth and smiled. "I get paid for my infinite knowledge of the criminal mind."

"Yeah, right."

"Speaking of Judge London, what's the scuttlebutt at the precinct on him?"

A dark expression came over Amos's face. "We catch 'em. He lets 'em go. The D.A. hates him with a purple passion, but lawyers love to get their clients before London. He's the guy who sentenced Jessie's husband to five years for capital attempted murder."

"London's wife and son are clients of mine as of

last Friday night. That's why I cancelled dinner."

"Yeah, I figured that out from what you told Jessie." Amos shook his head. "You trying to redefine stupid? London's trouble with a capital T. Deal me out on this one, buddy. I want to retire with a full pension. If I were you, I'd back off while I still could."

I peered across the table at my old friend. "You wouldn't if you'd met his family."

5

Noah's Home, Hebron, Wyoming

Tuesday afternoon the doorbell sounded, followed by an impatient knock. I opened the door and Jake Stein's solemn face stared up at me. "It's about time. I've been trying to reach you all day."

"Yeah, I tried to return your call a couple of times. What's up?"

Jake threw his coat on the tree by the door. "London pressed charges against you for breaking and entering."

"How did you find out? I haven't been served."

"I was at the courthouse and got wind of it. Told them I was your attorney and spoke to the D.A. He gave me a look at the tape from London's security system. Doesn't look to me like they have a case. They must prove intent to commit a crime. No evidence of that I can see." He stopped and stared at me. "You didn't take anything, did you?"

I shook my head. "Come on in the kitchen. I've got a pot of fresh coffee."

Jake followed and took a seat in the breakfast nook. "The D.A. agreed to a hearing before Judge Josiah Burns Wednesday morning at nine. He's the visiting judge the city uses when London isn't available. In this case, London is the alleged victim so Burns is sitting in. Burns is honest and he dislikes London even more than I do. That's off the record."

Jake accepted the coffee mug and took a sip. He rolled the coffee around in his mouth like a wine taster. "This isn't bad for Food Mart coffee."

"Thanks for the compliment, I think."

"Well, it isn't imported French roast, but it'll do, kid." He glanced around the room. "I like what you've done with the place. Is boring your style of choice or is this an accident?"

"What can I tell you? I'm a bachelor."

"So am I. That doesn't mean you have to live like a plebeian. White walls without accessories only work in a monastery. Really, Noah—"

I held up my hand. "Stop complaining. Grab your cup and come to the dining room. Maybe it will be more appealing to your refined sensibilities."

Jake shadowed behind me and pulled out one of the upholstered chairs at the dining table, his eyes alight with pleasure. "Don't tell me you did this?"

I shook my head. The area contrasted greatly with the rest of my home. The room had style with warmth that invited you in. Filled with rich colors and textures, the walls painted in a fashionable gold shade that accented the fabric in the drapes. "McKenna Thornton," I said.

"You should get her to do the rest of the house."

I glared at him, and he dropped the subject. He knew the history between McKenna and me.

He took the last sip of his coffee, and I returned to the kitchen and brought back a carafe to refill his cup.

"What are you going to do about your clients?"

"Our clients," I said.

"OK, what are you doing about *our* clients?"

"Trying to gather the information you wanted. It takes a little time to obtain all the records and get the doctor's report."

"Don't get defensive."

"I'm not—"

"You are. Tell me why."

I ran my fingers through my hair and stalked to the window. I hated the way Jake could read me. "I'm frustrated. I can't do anything but wait. Meanwhile, London is scheming ways to get his family back. Patience is not my long suit."

"How well I know. Just don't do anything stupid."

"I don't do stupid."

"You say that to the man who's defending you for a breaking and entering charge? Give me another word for that."

"Rachel needed the combination to London's safe. That's why I went there."

"Did you get it?"

"Yes."

"And you didn't take any money?"

"No, that's against the law. I just grabbed the combination for Rachel and left."

He shook his head "Breaking and entering is against the law. You're turning my hair white." With a final sip of coffee, he stood and walked to the door. "See you tomorrow."

I saw Jake out and returned to the kitchen. My coffee was cold, and I was still worried. My chosen profession got to me some times. I wasn't infallible. And mistakes in this case could hurt two innocent people. I couldn't mess this up.

❧❦

Hebron Courthouse

I arrived for my hearing on time, wearing an innocent smile and my best suit. Jake joined me outside the courtroom and we entered together. Even with Jake's confident smile, nerves gnawed a hole in my stomach lining like rats at a block of Limburger.

Assistant D.A. Walker Maddox, and a lackey I didn't know, represented the people. This would be an informal hearing, just the judge, D.A., bailiff, and court reporter.

Since Judge Burns was a visiting judge, he didn't have chambers in the building so we used the courtroom.

The spectator seats were empty. London was nowhere in sight. Must have decided not to grace us with his presence

A door behind the bench swung open, and the bailiff stood at attention as Judge Josiah P. Burns took his seat at the bench. "Take a seat, gentlemen, and we'll get underway."

The judge reminded me of my Boy Scout troop leader when I was ten. Tall, dark skinned, with closed chopped gray hair—regal in his creaseless black robe and no-nonsense attitude.

Judge Burns shot a look at both Jake and Maddox. "If you're ready, let's get started."

Maddox nodded and passed a single sheet of paper to the judge, and then handed a copy to Jake. "Your Honor, on Monday morning, December twelfth, Crown Heights patrol officers stopped Mr. Adams three blocks from Judge London's residence after someone breached his security system. We have the security disk from the judge's home, which clearly shows Mr. Adams inside the premises. We believe Mr.

Adams entered with the express purpose of burglarizing the estate but was frightened away before anything could be taken." Maddox paused as if waiting for applause. Judge Burns gave him an impatient wave to proceed.

The D.A. sucked in a quick breath. "We further believe Mr. Adams has a personal vendetta against Judge London. On Friday, December ninth, Mr. Adams placed a 9-1-1 call claiming he heard a child screaming in the judge's residence. The call resulted in the arrest of Judge London for child abuse. The charges were dropped that same night."

Judge Burns held out his hand. "Do you have the CD?"

"Yes, Your Honor." Maddox handed the disk over to the bailiff who opened a door at the back of the court and pushed a large television to the right of the judge's bench. He switched on the television, inserted the CD into the player, and punched play.

An urge to chew my nails overwhelmed me as I waited to see what the tape might reveal. Would I have to explain a sudden transporter room appearance and wait for the white jackets to show up? Jake had said the recording posed no problem, but I wasn't convinced.

The set buzzed, flickered, displayed thirty seconds of London's living room, and then a very fuzzy shot of me on the plasma screen. The time and date reflected in the right-hand corner.

I exhaled a shaky breath. It could have been much worse.

Maddox looked at Judge Burns and then me. "As you can see, Your Honor, the video irrefutably places Mr. Adams inside Judge London's home on that date."

Maddox turned to the clerk and pointed at the TV.

"You can turn that off." Maddox sat down behind the prosecution table.

The judge turned to Jake. "You ready to present your client's version of these events, Counselor?"

The clerk reached over to shut off the TV.

Jake raised his hand. "No. Leave it on."

He addressed the judge. "We move the charges be dismissed, Your Honor, due to lack of evidence. My client categorically denies these allegations, beginning with the security breach itself." Jake passed the judge and Maddox a sheet of paper. "This is a written statement from Arrow Incorporated, the security firm that covers Judge London's household and others in that area. In the past month there have been twelve unexplained false alarms in the Crown Heights community."

Judge Burns directed his question to Maddox. "Is this true?"

Maddox flushed. "I'll have to take Mr. Stein's word, Your Honor. We had no reason to question the validity of the alarm system since we had a picture of Mr. Adams inside the residence."

Jake continued. "Now as to the surveillance data, you will note, Your Honor, that everything in the room is crystal clear, the painting, the sofa, the Christmas tree, the fireplace—"

Judge Burns raised his hand. "We get your point, Mr. Stein. Get on with it."

"—except the one of Mr. Adams. You will notice that it is hazy compared to the rest of the film. Even more importantly, there are two cameras in that room, each of which takes random shots every fifteen seconds. Yet...the recording has only one shot of Mr. Adams, and it's on the TV screen. Why didn't the cameras get at least one image of my client entering the room? With two units, snapshots were taken less than every fifteen seconds."

The judge lifted an eyebrow. "Can you explain that, Mr. Maddox?"

Maddox shrugged. "Perhaps he was moving very fast."

Jake snorted. "Superman doesn't move that fast."

Jake had stuck in the knife; now he twisted the blade. "How my client's picture got inside Judge London's home, I can't say. The only reasonable explanation would appear to be that the CD has been tampered with."

Maddox sputtered to his feet. "We checked that. The recording was clean."

Jake passed another document to Judge Burns and Maddox. "According to the police report, my client's fingerprints were nowhere on the premises, and in the picture on the TV screen my client isn't wearing gloves. Your Honor, nothing was missing, and there were no signs of forced entry. In other words, Mr. Adams would have to have been invisible and floated through brick walls, leaving behind one picture of himself for posterity."

Seized with a sudden urge to laugh, I popped a cough drop in my mouth. Jake thought he was being funny, but I almost choked.

Judge Burns frowned. "We can do without the sarcasm, Counselor." He turned to Maddox. "Do you have an explanation for these anomalies?"

Maddox's confident expression slipped from his face. He blushed like a teenager on his first date and shook his head.

Jake turned his gaze to Maddox. "Again, Your

Honor, I respectfully request that all charges against my client be dismissed."

The judge's eyes narrowed, and he shot a hot glare at Maddox. Burns lived up to his reputation for having little patience for frivolous cases that wasted his or the city's time. "I have no alternative but to agree with Mr. Stein," Judge Burns said. "Do you wish to withdraw the charges, Mr. Maddox?"

Maddox stood, adjusted his suit jacket and expelled a heavy sigh. "Yes, Your Honor. The D.A.'s office withdraws all charges against Mr. Adams."

Judge Burns turned to me. "Mr. Adams, you're free to go."

Maddox snatched up his paperwork, stuffed the sheets into his briefcase, marched down the aisle, and out the door.

Harry London had slipped in during the proceeding and sat alone in the back row. He glowered at me and then rose and followed Maddox into the corridor.

I waited for Jake to gather his briefcase, and we left the courtroom together. In the hallway outside, I slapped my hand against Jake's in a high-five salute. "You are the man."

He grinned. "And don't you forget it."

My relationship with Jake is more like father/son than attorney/client. He has no children, and I lost my father at a young age. Jake feels it's his duty to keep me out of trouble. I wasn't surprised when he placed a hand on my arm and lowered his voice. "One thing before you go, Adams. I don't ever want to know how you pulled off that little shenanigan with the cameras."

After leaving Jake, I made a pit stop at the restroom. I stepped into the hallway and headed down the corridor to the elevators. Waiting for the next car was a red-faced Harry London, waving his arms and shouting at Walker Maddox. I backed out of sight, scanned the perimeter, went into furtive mode, and joined the group unobserved.

"That was the poorest performance I've ever watched." Harry's lips curled downward. "A first-year law student could have handled it better."

"I told you going in the evidence was too flimsy to get an indictment. Judge Burns looked ready to reprimand me. My office wouldn't have pursued this if you hadn't insisted. I'm not a miracle worker, Harry."

London worked himself into a towering rage, his face red, breathing hard. "I know how your boss feels about me. You didn't even try in there. You let the man who's holding my family captive get away."

"Harry, I did the best I could with the evidence I had, whether you choose to accept that fact or not." Maddox turned and stalked toward the stairwell.

On the drive home, a wreck on the interstate delayed my arrival. Traffic jams in Hebron are rare, and motorists never know how to react. They left their cars and made a social event of the delay. I wasn't in the mood to mingle, so I waited in my car and hid behind the steam on the windows. After a while, the traffic moved, and I pulled onto my street.

In a hurry to remove the suit, I rushed inside and pulled on sweat pants and a sweater, ready to work off the tension. A brisk circuit at the gym would take the stiffness out of my tense muscles.

Retrieving my car keys, I started out the door when the phone rang.

I debated whether or not to answer but then gave in to curiosity. I snatched the phone off the base.

A silky voice sounded in my ear. "Noah, it's McKenna."

She didn't have to tell me. Her voice was a melody that still played in my memory.

6

Hebron, Wyoming

I hadn't spoken to McKenna Thornton in more than two years. "Yes, I recognized your voice. It's been a long time. How are you?" That sounded lame even to my own ears.

"We need to talk. Meet me at the old place in twenty minutes." Guess she was too busy for small talk. She meant the park at the lagoon in the center of Hebron. Guaranteed, there would be no one else there this time of year.

Despite efforts to push it away, the old pain rushed back into my soul like a runaway train.

Four years ago, right after opening Adams Investigations, the district attorney's office hired me to do some investigative work. I arrived at their office early one morning to hand in my final report on a contractor doing business with the city. While I waited for someone to acknowledge my presence, a voice behind me called, "Noah, Noah Adams."

I turned to see McKenna Thornton walking toward me. Her cloud of dark hair stirred with the draft her athletic form created as she crossed the room. The sight made my mouth go dry just as it had in college.

Her luminous gray eyes glowed with pleasure. "Can you hang around until lunch? I'd love to visit with you. We can dis all our old college chums."

"Sure," I said with all the composure I usually had in her presence. "What are you—"

"Doing here?" She ran her arm through mine. "I'm the new star in the D.A.'s starting lineup." She laughed. "Of course there are only three of us. This is my second week."

Lunch turned into dinner, which turned into a daily habit. The summer passed, and the infatuation deepened. After four months, we shifted into another phase. We talked of marriage and a future together. Her intelligence, kindness, and ever-present sense of humor made me overlook the minor flaws of ambition and pride. The relationship progressed without a blip until the Saturday night she invited me to meet her parents.

Wearing a fresh haircut and a new dark suit bought for the occasion, I picked up McKenna at her apartment. On the way to her parents, she chatted about a new libel case the D.A. handed her. Her touch clued me into the importance of this introduction. Meeting her parents was a significant step for her.

Until the moment we drove though the gate, I hadn't realized McKenna's father was *the* Robert Thornton, mayor of our fair city, and the name on the bottom of my list as a future father-in-law. His identity never came up, and McKenna's touch only revealed her love for him. She probably assumed I knew.

Only a guardian angel with a sense of humor would have placed me in that scenario—in love with a woman whose father belonged to the local wing of the mafia.

Mind in turmoil, I drove slowly up the drive toward the mayor's home. Sitting at the end of the winding road stood a three-story mansion paid for with mob blood money.

McKenna also failed to mention this wasn't just a meet-the-family gathering. A full-blown social event was in progress.

Not bothering to ring the bell, McKenna stepped ahead of me and opened the door. She led me through a wide vestibule and down steps into the great room.

"McKenna, Noah, over here." Robert Thornton waved us toward a group near the entrance. He hurried forward, one arm outstretched. Thornton wore an expensive Italian suit, a two hundred dollar tie, and a Florida tan. According to the *Hebron Herald*, he'd just returned from a National Association of Mayors convention in Miami. He pumped my hand and then took my elbow. "I want you to meet some of our guests."

It saddened me that his handshake didn't show a reformed man—quite the contrary. If anything, the corruption ran deeper than at our first meeting two years before.

Thornton maneuvered us around the room like a couple of champion show dogs on parade, placing emphasis on my police and war medals. By the end of the evening, a number of guests promised to send their investigative work my way.

Their offers had one big drawback.

Most of the guys in the room were tight with the mob.

At the party's end, McKenna's mother grabbed a magnum of champagne and motioned us to follow her into the library.

Angie Thornton looked young enough to be McKenna's sister until I gazed into her eyes. They were brittle, cold, and tired. She wore good taste like a beauty queen's banner, as one would expect of the mayor's wife accustomed to a life of privilege.

Angie closed the door and pulled me into a faux hug. At our contact, flashes of a disillusioned life slammed into my psyche, revealing two fatal flaws—arrogance and alcoholism.

I didn't stand a chance with this woman.

She crossed to the bar and took three crystal flutes from the shelf, filled them with champagne, gave one to McKenna, then offered one to me. I declined. With a shrug, she took a long drink and released a breath of satisfaction.

She sat on the arm of a sofa across from us. "Tell me about your family, Noah. Do they live here?"

I took a deep breath. She was checking my pedigree. "I don't have any living relatives. Both of my parents died when I was young, and my grandmother passed away a few years ago."

Angie's hand trembled as she took another long sip of the sparkling liquid. She emptied the flute and leaned against the sofa's back.

"Have you and McKenna known each other for a long time?"

I gazed over at McKenna. Her mother must have already asked her these questions. McKenna gave me a quick glance and shrugged.

"Uh, yes, ma'am. We met at university in a study group. We crammed for exams and helped each other with individual weaknesses."

"I'm aware of what a study group does."

There didn't seem to be an answer to that, so I kept quiet.

"Are you clever, Noah?"

"In what respect?"

Angie waved an impatient hand. "In business, of course. I know about your police accommodations and war medals, but that doesn't necessarily mean you're intelligent." She was doing an excellent job of putting me in my place.

I answered truthfully. "No more, no less than most people, I should think."

"How disappointing. I've always wanted the best for McKenna."

"As do I, ma'am."

"Mother..."McKenna jumped in.

"Wasn't your family involved in a domestic tragedy some years back? I vaguely remember reading something about it in the newspaper." Angie's last question was a doozy.

My jaw clenched. She hadn't read it. She had me investigated.

"I guess you could say that." I didn't intend to satisfy her morbid curiosity.

"Your mother and brother were killed, is that right?"

McKenna gasped and jumped to her feet. "Mother, how could...?"

A gut wrenching pain seized my chest, but I wouldn't let Angie see the hurt. I held up my hand and signaled it was OK.

As we fled the inquisition chamber, I had the distinct feeling I'd flunked the interview. But so had she.

On the drive home, McKenna squeezed my arm. "Sorry about my mother. She means well, but she's overly protective." She rested her head against my shoulder. "I'm so proud of you. Father and his friends were very impressed. Those people can send you more business than you can handle. You'll have to hire a staff to take care of all the extra work. Isn't that exciting?"

I didn't know exactly how to approach the subject. This called for tact I wasn't sure I could muster. "McKenna, do you know that many of your father's guests tonight are crooks? Steve Clark is an east coast mob boss."

"Steve? I've known him for ages. He's totally harmless. Besides, if you want to talk about crooks, most of the CEO's in America are cooking the books these days." She spoke as if a correlation existed between gangsters and corporate crime. CEO's might murder your retirement fund, but they didn't take your life. At least, not literally.

I shook my head. "Some CEO's are crooked, but not most. Some good men are painted with the same broad brush as fraudulent bankers and insurance executives. You have to admit most CEO's don't kill people."

She looked at me and wrinkles formed on her brow. "You're going to have to be realistic. My father handed you a fortune in future business tonight. The least you could do is consider it. You can't afford scruples in the corporate world."

I couldn't hide my disappointment. "How can you say that? You're an assistant D.A."

"Like it or not, it's the truth."

"So in my business life, I'm supposed to park my ethics at the door?"

"That's not what I said, and you know it." She moved away from me and remained silent for the remainder of the ride home. When we reached her apartment, she jumped out and slammed the car door.

So much for my use of tact.

I watched McKenna enter her apartment building, and for a moment, I couldn't breathe for the tightness that filled my chest. I'd let myself believe we could share a life together—denying the burden my gifts placed on a relationship.

Had God determined I had to live a solitary life? Resting my head on the steering wheel, I prayed for strength.

That evening signaled the end of our *almost* engagement. One year later, McKenna married Alexander Clark, Steve Clark's son.

☜☞

Shaking off the past, I pulled into the parking lot at the lagoon. McKenna stood outside her car. She wore a hooded red coat and black boots, a lovely vivid contrast to the park's white setting. I walked over to her and she swung into step beside me.

"Want to talk in the car or outside?"

"Outside," she said.

We strolled to a nearby bench and sat down.

"I came to warn you." McKenna didn't look at me when she spoke, her gaze fixed on the frozen pond. "The district attorney told me to set warrants in motion for you and Rachel London for the kidnapping of Cody London."

I shook my head, numb with disbelief. Harry London didn't just want to continue the abuse of his family. He wanted to destroy me in the process. The state would pull my P.I. license. I took a moment to bring my indignation under control. "When?"

"Right after your meeting in Judge Burn's court

this morning. I called you as soon as the D.A. told me about the warrant." She turned toward me. "I'll delay the process so it takes a few hours for the police to get the papers, but they'll be looking for you soon."

"McKenna—" I didn't know how to say thanks. She'd risked her job to warn me. That meant that in some way she still cared about me. Love? Probably not. Just doing a favor for an old friend she trusted. Knowing I was incapable of kidnapping a child without a good reason.

Soft fingers pressed against my lip. She touched my hand with a quick soft stroke and stood to leave. "You needn't say anything" She took a few paces toward her car and came back. "Judge London is a friend of my father's. Do you know what I'm saying?"

I nodded. "I know."

"Then I don't need to tell you to be careful."

7

Hebron, Wyoming

Police would soon stake out my office and condominium. I needed a place to hide, to think, to plan for whatever else Harry London might throw my way. I stopped at my bank and pulled most of my cash from checking and saving. As I left the bank parking lot, I called Jake and gave him the update.

He shouted a few choice expletives in my ear. "You've got to be kidding me." The line went quiet for a moment. "OK, go to my cabin at the lake. Stay there until I can get a handle on what's happening." He swore again and added, "Let me call the D.A. and see what evidence he has. If it's something we can beat, I'll come to the lake and go with you so you can turn yourself in."

My blood pressure spiked. "Can't do that, Jake. I know where Rachel and Cody are hiding. They'd make me tell, or hold me in jail until Iran embraces Christianity. Turning myself in is not an option. At least not now. You know how things work downtown. Some of those guys would like nothing better than to get me alone in a cell." My special talents could get me out easy enough, but that would add jailbreak to my lengthening rap sheet.

Not good.

Jake exhaled a breath into the phone. "I hear you, kid. Hang out at my cabin until we unravel this mess."

He heaved another sigh. "Having you around certainly keeps my life from getting dull."

❧

Jake Stein's Cabin

Jake's place sat like a travel brochure on the placid shores of Pine Lake. I found the spare key just where he said it would be. No musty cottage here. It would have done an architectural magazine proud. The entryway opened into the great room with a massive corner fireplace. Lush green plants sat in stone urns in a room filled with rich leather furniture that beckoned, soft and inviting. Bookshelves lined the walls, packed with colorful book jackets and art objects.

A large cat, half the size of a mountain lion, lay on the hearth. He eyed me warily with a half-lidded gaze, and then returned to washing his face with one huge paw. Jake warned me about his feline friend. The cat had the run of the place. A caretaker came in to feed him, and a pet door took care of his other needs.

I'm a dog man myself.

A wide staircase led to the second floor where I located the guest suite, equally festooned with comfortable masculine furnishings. My scanty, recently purchased wardrobe looked lonely in the cavernous closet. I hadn't had time to pack.

Before leaving town, I made two stops. To the bank to withdraw all my cash and my office to pick up a few items, including the Armstrong file. I tossed the folder on the bed. The reports from Amos and Lincoln left some unanswered questions. I needed more information on Abigail's ex-husband.

I removed my coat and placed my gun with a laser

sight attachment on the bed beside the file. Even a trainee could hit the target, and I wasn't a novice.

I drew back the floor-to-ceiling drapes to an amazing view. Clear blue water melded into an azure sky, framed by tall, snow-covered cedars. The life of the rich and famous could grow on me.

A dust of white flakes settled on the wraparound deck and boathouse with a cabin cruiser tucked neatly inside. A getaway option if the police discovered my hideout.

Abigail's ex-husband had served time in San Quintin, so a call there would be less expensive, but experience had taught me people give the barest of details on the phone. They tended to be more forthcoming in person. California could hold the secret to Abigail Armstrong's abduction or murder. Risky, yeah. But I couldn't solve the case sitting on my duff at Jake's place.

A knock sounded downstairs, and my heart tried to leap from my chest. The authorities couldn't have found me that fast. Right? I stuffed the Glock back into the shoulder holster, picked up things I knew I'd need if I had to make a dash for it, and tiptoed to the window overlooking the entrance. A peek through the curtains revealed a gray-haired man dressed in a navy blue jumpsuit and heavy jacket.

The caretaker.

My heart resumed its normal activity.

Bounding down the stairs, I opened the door. The old man smiled and held out his hand. "Mr. Stein told me to expect a visitor. I'm Heath. I take care of the place."

I clasped his hand. "Noah Adams. What do I call the cat?"

He chuckled. "Ornery critter won't come no matter what you call him, but his name is Junior."

"Junior, huh? Guess he had to be called something."

"Yeah, he's a big'un all right. Eats like a horse, but Mr. Stein's right fond of him. I'll leave you be. Jest wanted to check in to see if you needed anything."

I shook my head. "I'm fine. Thanks."

With a slight wave of his hand, Heath left to do whatever he did.

I found the kitchen and made some of Jake's French roast. The refrigerator only contained cat food, which wasn't like Jake. Guess he didn't get down here too often. I'd have to do something about that. Heath could point me to the closest grocery store and restaurants. Both of which were in short supply in rural Wyoming.

Coffee in hand, I went into the cavernous den and tried to ignore the hunger pains.

I sipped the hot brew and ran through my options. Rachel and Cody were safe, at least for the moment. With the chaotic situation between the Hebron police and me, this seemed the perfect time to do a thorough search into Abigail Armstrong's past.

But first, I needed to call Rachel. I punched in the Hand-Me-Down number on my new cell phone, and gave Rachel the combination to her husband's safe.

"How did you get it so soon?"

"I've got people."

She laughed. "Sure you do."

"Don't go back to the house without me. I'm going on a short trip, and we'll go when I get back."

"Why? I can go while Harry's at work."

"It wouldn't be safe, Rachel. Just wait for me."

I considered keeping the bad news from her, but she needed to know. "Harry filed kidnapping charges against you and named me as an accomplice. There's a warrant out for both of us."

The line became silent. "H-he can't do that—can he?" She didn't wait for my answer—just burst into tears.

Seconds later Bill picked up the receiver. "What's happened?"

I explained the problem. "According to my attorney, what London did is legal. The only way to fight this is to take him to court. To do that we need proof he abused Rachel and Cody. Have Rachel contact the doctors Cody visited in the past for abuse-related injuries. Get copies mailed to a post office box. Then get the records to Jake Stein." I gave him Jake's number. "I'm flying to San Francisco tomorrow on another case, but I'll stay in touch."

I paused for a moment. "You know this could become a legal issue for you and your mother."

He didn't hesitate. "I know, but neither Mom nor I would put that family out now."

Bill jotted down my cell number and then disconnected.

After hanging up, I called Ted and asked him to look after the pups for a couple of weeks. No problem there.

I set the automatic coffeepot and eyed the cat food. Nope, not that hungry yet. Food could wait. I climbed the stairs wanting a warm bed and a good night's rest. Junior lumbered along the hallway behind me and skittered into the bedroom before I could close the door. For a fat cat, he could move.

Fine.

I ignored him, crawled into bed, and turned out the lights. Just as sleep began to weigh my eyelids, something big, warm, and hairy snuggled in close to my back.

Junior.

"Oh, no, you don't." I snapped the lights on, picked up his overfed body, set him outside the door, and closed it with a bang.

I don't speak cat lingo, but I'm pretty sure that fur ball called me a dirty name.

❧

In the early morning hours, I tumbled out of bed and showered. After dressing, I headed downstairs, my stomach as empty as Uncle Sam's pockets. Police would be looking for my car, so I grabbed a cup of coffee to go in a travel mug and borrowed the Jeep Jake kept at the cabin. I backed his vehicle out from the garage and moved my SUV into its spot.

From the trunk of my car, I retrieved a fake ID and business cards under the name, Sam Spade. I'd chosen the alias one day when business was slow and I'd spent the best part of the morning trying to kill flies with a dart. Google listed a hundred folks in the USA with that moniker, some of which were women, a shortened version of Samantha.

With ID in hand, I punched a button on the garage remote, and the door slid down the rail, concealing my car.

Police would be watching the regional airport in Hebron, so I made the four-hour drive to Salt Lake City's International Airport.

My stomach growled all the way into Utah, where

I finally grabbed breakfast in the airport food court. The flight to San Francisco turned ugly soon after the plane rose into the air. A young mother and infant took the seat across the aisle from me. The minute we left the ground, the baby started to cry. Passengers around me began to throw dirty looks at the mother. Finally, she sucked up her courage and glared back. It wasn't her fault. Babies and air travel aren't compatible. But I could empathize with my fellow travelers.

Matters more important than the baby concerned me. My stress levels reached maximum capacity over the current predicament. I'm not one to feel any situation is hopeless, always aware God bestowed my unusual powers for a purpose. I also believed He led me to people who needed my help. Quite often, however, I felt He overestimated my abilities.

This was one of those times.

Since I'd entered the picture, Rachel's problems had worsened, and the trail to Abigail's killer still lay cold as the dark side of the moon.

Lord, a little divine guidance here would be appreciated.

My flight neared its destination, and a view of the Golden Gate Bridge came through the window. The sight almost made the bad flight worthwhile.

Almost.

I hurried away from the still-crying infant and bypassed the luggage carousel. A rental awaited me at the agency counter.

Maneuvering my way through morning traffic to the outskirts of the city took two hours. Once on the interstate, the trip to the prison took less than an hour.

❧❦

San Quentin Prison, San Quentin, California

San Quentin, built in 1852, still held the title of California's oldest and largest prison. The grounds covered more than four hundred acres. A guard at the entrance pointed me to the reception area, where I gave my name and explained I would like to see the warden.

Inside the prison, another guard glanced at a computer screen. "Is the warden expecting you, Mr. Spade?"

I shook my head.

"I'm sorry, but he doesn't see anyone without an appointment. Would you like to talk to his secretary? She handles all his engagements."

"I'm a private investigator and I need some information on a former inmate. Is there anyone else I can speak to?"

His brow furrowed for a moment. "Let me check something." He held up a finger. "Just a minute." He rolled his chair around, back turned to me, and pings sounded as he punched in an extension number.

Seconds later, he hung up. "The assistant warden will see you."

After a short while, a fierce-looking biker type with a huge "Mom" tattoo on his forearm led me down a long hallway and knocked on a door marked, "John Tyler, Assistant Warden."

From the other side a gruff voice called, "Come on in."

John Tyler hadn't missed any meals lately. In his fifties, stout and balding, he had a hard time fitting his girth into the government-issue chair. I introduced myself and handed him my card. He scanned it and then looked back at me. "That your real name?" He chuckled, making his stomach ripple like waves rolling to shore. "Wasn't that a fictitious character in an old movie?"

"Yeah, Humphrey Bogart, *The Maltese Falcon.* What can I tell you? There are a lot of Sam Spades out there."

Formalities over, Tyler tucked the card in his desk. "Have a seat, Mr. Spade, and tell me what I can do for you."

With the most pleasant expression at my disposal, I explained the reason for coming. "I'm investigating the disappearance of Abigail Marshall Armstrong. Ben Marshall, a former inmate here, was her ex-husband, and it's my understanding he died in a riot some time back. Any information you can give me on the man would be appreciated."

"How far back? More than seven years?"

I nodded.

Tyler jerked his thumb at the computer on the credenza behind his desk. "Files are only stored on our computers for seven years after a death or release." He picked up the phone and asked someone to bring in Marshall's file.

We waited in silence until the biker-trustee walked in and handed Tyler a folder. He flipped through the papers and then slapped the file shut. "You're in luck. I don't need the documents to give you the details on this bird. I was guard captain back then. A meaner piece of humanity never walked God's green earth. The day he died they held a celebration in Hell."

"There's no doubt he died in the riot?"

"None at all. There wasn't much left of him after the fire, but we were able to match some of his fingerprints and his dental records."

"What did they send him up for?"

"He was a two-bit lawyer running a sleazy baby racket using pregnant teens and selling the babies for top dollar. He forced the girls to agree to the adoptions. After a while, enough of the women came forward to get a conviction. The state gave him ten years, and the California Bar jerked his license to practice law. I'm sure he was into other shady deals the state never nailed him for. He was living very high on the hog."

Tyler leaned back in his chair. "Prison turned out to be his element. He ruled the cellblock—terrorized and maimed the other inmates. No one mourned his passing."

"You couldn't stop the abuse?"

Tyler shook his head as if agitated by the memory. "Nobody would file a complaint. Without a viable witness, our hands were tied. The convicts knew what would happen if they squealed on him. The prisoners called Marshall and his three cronies the Four Horsemen, with good reason."

"What happened to Marshall's buddies? Are they still here?"

"Two were killed here and one escaped during the riot, Ralph Jenson. We never caught him."

"Marshall's ex-wife, Abigail, disappeared three years ago. Off the record, do you think Jenson could be responsible?"

"I wouldn't put anything past that guy." Tyler removed his glasses. He pinched the bridge of his nose with his forefinger and thumb. "I heard she divorced Marshall soon after he arrived here. He went on a rampage when he got the news. That might have been enough reason for Jenson to kidnap or kill her—to avenge his pal. Convicts have a warped sense of loyalty. But I'm surprised it took him so long."

"She moved to another state under a different name. Do you have a picture of Jenson?"

"Yeah, but it's an old one." He picked up the phone again. Minutes later, the trustee returned with the picture. Jenson's eyes in the mug shot were wild, crazy, and mean.

I thanked him, shook his hand, and returned to my car.

Driving away, I considered Jensen as Abigail Armstrong's murderer. It seemed a plausible lead. Had he really waited so long to kill her? Had it been an accident he'd found her that night, or had he searched for her? I doubted convict loyalty lasted so long, but I couldn't eliminate the possibility.

Before crossing the prison property line my cell phone jingled *The Star Spangled Banner*.

I'm a patriot. Shoot me.

Bill Hand's voice sounded in my ear. "The police arrested Rachel and took Cody. She's in the Hebron County jail."

8

San Quentin Prison, San Quentin, California

My worst case scenario had just happened. "Bill, where did they take Cody?"

Bill moaned. "They turned him over to his father. After you gave Rachel the safe combination, she wanted to get the money to repay Mom. We've told Rachel a thousand times we're providing Christian charity, but she's too independent to accept it. I let Rachel talk me into letting her borrow my truck. Cody begged to go with her, and she caved. It's my fault. I should have known better." Bill paused for a moment. "She used her one call to phone me. She opened the safe without any problems, but as she and Cody drove away, a squad car pulled her over. They were watching for her to come back."

"Did anyone get your name or ask where you live?"

"I gave my name, but they didn't seem overly concerned when I told them I was Rachel's pastor. They didn't ask for my address. They just seem pleased with themselves for having nabbed her." His voice choked. "Mom and I drove to the police station as fast as we could. She took my truck from the pound and drove it home. After they let me see Rachel, she became hysterical, knowing Harry had Cody. She stashed the money in Cody's backpack before the cops ordered her out of the vehicle. I stayed with Rachel until they made me leave."

I shifted the phone to my other ear. "They wouldn't let you post bail?"

"The judge refused to set bail."

"Did you call Jake? Couldn't he do anything?"

"I spoke to Jake after I'd talked to Rachel. He came down, but the judge still refused to consider bail. Jake said London is pulling strings to keep her there." The tone of Bill's voice turned harsh. "According to Jake, they can hold Rachel until the case comes to trial."

I glanced at my watch. "I'm on my way to the airport now. I'll get the first flight to Salt Lake. A friend owns a private plane, and I'll ask him to pick me up. I'll check on Rachel and then see what I can do about Cody."

"Won't that be dangerous since there's a warrant out on you, as well?"

"Don't worry. I'll be able to get in to see Rachel for a few minutes."

I couldn't tell Bill I didn't need help to get into the jail.

෯෨෧

Salt Lake City Airport, Utah

George Thomas waited for me on a spot near the runway when my flight landed in Salt Lake. He stood by his plane and tugged his ball cap lower over his brow. His skin was the color of rich, brown coffee beans, his eyes black as the tarmac. A wide grin, filled with gleaming white teeth, greeted me. "Hop in." George is a man of few words.

His sidekick, Too-Cute, better known as Tooie, jumped into the backseat when I climbed aboard.

George rescued Tooie, an ugly mixture of Boxer and Pit-Bull, after seeing him on an animal cruelty report on the local news. The mutt had logged more air miles than Charles Lindbergh.

We landed in Hebron thirty minutes later, and George drove me to a car rental agency. Jake's wheels still resided in long-term parking in Utah. I picked an inconspicuous Honda Civic, using George's credit card. He knew I'd be good for it.

My cash flow was dwindling fast after my flight to California, and I couldn't use my own credit cards.

On the way to the county jail, I took a chance and swung by my office to pick up a camcorder. If things went bad, it might be useful. Before I closed the office door, I touched the framed, printed slogan on the wall—Plan ahead. Pray ahead. A personal maxim that guided my life.

At least the pray-ahead part.

ॐॐ

Hebron County Jail, Hebron, Wyoming
Urgency squeezed my gut as I pulled into the empty slot at the county jail. Invisible, I hurried to the third floor ward.

The entry to the women's cells was long and rectangular, with the usual gray cement walls. Jessie Bolton sat at the guard desk on my left at the narrow end of the room. A coffeemaker and small refrigerator resided on a built-in counter behind the security station.

Inside the cellblock, I spotted Rachel in a corner four-bunk cell. On a lower bunk, a dirty, homeless woman lay asleep. Rachel huddled on the opposite bed, arms wrapped around her body, her eyes red and swollen. For the moment, she appeared OK. Relieved, I headed back to the exit, just as the block door clanged open. Jessie let Harry London inside. He strode down the aisle and stopped in front of Rachel. Jessie lingered near the cell entrance.

I stopped and waited.

Harry stationed himself in front of the unit, arms folded across his chest. "You look well, Rachel. Bars become you."

Rachel's chin went up. "I'm very well. Better than I've been since I met you, despite my new housing accommodations. I don't have to worry about my husband using me for a punching bag."

"We'll see how well you are after a few months in here with the cream of society. I can smell your roommate from here."

"I prefer her company to yours. At least she doesn't beat helpless children. Where's Cody?"

Harry's face turned apoplectic. "Safe at home with a sitter. You're very brave with the bars between us, aren't you?" His jaw clenched. "People have been known to die in jail. Did you know that? I can have people put in here that'll make your worst nightmares come true."

"You're my worst nightmare, Harry. And if you touch Cody again, I'll kill you."

His teeth bared in a faux smile. "How will you kill me, Rachel? I have the power to delay the trial however long I want, and you know it. You'll be here until I decide to let you go. Taking the money was a foolish risk. The police found it in Cody's book bag. It wouldn't have helped you, anyway. You can't run from me."

Rachel jumped to her feet, her body rigid. "Why don't you leave us alone? What is it with you, Harry, possessiveness, domination, what? You know I don't love you, and your son thinks you're Satan incarnate."

He looked down at his hands and back at Rachel, his voice soft. "Believe it or not, I need you. I've always needed someone who belongs to me."

"People don't belong to people, Harry. And you can save the pity act. Remember me; I've heard it all before." She turned her back on him.

Harry's body trembled with fury. For a moment, it looked as if he would try to get to her through the bars, but he saw Jessie watching. Red-faced, he whirled and stomped away.

What kind of childhood molded a man like Harry London? For some reason, I believed Harry did need his wife and son. He treated them miserably, but somewhere deep in his disturbed mind, he probably felt a need even he couldn't explain.

Whatever it was, I didn't have the answer and didn't care.

Harry alone was responsible for his actions, regardless of his childhood.

One thing I did know. I had to get Rachel out of jail before her husband carried out his threats.

During my short tenure on the Hebron Police Force, I'd seen ordinary citizens placed in custody for twenty-four hours and come out dead or scarred for life.

That would not happen to Rachel. I'd made her a promise not to let him hurt either of them again. A promise I intended to keep. At the moment, I just didn't know how.

Rescuing Rachel had just moved to the top of my

priority list. But first, I had to check on Cody.

∂∕∽

Harry London's Home

Praying the Crown Heights' twins were off duty or taking a long coffee break, I parked two blocks down from the London residence. As I exited from my car, my phone rang. I recognized the number.

"Noah, it's Jessie. We have a problem."

"What's that, Jess?"

"Rachel London is in one of my cells. Patrol just picked up two women high on meth and said they been instructed to put them in when Rachel."

That was fast work, even for Harry London.

"I know these women, Noah. They're bad news. Rachel wouldn't stand a chance with both of them."

"Can you help?"

"That's why I called." She paused for a moment. "I can't stand by and watch this. I have a plan. It's risky, but I think I can pull it off. Meet me at the back of the jail at seven thirty after the shift change. I'll bring Rachel to you. Once you have her, there won't be much time. You'll have to find a place to hide."

"Are you sure, Jess…?"

"I'm sure." She hung up.

Thank God for the Jessies of this world. That would solve my immediate problem. I could get Cody, and then pick up Rachel. Keeping them out of sight was my next problem.

Invisible, with a new sense of urgency, I hurried along the alleyway and went inside London's home. A woman who could moonlight as a female Sumo wrestler lounged in a recliner with the television blaring, a six-pack of diet soda, and a bag of potato chips at her side. The sitter, sitting.

I scrutinized the area more closely this time. My rescue might depend on knowing where all the exits were. The master suite lay on the opposite side of the house from Cody. I ducked in, snatched one of Rachel's hooded sweat suits from her closet, and stuffed it inside my jacket. Rachel would need to ditch the orange jumpsuit when she left the jail cell. Next, I went to find Cody.

The open area outside his room was unoccupied. I checked his door. Locked from the outside—key most likely in the dragon lady's pocket.

Mouth pressed close to the door, I whispered, "Cody, it's Noah Adams. Are you all right?"

A muffled cry came through the keyhole, a mixture of joy and fear. "Noah! Are you going to take me to my mom?"

"Shhhh." We couldn't afford to disturb the keeper of the castle. "I'll come around to your window. When you see me, open the transom and come out on the ledge. Jump and I'll catch you. OK?"

"Y-yes." His voice trembled. "I'm scared. Is Mom...?"

"She's fine, Cody. When I get you out of here, I'll liberate your mom."

The whine of a garage door opener echoed up the stairwell, followed by the sound of a car pulling into the garage.

My mouth went dry. Still in stealth mode, I wended my way to the back entry. Ryan and Duncan swung in behind Harry's Beemer.

I hovered behind Harry as the three men gathered beside the patrol car.

Harry leaned against the cruiser's door. "Keep a close eye on my home. I expect Adams to try something. If anything happens to my son, I'll hold you both responsible."

The two officers looked at each other.

I hurried back to Cody.

I inserted a quiet sense of urgency into my voice. "Cody, your dad's home. I can't get you out now, but I'll be back. I promise. Try to be brave. I'll return for you just as soon as I can."

"Don't leave me!" Cody's muted sobs came through the door.

Taking him while the Irish twins and Harry were around would put him in danger. I couldn't risk it. I felt like crap. Worse than crap. Cody needed me, depended on me, and I was walking away. The fact I was helpless didn't make me feel any better. I cared more about that kid than I wanted to. Getting involved personally with a client wasn't smart. But then I'd never claimed to be a genius.

Cody was terrified of his father, with good cause. I didn't think London would dare harm him now. The court would be keeping an eye on him since the recent charge of abuse.

As I pulled away from Crown Heights, my phone rang. It was Jessie.

❧❧

Hebron County Jail, Hebron, Wyoming

Mad at the world, I returned to the jail twenty minutes before my meeting with Jessie, and I scouted the area for a hiding place. With five minutes to spare, I scurried to the parking lot behind the building.

At seven thirty sharp, the back door open and Jess pushed Rachel outside. She was wearing Jessie's coat.

"Jess," I whispered.

"Not now, Noah. Get out of here."

Time wasn't on our side. I didn't know Jess' plan, but as soon as they discover Rachel was missing, the hunt would be on and the street would swarm with cops.

Part of my master plan included the use of an office building nearby. We could wait there until morning. I'd parked the Honda in the tower garage. We hurried down the sidewalk, and I threw a glance down Main Street. We had a two-block walk in plain sight to our destination. No cops yet.

The mist of falling snow dimmed the street lamps outside as Rachel and I sauntered to our sanctuary. Red bows and silver tinsel festooned the streetlights and lamp poles. In all the excitement, I'd forgotten there were only seven days until Christmas.

ॐ

Unitas Office Building

We proceeded from the cold into the lobby, then into the elevators. I jimmied the door of an office on the fourth level, a skill I picked up in my brief career as a cop. Once inside, we sat on the floor of a cubicle at the back of the room and waited for the adrenalin rush to pass.

I handed her the jogging suit. "Put this on in the ladies room over there." I pointed over my shoulder.

When she returned, we used the padded walls of the partition as a backrest, and settled in for the long wait for dawn. Rachel drew up her legs and rested her arms on her knees. Her face flushed with fear and excitement. She leaned toward me, a quiver in her voice. "Have you checked on Cody? Is he OK?"

"Cody's fine. I looked in on him. He's scared, but he's OK for the moment." I squeezed her hand. "I'll get Cody out once you're safe. Harry will be under close scrutiny by the juvenile authorities. He knows the court will have Cody examined before a hearing. He won't run the risk of abuse, not until the custody issue is settled." I shifted my position to watch her face. "We do have a problem. The police will notify Harry of your escape and suggest he move Cody. It may take me a while to find him."

She gave a wry smile. "You don't know Harry. He thinks he's invincible. He'll use Cody as bait to trap you. You'll have to be very careful. Harry's capable of murder."

"Don't worry about me." I grinned. "These hands are lethal weapons."

"Something tells me you might not be kidding."

Time for a change of subject. "We'll have to make ourselves comfortable here for the night. The search should spread outside the city by morning." I handed her a plastic-wrapped pack of cheese crackers with peanut butter. "This is dinner. Sorry. But the Shop-In-Grab-It didn't have *Chateaubriand* to go."

She chuckled. "What, no champagne either?"

"Nope, not even a soda. My pockets were full. But there's water in the cooler in the corner."

I sought Rachel's gaze in the dim lighting. "If we get out of this, I'll ask George to fly you to the ranch tomorrow."

"I'm scared. Visions of a life sentence keep flashing before my eyes."

I touched her arm. "They don't give you life for taking your own son. Don't be frightened. I said a prayer—I have connections in high places. We'll work through this. I had to get you out. Harry could harm you inside the jail. If you die, he automatically gets custody of Cody. We should be safe here until morning."

I studied her face. "How did you get mixed up with a guy like Harry London?" I already knew most of it.

She sighed and shrugged. "You wouldn't believe how many times I've asked myself that question. As I told you, I'm an orphan, one of the kids who was never adopted. When I turned eighteen, my grades earned me a scholarship at a small college nearby. After graduation, I came to Hebron and went to work in the courthouse. That's where I met Harry." She leaned back against the padded wall. "He was handsome and wealthy. All the girls in the office vied for his attention. For some reason, he chose me. The men I'd dated before had been about as deep as a salad plate. Harry made me feel special. No one had ever made me feel that way. Lucky me. At least, I thought so back then."

Her eyes fixed above my head. "He seemed to embody all I'd ever wanted in a husband. I suppose I wanted a father figure, and he was fifteen years older. When he asked me to marry him, I couldn't believe my good fortune. But the ecstasy lasted less than a week after the wedding. He became abusive right away— fractured my wrist two weeks later, and I soon found myself pregnant with no place to go." She shook her head. "Looking back, I realized there were signs of his dominant nature before we married—things I chose to ignore. He selected where we went, what we ate, and even made suggestions on how I should dress. I'd become accustomed to people at the orphanage controlling my life. His arrogance didn't register until it was too late."

"Were you aware he had surveillance cameras inside your home?"

Her mouth opened in a tiny gasp. "That's how he always knew when I planned to leave. I didn't think even Harry would stoop that low." She looked down at her hands. "There's something I haven't told you. My father shot my mother and then committed suicide. He was mentally ill. Harry insisted the courts would never give me custody of Cody with insanity in my family, and like an idiot, I was too frightened to take the chance."

"Your father's mental illness has no bearing on you or your ability to raise your son." I handed her my cell phone. "Call Bill. Tell him you're OK, and you'll be home tomorrow. Don't tell him where you are. If anyone asks, he won't have to lie."

She made the call and returned the phone. "Noah, helping me escape will get you into so much trouble and that poor guard. Why did she help me?" Tears pooled in her eyes, making them glisten in the semi-darkness.

"I was already in trouble, remember? Besides, they may not know I'm involved. As for Jessie, she had a husband like Harry."

She shook her head. "I don't understand why you've gone out of your way—put your life in jeopardy—to help Cody and me."

"Because I don't like bullies who beat up pretty ladies and little boys."

"Oh, Noah." Rachel moved closer to me and hid

her face against my chest.

Sudden sounds caught my attention. A murmur of voices moved in our direction.

I planted my hands on her shoulders and pushed her away. "Someone's coming."

9

Unitas Office Building

Motion suspended for a split-second. Placing a finger to my lips, I signaled Rachel to get under the desk. Her face drained of color, her eyes went wide with fear. I leaned close to her ear and spit out a fierce whisper, "Stay put. I'll be back."

Once out of sight and in furtive mode, I scurried into the small lobby outside the office.

A mass of human activity filled the halls. The manhunt had expanded to the tower's fourth floor. Mentally, I reviewed search protocol from police academy lectures. Within minutes, they would seal off the exits and move in—tighten the circle little by little, until there was no place to hide.

The Christmas lights on the tree in the corner chastised me. In the season of peace and goodwill, I was on the run for charges of kidnapping and had just committed a jailbreak. For a man who believed in the rule of law, I had broken more than my share tonight.

Cops entered each office and hastened down the corridor toward me—guns drawn. The elevator dinged and regurgitated two more uniforms into the melee. Within minutes, they would reach the office where Rachel was hiding. Our trackers moved fast, too fast, down the hallway toward me. Panicked, I searched the area for an escape route. Around the corner, I spied a door below a red fire exit sign—with a crash bar.

Thank You, Jesus.

I hit the bar like a bull through a rodeo gate. The impact set off the alarm above my head, threatening deafness. The angry blasts drove me back into the lobby toward the on-rushing horde of blue uniforms.

I hugged the wall as police trampled past in pursuit like a gaggle of angry geese.

Someone shouted, "She's headed for the stairs, radio Simmons to post guards at the bottom of the stairwell."

The corridor filled with curses from a burly cop close enough for me to touch. "If she, and whoever helped her escape, gets away, the chief will transfer us out to Fargo, North Dakota."

I was closer to panic than I wanted to admit, even to myself. But too much was riding on this escape to let these guys mess it up.

Still invisible, I bounded down the stairs behind the boys in blue and set off alarms at levels three and two until I reached the ground floor. More curses ensued as they split up and tried to cover everywhere at once.

As ordered, Simmons stood at the door like a Rottweiler on guard duty. I slipped behind him and my fingers found the perfect pressure point on his neck. He slid to the floor unconscious, but otherwise unharmed. A trick I learned from a SEAL I'd shared a hospital room with in Germany. While we'd waited for our bodies to mend, he'd taught me eight ways to kill or incapacitate a Tango—his name for the bad guys—with my bare hands.

Outside, my accommodating friends had left a couple of squad cars parked at an angle near the building and I hurried to the nearest one. Keys were in the ignition.

Too easy, but I wasn't complaining.

While Hebron's finest chased ghosts below the building's fourth floor, I slid into the car seat and fired up the cruiser. Within minutes, they would find Simmons and the search would go outside.

Operating from the seat of my pants was a bad practice. I had to come up with a plan. A good plan. Driving too fast for safety on the snow-covered streets, I plumbed my mind for somewhere to stash the much-too-conspicuous vehicle. I swooped past the park in the center of town. Like a flash, a mental picture of an old abandoned barn, where I played as a kid, came to mind.

Near the city limits, the headlights brought the decaying structure into view past a series of side streets. I pulled across the field, got out, jerked open the rickety doors, and then pulled the cruiser inside. As quickly as my cold fingers would allow, I disconnected the vehicles radio and GPS system, and then made the long trek back to town keeping in the shadows when not invisible.

In stealth mode, I entered the office building and traveled to the fourth floor. As I'd hoped, the area had cleared. The cops were now searching the countryside for the missing black and white.

I sometimes felt bad about the advantage my gifts gave me over pond scum like many of the men on Hebron's police force. But this was not one of those times.

Inside the office and back to normal, I whispered, "Rachel?"

She stuck her head out from under the desk. "Noah, where have you been? I thought...I thought they'd caught you."

I shook my head. "I had to draw them away from you. It was close, but we should be OK until morning."

"What happens in the morning?"

"You go back to the ranch, and I go get Cody."

∂∾∾

Temperature in the building had lowered overnight and the chill had seeped deep into my bones. Around six o'clock the thermostat snapped on spreading welcome warmth and awakened the smell of stale coffee stains in the carpet.

Rachel pulled up the hood on her jumpsuit and slipped on my sunglasses. We went in search of my car, our steps crunching across the snow that had blown into the double-tiered garage.

We entered the Honda in sub-zero temperatures. Shivering uncontrollably, I placed a call to George and told him to meet me at the airport. Soon, the heater pushed warm air upward from the floorboard. I maneuvered through alleys and side streets to the municipal airport where George kept his planes.

Authorities would post Rachel's photo over the media outlets, so driving to the ranch didn't seem a wise move.

I eased my car in close to George's twin engine Cessna with the plane between the control tower and us. George couldn't let them know the plane carried a passenger. I had explained the situation to him on the phone, and he didn't sound happy. He cast a disapproving gaze at me and then back at Rachel, unspoken concern in his eyes.

I shifted uneasily. Involving another friend in my

criminal activities bothered me. But my choices were few. The authorities would have checked the airport last night, so I needed to get her out of there fast before they returned.

"Can you fly Rachel to The Hand Me Down? I'll understand if you want to pass."

With a tug on his ball cap, he paused to consider and then gave me a weary nod. "I'll take her."

He helped Rachel into the backseat. "Stay down until we get into the air. As far as the tower is concerned, I'm flying solo."

Rachel nodded. She turned back to me. "I want to come with you to get Cody."

That wasn't going to happen. "You can't. You'd be a liability. Every cop in town has you on their radar. They don't take kindly to people who make them look foolish. I'll bring Cody to you. I promise."

Her eyes narrowed as she processed what I said. Then she handed me Jess's coat and ducked down behind the pilot's seat. George covered her with a blanket.

Standing beside my car, I watched the plane as it rose into the air. Satisfied Rachel was safely on her way, I started the Honda and switched on the radio. A reporter on a Christian music station compared Rachel's escape to that of Peter's release from prison by an angel of the Lord.

The police didn't like that explanation, although they didn't have a better idea for the daring getaway. The security cameras had failed to pick up any portion of her escape.

The security tape revealed just one visitor to the women's section that night—Harry London. *The Hebron Herald* suggested it had been an inside job, and the police should question Judge London about his wife's break out.

The irony of the situation was perfect.

Next stop, Crown Heights. I had a promise to keep.

৵৽৽

Harry London's Home

The ideal time to pick up the boy would have been while Harry sat in chambers, but a daylight rescue would be too risky. Jake told me he played cards at the club on Friday night with Harry. As I turned onto Cedar Hills Drive, I prayed the poker game was a standing engagement. I scanned the driveway for Harry's car. Nothing—no Crown Heights squad car lurked nearby.

By God's grace, it looked like I'd caught a break.

Invisible, I entered the kitchen and located the lady wrestler on duty. The sitter placed a cheeseburger and chips on a tray. My mouth watered. I'd only one meal in the last twenty-four hours, if I didn't count the package of peanut butter crackers I'd shared with Rachel.

Tray in hand she mounted the stairs with me in her wake. She unlocked the bedroom door, lumbered inside, and placed the meal on Cody's desk.

I caught a quick glimpse of the boy. He watched cartoons from a cross-legged position on the bed—chin in his hands. Sad, but apparently unharmed.

Without acknowledging the boy in any way, the woman turned and left the room. The Amazon locked the door and retreated down the hallway.

I whispered through the keyhole. "Cody, I came

back for you."

Cody placed his mouth close to the lock. "Noah?"

I'd never heard anyone put so much joy into the sound of my name. "Yep, it's me. I'm taking you out of here and to your mom. We'll try the same drill as before. When you see me outside your window, come out on the ledge and jump to me." I lowered my voice. "Be very quiet. We don't want to disturb your sitter. Will she come back to pick up the tray?"

"No, she leaves when Dad gets home." Cody's voice sounded through the keyhole. "She'll clean up the room in the morning."

"Good." They might not miss him until the next day, and we needed as much of a head start as we could get.

The D.A. said there were no cameras outside, and I prayed the situation hadn't changed since I was now flesh and blood. If London had installed an outside security system, this time the D.A. would have proof of kidnapping.

Sounds of an automobile in the alley brought me up short. All the homes in the area had back entrances to the garage. The car stopped and the door closed with a loud *crack*. I couldn't tell which direction the noise came from.

Dear God, not again.

Cody came to the window, unlocked it, and raised the sash. I motioned him back. His eyes widened in panic. I watched as he whirled toward the bedroom door. From my position under the ledge, I couldn't see what happened inside his room. The bedroom door opened, and seconds later, closed again.

I charged around the corner, expecting to see Harry or the twins with guns pointed at my heart.

Instead, chatter from two females next door greeted my ears.

Before this night ended, I would die of fright.

Back to the spot under Cody's ledge, I searched for movement in his room. He wasn't there. I imagined every terrible possibility. Had Harry come home? Had he taken Cody? I checked my watch. Almost ten minutes before I could become invisible again.

Urgent steps brought me to the tree near Cody's window. I struggled up to the limb nearest his bedroom—five feet from the open transom.

I climbed the western river birch to the second level, grabbed a naked branch above my head with both hands and began to swing. The cold, rough bark cut into my palms as I stretched full length and tried to get a foot inside. And missed.

I also missed the next three attempts.

I returned to an upright position on the limb, my hands stinging. Teeth gritted, I tried once again. This time I landed both feet hard inside Cody's room. My leg grazed his dinner tray and it crashed to the floor. My invisibility kicked in just as the door jerked open.

Harry stood in the doorway. "What was that?"

Cody peeked around his father into the room. "My tray fell. Where are you taking me?"

"You're moving down to the end of the hall. I'm planning a surprise for your friend, Mr. Adams, when he shows up."

Cody braced against the wall, his fists clenched like a fighter ready for the bout of his life. "I won't stay here. I'm going to my mom."

Face red, Harry turned toward the boy. "You'll do what I tell you."

"No, I won't!"

Harry swung his right hand at Cody. Before I could reach Harry, something amazing happened. With a fast judo move, Cody stepped forward into the blow, grabbed his father's arm and using Harry's weight as leverage, threw him to the floor. Cody's eyes widened in surprise.

Riding wasn't the only thing Bill Hand taught the boy.

Harry rose from the floor and charged, his face contorted with fury. Cody pushed over a chair in front of his father, blocking the path. In a desperate attempt to avoid Harry's grasp, Cody grabbed trophies and bric-a-brac from the bookcases, hurled them at Harry, and made a frantic dash for the stairway.

As Cody rounded the curve in the flight of steps, Harry rushed toward the landing in pursuit. I stuck out an invisible arm and close-lined Harry, catching him solid across the throat. He went down like the Berlin Wall. He rose to his knees, slowly, one hand on his throat, the other feeling the air, face immobile, mouth open. I reached behind him, snatched a vase from the floor, and banged it hard against his skull, hard enough to keep him off our trail for a while.

I promised myself someday soon, very soon, Harry London and I would meet one on one. Then I wouldn't hide behind my invisibility, and he couldn't hide behind his cowardice.

For the present, we had to get out of Dodge before someone else showed up. Outside and normal again, I rushed to find Cody. He slammed into me as I rounded the corner near his window. With a soft yelp, he staggered back and almost lost his footing.

I reached to steady him. "It's OK. It's me."

Cody leaned against me, trembling. "D-Dad . . .?"

"He won't bother us for now."

Adrenalin pumping, Cody and I headed west toward the Hand Me Down and to his mother. We made one stop on the way for dinner to go.

⧫

Hand Me Down Ranch

The reunion at the ranch played like a Walt Disney movie. I swallowed the boulder lodged in my throat as mother and son cried and clung to each other.

Over Cody's shoulder, Rachel mouthed, "Thank you," tears streaming down her face.

Cody released his mother and swiveled to face Bill. Excited, the boy danced from foot to foot like a prizefighter, his face bright and animated. "I used the trick you showed me, Bill. I threw my dad on the floor." Cody plopped down on the sofa and exhaled. "I couldn't believe I did it."

Bill tousled the boy's hair. "Good for you, Champ. Did you remember the most important part where you're supposed to run for your life when your opponent is down?"

He nodded. "Just like you told me."

Bill's voice grew husky. "You have more courage than many grown men I know."

Cody had blossomed under Bill's gentle tutelage—learning not all men were like his father.

I gave Emma and Bill a wave and then slipped away.

On the drive back to Hebron, I flipped open my cell phone and called Jessie at home. She answered on the first ring.

"Are you OK?" I asked.

"Yeah. I'm good so far. I drugged the coffee, and it left me with a sleep hangover."

"How did you get around the security tape?"

"I worked in editing at the TV station in Cheyenne before I moved to Hebron. I spliced out the incriminating parts. They can tell it's been tampered with, but they can't prove it was me. I'm leaving in six months anyway. Taking the boys to Florida. They'll like it there."

"I have your coat. I'll give it to Amos. I don't know how I can repay you, Jess."

"You already did. You put my husband in jail. That saved my life."

10

Hebron, Wyoming

As I drove back to Hebron, the gravity of Rachel's situation weighted on me. I had no idea where this case was going. London held all the cards. His family had evaded his grasp this time, but there were no guarantees about the next confrontation.

When I reached Jake's cabin I sat in the Jeep and closed my eyes. No bright flash of light occurred with the answer. I started the vehicle and drove back into the city.

After doing some shopping, I called George. "I need a ride to the ranch, you free?"

He chuckled. "You got money?"

Wearing my everyman outfit, baseball cap and down jacket, I arrived at the airport to meet George. He led me to his latest acquisition, a Velocity XL RG. A sleek white jet with four seats, and two doors that opened from the bottom like an extra pair of wings.

I whistled my appreciation. "Wow, when did you get this?"

He ran his hand along the aircraft's smooth sides. "It arrived this morning. I have a few special clients I fly on business trips. Think this'll impress 'em?"

"It impresses me."

George climbed into the cockpit, his face that of a child who just received the latest electronic gadget for Christmas. He waved me aboard. "Want to try it out?"

"You bet." I hopped in beside him. "I didn't expect a classy ride this morning."

George eased the sleek bird into the sky, and we flew west as the sun broke behind snow-covered mountains. The V-XL sliced through the strong headwinds like snow skis on a downhill run. He only charged me for the flight fuel, which I could barely afford with the rising fuel costs even with the Armstrong money coming in. But I couldn't risk driving to the ranch again. I kept an eye out for a tail. Hadn't spotted one, but I wasn't infallible.

When we'd been in the air a few minutes, George turned his dark gaze my way. "You in trouble, Noah?"

I hedged. "Not doing anything immoral."

He nodded and fixed his gaze on the instrument panel. "Maybe not immoral, but how about illegal?"

I adjusted my sunglasses and stared out the window. "Sometimes, George, things that are legal are immoral. Take abortion, for instance. That's as immoral as it gets, and it's legal."

He grunted. "Just cover your backside, my friend. You can't save the world."

No, but I could try.

As the plane banked for landing, light rays bounced off cotton clouds below. We descended through the white mist, and the ranch house came into view, a tiny dot in the valley's landscape. George set the bird down on the blacktop road leading to the ranch house.

The plane taxied to a stop, and Bill met me when I stepped to the ground. I introduced him to George.

Bill shook George's hand. "Come on back to the house. I'll fix you guys some breakfast."

Bill eased into step beside me "I have to check on

the sheep herders in the mountains today. They'll be running low on supplies about now. Want to come along? I need to talk to you."

Bill and his mother had put their lives in jeopardy to help Rachel and her son. It seemed only fair to give Bill a half day of my time. "I'll be glad to if you'll loan me some warm gear. I'm not dressed for a ride in the mountains."

He nodded. "I can do that. We'll leave after breakfast."

We entered the kitchen and Rachel emerged from the den. Her eyes twinkled with pleasure as she crossed the room and wrapped her arms around my chest with a tight lingering squeeze.

I looked down at her. "You doing OK?"

She shrugged. "As well as can be expected for a fugitive from justice."

She gave George a hug. "Thanks again for yesterday."

Over breakfast, Bill told Emma about our trek to the sheep camp. "We should be back before supper."

Cody's spoon stopped halfway to his mouth. He wiggled like he had ants in his pants. "Can I go, Bill, please?"

Bill shook his head. "Not this time, champ."

Cody lowered his gaze, his mouth turned down at the corners.

Bill lifted Cody onto his lap. "You know I'd take you if I figured it would be safe. But you're not a good enough rider yet for such a long trip. I'll take you hunting when we get back. OK?"

Cody's eyes focused on Bill, shining with admiration. He wiped away an escaping tear with the back of his hand. "Really? Will you really let me hunt with you?"

"You bet. I promise. As soon as I get back, we'll go track down a moose. If Noah's good, we might even let him tag along."

I shook my head. "Over my dead body. I have a pact with the wild animals. I don't bother them, and they don't bother me."

Bill turned to George. "What kind of plane is that? I've never seen one like it."

And George was off on his favorite subject.

After breakfast ended, I handed Rachel a shopping bag I'd brought with me. "I purchased some things for you in Hebron. See what you think."

She took the sack, and a smile of anticipation touched her face. One by one, she removed brown contacts, hair color, fake eyeglasses and a blue dress.

"Hopefully, the disguise will help when you visit the doctor."

She replaced the items in the bag and turned to leave. "Thanks, Noah."

Bill found some thermal clothing for me. We stuffed our gear into saddlebags and set them beside the door in the den, reluctant to leave the warmth for the cold ride ahead.

Bill picked up the fire poker and shifted the logs in the hearth. "Anything new with London?"

I shook my head. "Nothing. Have you gotten back all the doctor's reports?"

"We have Dr. McCall's report and X-rays back. He's the local doctor at the clinic here." Bill said. "Doc Moore is semi-retired. He's been our family doctor all my life. I explained Cody's situation." Bill placed a booted foot on the hearth. "He agreed to testify if we need him. The X-rays prove ongoing mistreatment—

six broken bones in a child Cody's age aren't normal. Unfortunately, the films don't prove who's responsible. I'll take Rachel as soon as the doc can see her."

"You've done a good job, Bill. But I'm beginning to regret pulling you and Emma into this mess. Things could get worse before this is over. You could both be in serious trouble for harboring fugitives if the sheriff shows up."

Bill's mouth formed a grim line. "We wouldn't have it any other way. If decent people don't stand up for what's right, the Harry Londons of this world win. Before I let him get his hands on this family again, I'll send them to a mission camp in Mexico. London couldn't find them there." Bill punched his hands into his pockets. "What can I do? Waiting around for London to pounce drives me crazy."

"Waiting is always the hardest part. Try to reassure Rachel as often as you can. Keep her spirits up. I've had to play this as I go. Jake Stein tells me there's nothing he can do with the kidnapping and jailbreak charges, at least, not until we can prove Harry abused Cody. When we have proof, hopefully Jake can work a legal miracle."

I'd lost the advantage of sending the cell phone with Howie. London now knew Rachel hadn't left the state.

Bill poked the log again, sending sparks up the chimney. "I don't do patience well."

The rustle of fabric attracted our attention, and Bill and I spun toward the sound.

Rachel, framed in the doorway, wore the blue dress with small white flowers and a white collar. Tortoise-shell eyeglasses perched on her nose, her hair now a dark auburn. Nothing could hide her beauty, but the change was miraculous.

"Well?" Rachel said.

I surveyed her appearance. "I don't think even Harry would recognize you in that getup."

She turned to me with an impish grin. "Remind me never to let you shop for my clothes. No woman I know would come near this dress."

"I never claimed to be a fashion expert. That's the kind of thing my grandmother wore."

She nodded. "Exactly."

I got the picture and changed the subject. "Where did Cody run to?"

Bill paused, his gaze lingering on Rachel. "Uh...I think he's in the barn with a new foal born yesterday. He carries on like he's the mother."

The door slammed and Cody rushed in, cheeks bright red from the cold. He did a double take at his mother's new look.

Rachel twirled around. "Well, what do you think?"

Cody shrugged. "I liked you better the old way."

She laughed. "So do I, but extreme situations call for extreme measures."

He reached and grabbed my hand. "You wanna come see the new foal? Did you see the Christmas tree?"

"I can only answer one question at a time. I would love to see the new baby, but not now. Bill and I have to leave. And yes, I saw the tree through the window when I drove in."

Cody dragged me into the living room. "Bill and I chopped it down in the forest all by ourselves!"

The eight-foot tree sparkled in front of the picture

window, decorated with traditional red and gold ornaments.

"Isn't it beautiful?" He gazed at the tree. "It's much prettier than the one we had at home." He let go of my hand. "Do you think Mom's happy here? I sure hope so. This is the best place I've ever lived."

"Your mother has a lot on her mind right now, Cody. But I know she likes living here as much as you do. She told me so."

"Good, because I want to stay here always." His small jaw clenched. "I'm never going back to my dad...not ever."

❧

The Unitas Mountains

Two words described the ride to the sheep station: long and cold. The temperature dropped incrementally as we climbed upward into the shadow of the mountains. The land belonged to the state Bureau of Land Management, leased to Hand ancestors for almost a century—handed down from father to son.

Shouts of welcome greeted us as Bill and I rode into the small valley. Amazed, I watched as three hundred or more sheep swept over the hill—rolling waves of white wool undulating down the mountainside. Two herders in their midst led the sheep into a makeshift pen.

They dismounted and Bill met them halfway to shake hands, their native language rolling off his tongue like a true Latino. Bill introduced me to the two brothers. Federico and Juan smiled affectionate, toothy grins, and both talked at the same time.

As a group, we moved across the clearing toward

a wooden shack on wheels. Smoke poured from the black stovepipe sticking out of the tin roof, covering the stench of the herders for the moment. In winter there were few opportunities to bathe.

We unloaded the grub, and Bill went to work preparing canned beans, bacon, and corn fritters on a generous campfire. The men teased Bill about his cooking—company a rare treat for the herders.

Perhaps it was a masculine gene-thing to want to bond with these pleasant men and to experience nature in the rough. A peaceful solitude eased into my soul, removing the concerns that lay back in Hebron, if only for a brief period.

"If you'll put plumbing in that shack, I'll come up and work for you," I said, half seriously.

Bill shook his head and chuckled. "Putting the plumbing in is the easy part, finding water and sewer lines to connect them to are the hard part."

"I knew it sounded too easy. I could get accustomed to this life."

"It's harder than it looks. If you came up here in the dead of winter, you'd change your mind. You think it's cold now. You should see it in January at forty below. It can also be dangerous. I lost a man eighteen months ago."

Stunned, I asked, "How?"

"Armando, Federico's older brother, was struck by lightning. One bolt killed him, his horse, and thirty sheep that were around him when it hit. The metal shoes on the horse's hooves apparently drew the electricity. You never forget a sight like that. Armando and his horse lay in the most perfect circle you can imagine surrounded by dead sheep." Sadness clouded Bill's eyes at the memory. "Federico rode about a hundred yards behind or he could also have died. Armando left a wife and five kids back in Mexico."

Suddenly the lives of the herders didn't seem quite so romantic.

We cleaned up the dishes, picked up their supply list, and headed home. Christmas lay only days away, and these two men reminded me that contrary to popular myth—shepherds had the world's oldest profession. God chose to send angels to announce the birth of the Messiah to such men as these. Not the rich and mighty of that time, but to men on the lowest rung of the social ladder—the first to worship the Christ.

The welcome sight of The Hand Me Down came into view in late afternoon, nestled in the valley below. Cold and hungry, we spurred the horses toward the warm food and comfort that awaited.

Emma opened the door with a smile. "You're just in time for dinner."

"Food is the magic word. I could eat a saddle."

She laughed. "I think we can do better than that."

George flew me to the Salt Lake International airport later that evening to pick up Jake's Jeep. On the long drive home, despite the heaviness in my chest, I took the positive approach. Any day Harry London didn't find Rachel and Cody was a good day.

11

Jake's Cabin, Pine Lake

The trek home was long, and I arrived at Jake's cabin as a wild snowstorm struck. Gale-force winds bent full-grown trees almost to the ground, nature bowing to the preeminence of God.

Safe inside the dry, warm cabin I was heartened to find Heath had stocked the refrigerator and pantry. I loved Jake Stein.

I threw together a roast-beef sandwich and poured a glass of milk. As I took a mouthful, Junior's large feline face loomed over me from the breakfast bar, keenly interested in my meal.

I grumbled. "Cat, I'm in no mood for company."

He didn't care. Just continued to covet my sandwich.

"Oh, for the love of Pete." I grabbed a piece of beef from the platter and held it out to him. A dog would have gobbled it down and panted for more.

Not Junior.

He drilled me with gray-green eyes as if to say *barbarian*, so I placed the meat on the counter where he daintily ripped it to shreds.

Unaccustomed to long rides on horseback, every bone in my body ached as I climbed the stairs to the guest room. After a hot shower, I fell into bed and stretched out on the firm mattress. My sleep mirrored the tempest that still raged outside, and the nightmare drew me in.

I peek around the alcove into the kitchen. My mother pleads with my drunken stepfather. "Sit down and eat, Craig. You'll feel better after you get something in your stomach."

Craig screams, "You want me to eat this? It's slop! I wouldn't feed this to a dog." He picks up the dinner plate and hurls it against the wall. Food smears down the painted surface, and broken glass bounces onto the tile. He thunders to the stove, jerks up each pot, and dumps the contents among the shards on the floor.

He continues to rage. "I'm tired of you and tired of your son I can never find. If I ever get my hands on him, he'll be sorry he ever heard my name."

Mom looks at him with narrow, hate-filled eyes. "I think you've already achieved that."

Craig draws back his fist and slams it hard against her jaw. Her head bounces back against the wall, and she folds to the floor.

Invisible, I snatch one of the heavy pots from the floor and swing it like a baseball bat into his gut. Air leaves his body with a whoosh. A look of astonishment flashes across his face, and he crashes backward onto the floor. Too drunk to comprehend, he shakes his head and chokes as he struggles to replenish his air supply. Then like the coward he is, he rises and stumbles to the door.

"I'm going down to the Hitching Post to get some real food." Craig stands in the entryway, his face red, contorted with anger. "Clean up this mess before I get home." He puts a hand to his midriff and bursts out the door. Minutes later, his car roars away.

Dazed, my mother's gaze searches the room. She knows about my gift. She doesn't understand, but she knows. "Noah?"

I materialize and grab a dishtowel from the drawer, put ice in it, and press it against her swelling jaw.

Her fingers touched my now visible cheek. "You shouldn't have done that."

I shook my head. "I should have done more. I can't stand by and let him beat you."

"Noah, I don't pretend to understand how or why you can do the things you do. But I do know God bestowed the powers for a reason. The one thing I'm sure of is you are not supposed to hurt other people just because you're special."

Our eyes lock. "Mom, I couldn't take him on without the invisibility. He'd just beat up both of us. We have to get out of here tonight. He'll be back, and he'll hurt you again. Let me call Grandma. She'll come pick us up. Please, we've got to leave now."

She reaches out, tears shimmer in her eyes. "Tomorrow when he goes to work, I'll pack our things. We can't leave in the middle of the night."

Even my child's mind knows waiting is a bad idea.

A loud knock pulled me back from the dream's shadows. Dazed, I shook my head to dispel the cobwebs. Morning had come, but the storm still raged.

With a jerk, I pulled on my clothes and stumbled barefoot down the stairs. Who in their right mind would come out in this weather? The lock slid back smoothly, and I eased the door open. Snow-filled wind blew me back into the entryway along with Amos Horne.

Shoulder against the portal, I heaved the door shut. "What brings you out in this blizzard?"

He shook the snow from his coat, tossed it on the rack by the door, and scowled at me. "You left me a message to come, remember?"

"Yes, but I figured you were smart enough not to

risk your life."

He shrugged and followed me into the kitchen where he drew out a barstool at the island. He gazed around the room. "You're living the good life, huh?"

"It helps to have rich friends." I poured us each a cup of coffee and shoved one across to him.

He blew a breath into the cup and took a sip. "What's up?"

After a moment's hesitation, I quelled my conscience. I left the room, returned with the photograph of Ralph Jensen, and placed it in front of Amos. "Take this to Sally Benedetti in the crime lab. Tell her to age it ten years. She'll do it. She likes me."

His craggy brow creased. "Imagine that, somebody who actually likes you." He dropped his head and then looked up at me. "We could get in a world of trouble if anyone finds out we know where you are, much less helping you. I've never seen London so mad. He storms through the courthouse corridors looking for scalps, and he's not particular about whose he takes."

I placed my cup on the bar, searched for signs of reluctance in his expression, and found none. He was only venting.

"The picture belongs to Ben Marshall's cellmate at San Quentin. I've taken advantage of our friendship, and I wouldn't have if I could handle this personally. The picture is the only lead in Abigail Armstrong's disappearance. I'm hoping you want to see the case solved as much as I do."

Amos took the picture and placed it in his jacket pocket. He was a friend, but more importantly, he was a cop. He would take the snapshot to Sally.

"You need to get this London thing under control.

Internal Affairs has brought charges against the guard on duty when Rachel London escaped.

That made me feel lower than pond scum. "Tell Jessie to claim somebody drugged her. Also, tell her to give Jake Stein a call. He'll represent her. I'll call and set it up with Jake."

Amos stared at me as perception dawned in his black eyes. "And how did you know Jessie was the guard?" He smashed his fist hard on the counter. "Noah, did you help that woman escape?"

"You don't want to know the answer to that question."

"You're right. I don't." He shook his head, and a grin turned the corners of his mouth upward. "But someday, after I retire, you're going to have to tell me how you pulled that off."

"That's something else you don't want to know. Have you eaten?"

He shook his head.

I refilled his coffee cup. "Let me put on some shoes, and I'll whip up some breakfast burritos."

Thirty minutes later while we were finishing the last of the burritos, Amos stopped in mid-chew, his gaze pensive. "You ever ask yourself why you do what you do? I mean taking on a crooked judge like London with city hall behind him?"

I shrugged. "Yeah, in times like this when the bad guys have the upper hand."

"Why do you keep doing it?"

That question often crossed my mind, and I paused for a moment before responding. "The short answer is there's too much injustice in the world. Too many like Rachel and Cody with the system skewed against them. The real reason is, I think of myself as a leveler—making the odds even so regular people get an even break."

His jaw tightened and he looked away. "If I had a hero, it would be you, Noah. You got more guts than brains."

Embarrassed, I laughed to cover the discomfort. "I'll remember you said that when we're sharing a cell in the federal prison in Rawlins."

Amos drove back to the city, and I tidied up the place.

Later that afternoon, the weather cleared, and I grabbed a sandwich at a burger shack near the lake. As I paid the cashier, my cell phone trilled its patriotic melody. It drew the attention of nearby customers. I think they felt a need to stand and place one hand over their hearts.

"I'm driving into the city tonight. I need to talk to you." It was Emma's voice on the phone

I pocketed my change. "Sure, anything wrong at the ranch? You haven't heard from Harry London, have you?"

"No. If he's traced Cody's call, we don't know about it. Things are quiet, but Rachel's still nervous."

"How about I take you to dinner at Chateau Bennett when you get to Hebron? Mabel's a friend of mine, and the food is great. She'll give us a private room. I'll meet you there at six thirty."

"Isn't it dangerous for you to be seen in Hebron?" Her words were slow, tired.

I must have lost my touch. Women I invited to dinner didn't usually sound depressed. "It'll be OK. Mabel knows about my situation. Wait until you see my new disguise, a scruffy look, eleven-day-old beard and all. Girls love it. You may not recognize me."

"I'll recognize you."

❧

Chateau Bennett, Hebron

I arrived early. Mabel opened the restaurant's back door and led me to the private room we'd pre-arranged. "You do like to live dangerously, don't you?" She wiggled her eyebrows at me. "Important date?

I laughed. "No, just dinner with a friend."

"You're no fun." She brought my iced tea and returned to her post at the entrance.

The dinner crowd hadn't arrived yet. Through the small one-way mirror to the left of the table, I watched waiters scurry under tiered chandeliers, checking tablecloths and flowers at each station. Savory steak-on-the-grill aromas drifted from the kitchen. Someday, I had to ask Mabel about that window. There had to be a juicy story there.

Through the window, I saw Mabel weave her way through the dining room toward my hide-a-way, Emma in tow.

Usually attired in jeans and boots, tonight Emma wore a simple black dress and heels. I held out a chair for her. "You clean up real good."

She almost laughed.

Seated in the nook at Chateau Bennett, I asked the question on my mind since her phone call. "So, what's the problem? You sounded down earlier."

Emma regarded her nails for a moment, seeming to search for words, and then blurted, "You need to find another place for Rachel and Cody. I know I said they could stay as long as needed—I've changed my mind." She dropped her gaze back to her manicure.

I patted her hand. "Don't look so depressed, Emma. I told you that you have the prerogative to back out of the deal anytime. Besides, we still have the problem Harry might trace Cody's call. It could be a good move to find them another safe house."

Her eyes welled up. "I *do* feel bad. I love Rachel and Cody..."

"What's the problem, Emma? This is Noah—you can tell me."

Her jaw muscles tightened and her lips narrowed as she pressed them together. "It's Bill. I'm afraid he's fallen in love with Rachel—a married woman. Bill's a preacher, for heaven's sakes. I know how much his faith means to him. I can't watch him ruin his life."

"Have you spoken to him?"

She shook her head. "I'm afraid to. I don't know how he'll react. I'm not a meddlesome mother..." Misery lined her face.

"Emma, you need to discuss this with him. Maybe he has feelings for Rachel; maybe he doesn't. I don't know. But he's a pastor first. He'll make the right choices. You did a good job raising your son. Sit down and talk with him. In the meantime, I'll look for a place to move Rachel and Cody."

She fingered the silverware. "I feel so bad about this. I made a commitment, and now I've backed out on you. You saved my ranch, and I can't even do a simple favor." Tears slipped from under her lashes.

"Stop it, Emma. We've been through this. You paid me well for the job I did. You don't owe me anything."

She relaxed against the back of the booth and expelled a deep breath. "Rachel's a sweet, wonderful woman. I just don't want to see Bill walk away from the job God called him to do."

"Don't borrow trouble, Emma. You may be worrying needlessly. I have a place my grandmother left me. I'll need to tighten security around the old homestead, make sure things still work, but it won't take more than a couple of days. That shouldn't be a problem. I didn't take them there that first night because Harry could have traced them through me."

Emma's face tightened. "Are you sure? If anything happened to Rachel and Cody after I'd sent them away, I could never..."

"Don't worry so much. This really isn't your problem. You took them in when you didn't have to. Besides, if Harry intended to check out my old homestead, he would have done so by now. They'll be safe there."

"Is that a promise?"

I hedged. "There are no guarantees in life, but I wouldn't leave them unless I felt confident of their safety. I have to go out of town tomorrow, but I'll make arrangements to move Rachel and Cody when I return."

As we readied to leave, I slipped cash between the folders of the check presenter and handed it to Mabel. "Thanks for setting this up, Mabel. The food was outstanding, as usual."

She winked and squeezed my arm. "Anytime, neighbor."

I followed Emma back to her hotel and made sure she entered the lobby safely. As I drove away, thoughts of moving Rachel and Cody troubled me.

My grandmother's home sat on a ten-acre tract in a rural community outside Hebron. Built by my grandfather during a flush period in his accounting firm—his wife's dream home. A gracious two-story frame they'd hoped to fill with grandchildren. When my father died in the last days of the Vietnam War, the dream ended. I couldn't bring myself to sell the homestead. Too many memories haunted the rooms and hallways, mostly good ones.

I'd put on a face of assurance for Emma, but it was risky. The house was isolated and exposed. Even more important, Bill Hand wouldn't be close by to protect them.

12

Noah's Home, Hebron, Wyoming

I returned to my condominium after following Emma to her hotel. Not smart, but I needed additional clothing and wanted to check on the pups. According to Amos, the HPD had suffered budget cuts and was short on manpower. With luck, they'd given up waiting for me to show.

After a couple of passes down my street, it looked safe. If the police were still around, they wouldn't recognize Jake's Jeep. A thin sheet of ice covered the streets, sidewalks, and gutters, a present left by the recent snowstorm. Before pulling into the alley behind my house, I parked four houses down and watched.

The dimly lit neighborhood sat quiet, lined by stark, nude trees. I scanned the block for strange cars. The Buick was conspicuous by its absence. Things appeared normal enough. All sane people would be inside by the fire. I pulled the Jeep into the alley and crunched through the snow to my back entrance.

Another one of those bitter, wintry days I should be used to by now, days when hard cold winds whipped down from Canada, lashing my skin and stinging my eyes. I snuggled down into my jacket and tugged the hood tighter around my head.

As I reached my backdoor, a crash against the stockade fence beside me sounded like a mad rhinoceros on the move.

Car keys fell from my hand, and I searched wildly through layered clothing for my Glock. I clutched the gun in shaky hands and turned.

In the moonlight, a huge head reared above the fence, fangs bared.

I sucked cold air to steady my nerves. "Attila, you satanic mutt..."

Good ol' Attila, the Doberman next door, had a blood lust for my type: O-negative. I considered shooting him, but it would wake the neighborhood. I'm a dog lover, but Attila was an exception. I sheathed the pistol, retrieved my keys from the snow, and unlocked the door. The fragrance of pine drifted into the kitchen, brought in by the cold breeze that whipped down the alley like a wind tunnel.

Brutus met me with a whine.

Something wasn't right.

As a rule, the pups don't whine, and Bella was missing.

Without flipping on the lights, I followed Brutus through the house and downstairs to the basement.

The glow from the television flickered across a body on the floor.

Bella lay with her head on Ted's stomach—his broad face covered in blood. "Ted!"

Heart hammering like a manic jackhammer, I dropped to his side and jerked off my gloves. Cradling his head in one arm, I searched for a pulse in the carotid artery. Warm, sticky ooze covered my fingers, but the strong throb told me he was alive and reasonably stable. Blood flowed from a large bump on his skull, still wet. Someone hit him hard, and not too long ago.

The pups raced me to the top step as I clambered

upstairs to the medicine cabinet.

At the landing, Brutus pushed past me, turned, and flashed an open-mouth grin. Red stained the white fur around his muzzle. Drops of blood led through the kitchen to the front door.

Brutus had grabbed a piece of the attacker before he'd gotten away.

I snatched towels and my first aid kit and hurried back to Ted. With shaky hands, I dunked the towel in cold water in the basement bathroom, and squeezed it dry. On my knees again, I washed the blood from Ted's ashen face, put his head on a pillow, and covered him with a blanket. With a low moan, his eyes flickered and opened slowly.

Ted stared up at me, gaze wide with fear. "Noah...my head hurts. Why did the man hit me? Didn't he like me?"

"He thought you were me. Did you get a look at him?"

Ted nodded and then winced in pain.

"Did you recognize him?"

"No. I didn't know him, Noah. Don't know why he hit me if he didn't know me."

I patted his hand. "Too dark down here for him to see."

I struggled to push back the rush of emotions that engulfed me. The effort failed. Why were the innocent among us the victims of the most evil among us? My hands ached to get hold of the guy, but I talked myself down. Ted needed attention. Anyway, whoever hit him had gone. Brutus took care of that.

Crossing to the phone, I called Mabel. I pushed heavy air from my lungs, relieved. "It's Noah. I was afraid you might not be home yet. Can you come to my place? Ted's been hurt."

She inhaled an anxious breath. "How?"

"I don't think it's serious, but I'd rather not discuss it over the phone. We probably need to get him to emergency. Have him checked out just to make sure."

Her voice cracked. "I'm on my way."

I went upstairs and opened the door.

Mabel crossed the street and swept past me into the entryway. "Where is he?"

In the basement, she rushed to Ted's side and cradled his head in her lap. She stared at the gash on his head and tossed me an angry glare. "What happened?"

"An intruder struck him. I'm sorry. You know I wouldn't knowingly place Ted in danger. I love him almost as much as you do."

The lines around her mouth softened. "I know that." A lone tear rolled down her cheek. "He shouldn't have been watching TV here, anyway. I think it makes him feel grownup to be here alone. It's just...if Ted were seriously hurt, I..."

"I know...I know." I put my arms around her shoulders. "The cut doesn't look serious. He'll be fine."

She wiped her eyes and straightened. The steel was back in her spine. "I'm OK. I can do this. I'll call 9-1-1. You know they'll bring the police. What should I tell them?"

"The truth, except the part where I found him. Someone jimmied the front door so that will match the intruder theory. Just give me ten minutes to get away before you place the call. Maybe later, Ted can pick out the thug from the station's mug shots."

I gathered up jackets, sweaters, snow boots, and wrote my throwaway cell number on a business card. I handed her the number and squeezed her hand. "Let me know what the doctor says. I'll call and check on him."

She gave her watch a quick glance. "You best get going. We've had more than one visit from the police since you left. They stopped Ted while he walked your dogs. An officer asked him to call if you turned up." Mabel smiled. "Ted told them he wouldn't call. You were his friend."

"Thanks, Mabel. I'll have the kennel pick up Bella and Brutus for a week or so, just until Ted feels better. He can take over again whenever he wants. The kennel guy will be here tomorrow. We've done this drill before. He won't need a key since the locks broken. I'll have a locksmith come out and take care of it and leave the key with you."

She nodded and pushed me toward the stairway. "Get going. Ted will be disappointed, but it's best, at least until this situation blows over."

God willing, it would take the authorities fifteen minutes to get to my place. At the Jeep, I opened the door and threw the clothes into the backseat. Before I could get in, a car swung in behind me and jammed the bumper against the Jeep's backend.

The police couldn't have gotten here that quick. Unmarked car. Perhaps a detective, but they didn't roll on minor cases. I leaned inside the jeep, pushed my gun under the seat, and eased away from the door, arms away from my body, hands open.

A goon with the face of a bad prizefighter withdrew from the vehicle. A bloody handkerchief encircled his left hand—red stains smeared down his jacket.

This clod didn't work for the city. He was the

lowlife who had attacked Ted—the owner of the blue sedan.

An inch shorter than me, he reached into his jacket with his good hand and pointed a .40 Beretta at my heart. "Hold it there, Adams." As I stared at the gun, he looked much bigger. "I've been waiting a long time for you to come home, and I don't like to wait, especially in the cold." He moved in close. The gun never wavered.

"Why? Did you run out of handicapped kids to pistol whip?" Wrong thing to say to a man holding a gun.

He lunged forward and brought the gun butt down, aimed at my skull.

I ducked and caught the blow on my right collarbone. Hot pain soared through my arm and my collarbone crunched like someone stepping on dry twigs. I hit the ground.

The goon stepped back and growled. "I want to know where you've stashed London's kid."

"I don't know what you're talking about," I said through clenched teeth.

A sinister grin spread across his ugly face. "I think you do." He stepped forward, put his foot on my wounded shoulder, and pressed down.

Waves of pain like hot knives ripped down my arm and flooded through my shoulder.

The goon stood over me, poised to rain another savage blow on my head, when blue and white strobe lights flashed into the street. The ambulance, soon to be followed by the cops.

The thug jerked around. The lights moved into my front driveway. His posture tensed, and he turned back to me.

I raised my good arm to evade the blow that would follow. Instead, he drew back his foot, and aimed at my upper body. In mid-swing, I grabbed his shoe, almost knocking him down. He recovered quickly and before I could block the next move, pain flared as the gun butt connected with my skull. I slid back onto the icy ground and welcomed the darkness that followed.

⤙⤚

Somewhere Outside Hebron

Consciousness returned in small increments of awareness. As the fog in my brain cleared, I realized I lay folded into a fetal position, my head jammed against my knees in the trunk of a small automobile. Claustrophobia pressed the trunk closer, closing in on me.

The car wasn't moving and stale, sour air inside the trunk assaulted my nostrils—familiar odors of oil and fuel.

Pain and cold metal were my next sensations although the top of the trunk lid felt tepid. Sunrays seeped through rusted holes like tiny flashlight beams in the dark space. I must have been out for a while. The light confirmed it was daylight and that the car sat somewhere in the open.

My body throbbed with the ache in my head and my shoulder felt as though the thug continued to beat me with the butt of his revolver. I tried to move, but the small space left no room to maneuver. I focused on becoming invisible, tried to summon my power. It didn't work. The gift had never failed me before. The pain in my body wouldn't let me concentrate, and the tight space became unbearable. Blackness enveloped me once again.

When I next awoke, my head pounded and the misery in my shoulder remained as severe as ever. A chilled darkness emanated from the metal hull.

Night.

My tin coffin grew colder as the temperature dropped. As a rule, tight places don't bother me, but there was far too much of me, and much too little space in the trunk. I tried to fight the panic that filled my chest, as silent screams choked off my breath.

The terror must have been the stimulus my tortured psyche needed. Like the answer to an unspoken prayer, I found myself free outside the car, invisible and sucking fresh, cold air into my lungs. Weak, I slid painfully to the ground.

The pungent odor I'd smelled earlier was a junkyard. My assailant had locked me in an abandoned car on the outskirts of Hebron.

With stiff feeble movements, I climbed into the backseat of the rusting wreck. I stretched out as much as possible, and welcomed the comfort the dirty seat covers provided. My body needed rest—until it could heal itself. A warm blanket would have come in handy.

As I lay in the frigid darkness, my arm felt a familiar bulge in my coat pocket. My cell phone.

In his haste to leave, my attacker was in too big of a hurry to check my pockets. Now if I could just get bars. Yes!

I called George.

ॐॐ

I stumbled outside the junkyard and sat on a cement retaining wall. As best I could figure, it was late Tuesday night.

George's truck slung snow sludge as he barreled down the narrow lane and slid to a stop in front of me. He got out, opened the passenger door, and helped ease my bruised carcass into the warmth of his pickup. "What happened? You look like the loser in a kickboxing tournament."

The heat in the cab stopped my chill, and I relayed the one-sided battle with the mugger, leaving out how I'd escaped from the trunk. It eluded me how the thug evaded the police and why he didn't just shoot me. Perhaps he wanted my death to be a slow process since I hadn't divulged the information he wanted.

Nice guy.

The truck roared into action, and George glanced over at me. "I know I owe you my life, but saving your hide is getting to be a habit." He went quiet for a moment and then nodded as if reaching a conclusion. "I have an old Marine buddy who's a medic. We'll get you fixed up."

He picked up his cell phone and made the call.

❧⟨

Twenty minutes later, we entered a small frame house in the suburbs. George's Marine buddy, Gloria Burke, was a pretty woman with caramel skin and bright hazel eyes. She opened the door at our knock.

Without fanfare or introductions, George nodded at her. "This is the package I called you about."

She stood back and opened the door wide. "Bring him in."

The pain was almost unbearable. George helped me inside and led me to a sofa. Sweat beaded on my brow, and I leaned against the cushions.

Gloria prodded my head with the gentle touch of an angel. "You've got a big goose egg here, and your right eye is dilated, so looks like you've got a concussion."

She helped me off with my shirt. More pain.

"Ohhhh, I bet that hurts," she said. "There's swelling and the skin is broken in several places. Without X-rays I can't say for sure if the collarbone is broken, but it sure looks that way." She washed the wounds with alcohol wipes and smeared on an antibiotic gel.

I gritted my teeth and tried not to embarrass myself by fainting. Tough guy to the end.

She removed a prescription bottle from her bag and handed me two pills. "This will help with the pain, but it might make you drowsy. Keep the rest."

I fell in love with Gloria Burke.

"If the bone is broken it will take five to six weeks to mend," she said in a boot drill sergeant tone. 'Your collarbone doesn't appear to have a clean break, but it could be fractured. You should really see a doctor and get it X-rayed. The sooner, the better."

I wouldn't see a doctor. They'd asked questions I didn't want to answer. Another anomaly of my physical structure—broken bones healed at an accelerated rate. I would be whole again in a week.

Gloria encased my arm into a sling and stepped back. She nodded her satisfaction. George helped me to my feet and I tried to pay her.

"Forget it," she said. "You can repay the favor sometime."

George took me to his home and put me to bed. Good friends were God's answer to prayers.

13

George Thomas's Home

"Norma takes better care of you than she does me." George feigned a wounded look at his wife.

I winked at Norma. "Yeah, I think I'll sell my place and move in with you guys. Norma's a great cook. She fluffs my pillows, makes me breakfast, and brings me coffee. This is better than the Hilton."

George's right eyebrow lifted. "Exactly why is it you make him an omelet and hash browns, and I'm lucky to get a cold biscuit?"

"That's easy." Norma tossed a grin over her shoulder. "He's prettier than you are."

As she left the room, George called after her. "Girl, you need glasses."

After breakfast, George walked me around the property, Tooie at George's heels. The dog carried a slight limp in his right back leg, a gift from his previous owner.

I scratched behind Tooie's ear. "How's he doing?"

Pulling a doggie treat from his pocket, George grinned. "He's healthier than I am."

Tooie was a rescue dog George picked up, half-starved and crippled, at a shelter. The dog had needed a lot of love and affection before he started to trust people again. The two had been inseparable ever since.

I enjoyed the easy camaraderie of George and Norma's home for a day. It took that long to regain my strength and adjust to life with one good arm, but I was getting better by the minute.

Pain in the shoulder had almost ceased. It wouldn't take long to heal, even if it the bone had fractured.

❧

Hebron, Wyoming

Back at Jake's place, I called Rachel. Nothing new. The situation remained stable. That was a good thing. I avoided the subject of my injury. She didn't need the extra worry.

Next, I dialed Mabel and asked about Ted. She laughed. "I've always figured he had a hard head, now I know for certain. He hasn't even had a headache."

Still one more call to make. I punched in Lincoln Armstrong's number. He didn't answer so I left a voicemail about my trip to San Quentin.

Later that morning, I flew back to Frisco to check out Abigail's old neighborhood.

Holiday traffic cluttered the road, and weary travelers packed the airport. Only three shopping days until Christmas.

Onboard my flight, I found myself sandwiched in the middle seat between a talkative valley girl and a man who kept the flight attendant busy bringing rum and Coke. And I paid a small fortune for the privilege.

❧

San Francisco, California

After we landed, I grabbed a taxi. I was too much a coward to drive in freeway traffic with one arm.

Abigail's last known address lay in one of the city's high-rent districts, a gated townhouse community with well-tended lawns and bright tropical flowers. A salty mist in the air confirmed its nearness to the sea. My ID and gift of gab got me past the female guard at the entrance, and I started with the neighbors on each side of Abigail's old address.

At my first stop, a smiling cherub doorknocker greeted me. An elderly woman with a permanent frown imbedded on her brow answered my knock.

I smiled. "Good morning, I'm—"

"How did you get in here? Solicitors aren't allowed. Didn't you read the sign at the gate?"

"Ma'am I'm not selling—"

The little cherub bounced violently when its owner slammed the door in my face.

That could make even an angel frown.

Undeterred, I marched on to the next winsome cupid and dropped the knocker on the metal pad. The cherub's smile seemed to brighten.

The woman who came to the door looked about forty, except for age spots on her hands. I guessed her to be in her early fifties. Attractive in the way of many California women who aggressively pursue the fountain of youth.

Reaching inside my jacket, I pulled out my card, and handed it to her. After a slight hesitation, she scrutinized it and introduced herself as Goldie Marks.

"I'm looking for information on Abigail Marshall. She lived next door about ten years ago."

She paused. "I knew Abby well. Is something wrong with her?"

I shrugged. "She disappeared three years back. Her husband asked me to find out what happened."

Goldie's eyes widened. "Why did he wait three years to hire a detective?"

"It's a long story. Basically, he let the police handle it until he determined they'd stopped looking."

She eyed my injured arm. I could almost see warnings of stranger-danger flash through her mind. She must have decided she could take me if I tried something. She stepped aside and allowed me to enter.

Inside, she led me through the entryway to a low-to-the-ground white sofa. "Would you care for a cup of green tea? I can make coffee, but the tea will be better for your arm. It has loads of antioxidants."

I opted for the coffee. She excused herself and left for the kitchen, giving me a moment to explore the surroundings.

The living room offered a wide expanse of marble tile with a spectacular view of the Pacific Ocean through floor-to-ceiling windows. That panorama of sea and shoreline must have cost a mint, considering property values in the Bay area. I could buy a three-story mansion in Utah, complete with tennis courts and pool, for what she must have paid for the condominium.

Modern décor never appealed to me, but the room was striking. A white twelve-foot Christmas tree, adorned with red birds and bows, stood in the corner near a marble fireplace.

A collection of colorful porcelain and pottery decorated one wall. I'm no art connoisseur, but even my untrained eye recognized these were valuable. I rose from the sofa and strolled over to an alcove. Inside the hollow sat a white porcelain vase painted with tiny blue flowers.

While I studied the pottery, Goldie returned with a

silver tea service.

She set the tray down and then came up behind me. "You have a good eye. That's the most expensive piece in the collection. It's a plum blossom vase from the Yuan Dynasty. It's more than seven hundred years old." She spoke with practiced ease, her face alight as she related the historical pedigree of her treasures. "Do you know anything about antique porcelain?"

I shook my head. "No, I was just attracted to the lines and color."

"My late husband was an avid collector. Most pieces here are museum quality. He also collected porcelain figurines." Goldie waved at the opposite wall brimmed with delicate dolls in various 18th century costumes and poses.

"Come, let's drink the coffee before it gets cold."

We returned to the sofa, and when I sat, my knees almost touched my chin. Low furniture did that to men of my height.

She poured the liquid into tiny cups too small for my fingers. I fidgeted with the handle, holding it with care between thumb and forefinger.

She opened her mouth as if to say something when her gaze fell on my predicament. She laughed, and almost spilled her drink. "Are you as uncomfortable as you look?" She laughed again. "Let me get you a bigger cup."

I tossed her a grateful grin. "Thanks."

Still smiling, Goldie took the tea service away and returned with two large mugs and a carafe. "I should know better than to bring the china out except for ladies' luncheons."

I settled back on the couch. "What can you tell me about Abigail Marshall?"

Relaxed in the curve of an oversized chair, Goldie folded her legs beside her. "Abigail was the most beautiful woman I'd ever seen. She could have made a fortune modeling, but she didn't have time for a career. She had a full-time job just to keep herself and her son alive. Abby married a monster. Many nights, when Ben arrived home in a rage, she and Joey came here to sleep—afraid to go home. Her prayers were answered when Ben went to prison. Unfortunately, it wasn't soon enough to keep him from killing her son."

"Marshall killed his own son? The boy didn't die in a car accident?"

"Oh, Ben didn't drive the car that ran Joey down, but he was as guilty as if he'd been behind the wheel. "That day, Abby and I stood in the courtyard watching Joey ride his bike. Ben came home and called him to come inside. Terrified of his father, Joey froze. When he didn't come immediately, Ben charged at Joey in a fury, and the boy rode his bike into the path of an oncoming car, trying to get away. The driver wasn't moving fast, but he didn't have time to stop. Joey died instantly. I'll never forget Abigail's scream. It still haunts me. Joey was the best-behaved child I'd ever met." Goldie's eyes clouded, and she glanced at the antiques. "He loved to look at the figurines. He never tried to touch or hold them. He just sat on the floor with his toys and stared for hours."

She shook her head as if to erase the vision she'd resurrected. "Abigail sold her home and moved in with me after Joey's death. She was a wreck for six months. I believe she would have killed Ben if he hadn't gone to jail. She waited until the trial ended and they shipped Ben off to San Quentin. Almost a year later, Abby was gone. She left a note that she needed to start over. At first, I received a few calls and then nothing. She never returned. I suppose there were too many bad memories here."

I pulled out the retouched Ralph Jensen picture Amos had given me. "You ever see this guy around here?"

She studied the photograph for a moment. "No, I don't think so, but he does look familiar. Who is he?"

"An old friend of Ben's—perhaps responsible for Abigail's disappearance."

She shivered. "I hope you catch him. Abby deserved a lot better than she got." Goldie stood and picked up our cups. I rose from the sofa with her.

"I have some photos Abby left. I'll dig them up. I didn't want to throw them away. The pictures were her prized possessions after Joey's death. She left in such a hurry...I think she just wanted to leave the pain behind. Perhaps you could take them to her husband. Would you like to stay for dinner? You really don't need to be driving around the freeways looking for a restaurant with that arm."

The eagerness in her invitation showed a vulnerability I wouldn't have suspected–an unexpected side of her personality. Wealth had never been a cure for loneliness.

I accepted the dinner invitation but admitted I'd arrived by cab. She would probably give me tofu and rabbit food, but I could live with it for one meal. I've always had a weakness for older women who try to mother me.

After we finished the coffee, Goldie left the room. She returned with a gift box filled with photographs. "These weren't as hard to find as they might have been." She set the carton down and looked at me, eyes wide, puzzled. "Why do you keep popping up and down like a jack-in-the-box every time I come into the room? That must be hard on your arm."

I grinned. "It's a lifelong habit I can't seem to shake. My grandmother taught me to stand whenever a lady is standing."

She gave me a wicked grin. "Who told you I was a lady?"

I returned the smile. "I always assume the positive."

She motioned for me to sit. "It's charmingly gallant, and it makes me feel kind of special." She glanced down at my hand. "How come a sweet man like you isn't married?"

I shrugged. "A personal choice I made some time ago. My job can be dangerous, and it would be hard for a wife and kids to cope with the fluctuations in my income. Its steak one week and tacos the next."

While the meal cooked, Goldie placed the box on the sofa between us. She pulled out photos of Abigail and Joey, giving details of time and place on various shots, reliving the memories. There was a regal loveliness about Abigail Armstrong. I understood why her beauty captivated people.

Happily, the evening meal turned out to be great. Grilled salmon steak, rather than tofu. Over the salad, Goldie spoke of the past with Abigail. "Abby spent many nights in the emergency room from beatings she received at Ben's hand. Even worse was the damage he did to her self-esteem, making her think the abuse was her fault." My hostess sat silent for a moment. "It's a pity that women like Abby continue to suffer. Giving domestic abuse national attention would certainly help."

"The real issue is authorities aren't notified until it's too late. And when they are notified, unfortunately, the cases often fall through bureaucratic cracks."

Her eyes reflected an inner struggle, perhaps between good manners and conviction. Conviction won. Goldie dropped her napkin on the table. "Yeah, it seems Abby fell through the cracks. Her husband goes to prison and dies, yet he still manages to get to her from the grave. That makes me mad."

"Whoa," I said, unable to believe she'd taken offense at my comment. "I agree with you. It's obscene that a woman can take all the precautions and still wind up dead. I just don't see how federal intervention would have stopped it. The government breaks more social programs than it fixes."

A bright pink flush covered her cheeks. "Well, somebody needs to protect abuse victims."

I nodded as I picked at the salad. "You're totally right, and I think you have the answer and just haven't seen it."

She didn't speak right away. Instead she busied herself removing the salad plates. Shortly she returned with the salmon and grilled vegetables, and placed the food in front of me.

She took a seat and snapped her napkin onto her lap.

I raised both hands. "What I mean is that you stepped in to help Abby. That's what everyone needs to do. When we see or suspect domestic violence, report it. Don't just turn a blind eye to the situation."

She nodded and a grin teased the corners of her mouth. She stared at me for a full minute. "You have way too much charm for my own good."

We finished the meal in amicable silence. I stood

and looked into her eyes. "Are we still good here?"

Had I been a jerk? To make amends, I helped carry the dishes into the kitchen. "The fish was great. Normally I find salmon too dry, but yours was moist and the flavor was excellent."

She smiled. "It's the magic of my herb marinade."

"You did good, Goldie, and it was probably good for my health. My system may go into shock."

Ripples of laughter filled the kitchen. "You can thank me when you're ninety-two."

While she put away the leftovers, I noticed a metal cross, enclosed in a silver shadowbox on the wall. "That looks old."

She walked over to my side. "It's very old, from the First Crusade, somewhere around 1095-1099 A.D.

I drew closer to the ancient artifact. Delicate engravings on the metal looked worn, but still impressive. "Are you a Christian?"

She rolled her eyes. "Hardly."

"Perhaps we need to talk about that sometime. It's better to live life as though there is a God, than to live life as though there isn't...and die and discover otherwise."

Goldie shrugged and then hooked her arm through mine. "Come on. I'll drive you to the airport and save you cab fare."

On the flight home, haunting images filled my mind of a beautiful woman and her freckle-faced son—the sorrow they shared in a life all too short. My own memories surfaced, and the wind whispered a reminder.

It seemed to me, God sometimes called the best of us home early.

14

Jake's Cabin, Pine Lake

"You have one message, and two saved messages," my voicemail system announced in a serene voice. "First message, 9:02 am"

The call was from Amos Horne, his voice strained and almost unrecognizable. "I need to see you right away. Something important has come up. Meet me at the summer place, the usual time."

I cleared the message and glanced at my watch. One o'clock. I'd have to hurry. The summer place was his boat slip on the opposite side of the lake from Jake's cabin, and the usual time, two o'clock. Backing the Jeep from the driveway, I turned north toward the dam.

Summer weekends, Amos and I met there and took out *The Cherokee*, his small cabin cruiser. Amos fished. I cooked.

Patience had never come easy for me. Always been too antsy to wait for fish to bite. I got exasperated and wanted to shoot them, but Amos said it would be unsportsmanlike.

❧

Pine Lake

My friend paced the parking lot behind his truck as I pulled into a slot beside him. He wore a knitted stars and stripes cap pulled down low over his ears.

"What happened to your arm?"

We climbed into the warmth of Amos's truck. The smell of onions and fried food hit me before I could close the door. Soon, a foggy mist covered the windows caused by the warmth inside and the extreme cold outside. I explained my clash with the thug.

"Did you get a good look at the bum?"

"Yeah, but I didn't recognize him. With my current circumstances, I can't go to headquarters and look at mug shots. My neighbor has probably looked through your files by now. The thug pistol-whipped him." I unzipped my jacket. "What's so important you couldn't relay the message over the phone?"

"My office ran a check on your cell phone and credit card records. Thought you'd want to know. There's also another problem. Because it's a kidnapping, the fibbees are on the case now. They met with the chief today. Scuttlebutt says they have your name as well as Rachel London's. You know what this means, Noah. These people can find you. They have technology the Hebron police don't even suspect."

"When did all this come down?"

"Ten minutes before I left you the message."

"I haven't used the credit cards anywhere near the ranch. I assumed your guys had already checked my phone and cards. What took them so long?"

"My buddies working on this didn't want to fink on one of their own. When the pressure came down, they had to."

I issued a long breath. "When they checked my phone records, they must have found your number listed. You'd better come up with a cover story. Be careful how you call me. I don't want to pull you any further into this than I already have."

He produced two greasy paper bags from the back seat and threw one to me. He'd picked up burgers on the way. "We should be OK...for now. I called your unlisted cell from a pay phone. When you didn't answer, I took a chance on calling the office number, also from the booth. I tried to disguise my voice." He swallowed a bit of his burger. "What will you do?"

"I'll have to try to survive with limited cash flow or figure some way to get a card that can't be traced to me. Armstrong might help. He's something of a maverick. He's on the up and up, but he likes to take risks. How about you? Will you be OK?"

Amos nodded. "I should be. A few of the guys in the department know we're friends, but I don't expect them to squeal on me. They don't think you'd ever harm a kid." A lopsided grin curled his lips. "When you worked in the precinct the guys called you 'the pope.' Plus, they know London by deed and reputation. Add the fact there's a lot of jealousy between the locals and the federal boys—I figure they'll give me a pass as long as it doesn't jeopardize their jobs."

Amos pulled a thermos from under the seat and poured two cups of coffee, crumpled his bag and tossed it on the floorboard. He reached over and helped himself to my fries. "Any chance you can close this case before we get those adjoining cells?"

"After he received Cody and Rachel's X-rays, Jake drew up the divorce papers, citing abuse. But he'll make sure he has every jot and tittle in place before he files the case. I can't say when it'll happen, and the Feds will probably have his phone tapped and check out his cabin soon. I'll need somewhere to stay. I'll get to Jake and fill him in as soon as I can. The FBI involvement adds a new sense of urgency Jake needs to know about."

"Can you find a safe house somewhere?"

I nodded. "The possibility the authorities would find out about Jake's cabin has always existed, and I've given moving some thought. There's a retreat my church uses for summer camp. It's in the mountains and deserted this time of year. The only way in or out is by snowmobile. The facilities are rustic, but it has plumbing and electricity. I can manage there for a while."

"You can use my snow rig. Its old, but it still covers the ground pretty fast. Just tell me where to meet you."

"I appreciate the offer, but Jake has all the equipment I could ever want. I'll just borrow his." I extended my hand to Amos. "Thanks, buddy, for the warning."

He swallowed hard. "Don't mention it."

I finished off the burger and handed the bag to Amos. He tossed it on the floor with his. I shook my head. "Man, that's just wrong."

He only shrugged.

Climbing out of the truck, I called, "Merry Christmas."

His face went blank for a moment. "Oh yeah, Christmas is Monday. I forgot since the kids aren't here..."

Amos's wife left him four years ago and took their two little boys back to South Carolina. Women not born here or in a similar climate could never seem to get use to the cold and the absence of shopping malls. Too bad. Amos missed those boys.

On the way back to Jake's cabin, I called

Armstrong. He invited me to dinner at his place. It seemed a good idea. I needed to talk to him, and two lonely bachelors wouldn't have to spend an evening alone.

The drive to the cabin resurrected memories of holidays spent with my mother, flooding my mind with visual images. They weren't warm recollections.

My stepfather used the Christmas season as an excuse to get drunk. Not that he needed an excuse.

While he caroused, my mother gathered Tommy and me into her bed and sang to us in her sweet soprano voice a melody I've never heard since, perhaps something she wrote. I could only remember the chorus.

> *Holy Child this vow I give you,*
> *As I offer up my praise,*
> *To remember Christ is Christmas,*
> *Every Christmas Day.*

The sight of Jake's cabin jerked me back into the moment. Getting packed was the first thing to tick off my to-do list. Heath, the caretaker, insisted on helping me stow the snowmobile in the Jeep. My arm had almost healed, but I accepted the offer.

I was going to miss Junior. Not.

Gear packed, I drove to Armstrong's place.

☙❧

Lincoln Armstrong's Home

A handsome oriental butler opened the door. The foyer looked larger than my first floor, and the flowerpot in the center, overflowing with poinsettias, covered more square feet than Amos's boat. The houseboy ushered me through the reception area into the library.

Armstrong sat in a green leather chair by a generous blaze in the hearth. He stood and greeted me with a firm handshake. "Come on in by the fire. That wind is brutal. Dinner will be ready in about twenty minutes. Gregory is preparing something special tonight—roast duck, I believe. I promise it will be worth the wait. May I get you a drink?"

I passed on the drink and took the hot apple cider he offered as a substitute, sat in a second chair in front of the fire, and glanced up at the large oil painting above the fireplace. I recognized the woman as Abigail Armstrong from her pictures. Indeed, she had been beautiful.

Armstrong's gaze followed mine to the portrait, and he smiled. "I never tire of looking at her. I had that done right after we were married."

I nodded. "I met a friend of your wife's in San Francisco yesterday. She gave me some old photos Abigail left behind. I'll turn the box over to you when I've finished going through them."

He nodded and swirled the golden liquid in a crystal brandy snifter. I related the things Goldie told me about Abigail's abuse and Marshall's indirect responsibility for the boy's death. Armstrong's eyes hardened like steel. He gripped the arm of his chair, then rose abruptly and stood in front of the fire. After a minute, he turned to me, his face smooth and composed—a look he no doubt used in board meetings.

"Lincoln, I need a favor. I have a client who's involved in a situation very similar to Abby's. She has an abusive husband and a son. She wants to get out of the marriage before he kills both of them. He's filed kidnapping charges against her and had her arrested once. The warrant also includes me. The husband is a judge, which makes the circumstances more tenuous. I understand the FBI also may be looking for both of us. They can find me through my credit cards. I need a card that can't be traced back to me."

His expression didn't change. He had a good poker face. "And I should help you because...?"

"I'll be more than glad to give you the title to my home as collateral. Of course, any charges I make unrelated to your case, I'll repay. Or you can deduct the amount from my salary, provided you still want to retain me."

"What makes you think I won't tell the FBI where to find you?"

I shrugged and grinned. "A professional hunch."

He chuckled and returned to his seat. "Your name came up over dinner last night at the club. The mayor let it drop that the police were looking for you. He appeared quite agitated; asked if I'd hired you. I said no, of course, told him I'd wanted to handle the investigation within my firm. I'm glad you're being forthright with me. Is this Judge London's wife, the woman whose picture has been in the news?"

I nodded. The man didn't miss much.

"As I told you when we first met, I checked you out thoroughly before I hired you. Don't take offense; I do that with everyone I place on my payroll. I don't like surprises, and it's a good business practice. You have a reputation for honesty to a fault—taking cases that are more community service projects than lucrative business transactions." Armstrong shrugged and smiled, a light burning deep in his eyes. "The Hebron police wasted three years of precious time blaming me for Abby's disappearance and almost succeeded in destroying my reputation. They also caused me three years of misery. You'll have the card by noon tomorrow. Tell me where to send it."

I swallowed the lump in my throat, stood, and gave him the business card with my fake ID and a post office box number.

"Let's eat. I'm hungry." He patted my shoulder like an indulgent father and led me toward the dining room.

He was right. The duck exceeded my expectations.

After dinner, we returned to the library with mugs of hot apple cider. I lifted my cup. "To mothers."

Melancholy washed over his face briefly before he raised his own mug. "To mothers."

かしゃ

Bridger Mountain Lodge
Unloading the snow jet proved easier than anticipated. I pushed it from inside the Jeep with my legs and it landed easily in the foot-deep powder.

I arrived at the campground before midnight, cold and tired. I hate the cold. My trusty skeleton key opened the lock. A blast of arctic air hit my nostrils as the cabin door creaked open. No need to worry about strangers lurking inside—too frigid to harbor humanity.

The flashlight beam helped me locate the furnace. I sucked in an anticipatory breath as I flipped the switch. The quiet hum answered a prayer. My guardian angel had come through one more time.

I found the light switch, and shrugged. Jake's place, the Trump Towers, the lodge, a cheap motel. Complaining? Well, just a little. But the church had stocked the pantry with staples. A plus I didn't expect. This I could live with.

Early the next morning I woke to the trill of my cell phone. A number I didn't recognize glowed on the tiny screen. Guarded, I answered, "Hello."

"I think I have something you want, Adams."

The static-filled connection faded in the tree-covered mountains, but I recognized the voice as Hebron's mayor, Robert Thornton. "How did you get my number?"

"McKenna," he said.

I'd forgotten about giving it to her.

"Meet me at my boat in an hour. We'll discuss it there. You know where it is."

"Give me two hours. I have a long way to drive."

"Fine." The line went dead.

Great. I should have published my cell number in the *Hebron Herald* along with my itinerary. With two rendezvous at the marina in two days, the Feds could just patrol the lake if they really wanted to find me.

Curiosity piqued, I grabbed snow pants, boots, and a thermal jacket from the closet. Dressed for the weather, I started the snowmobile. Wind and flakes slashed like icy needles biting my face as I slithered down the mountainside, wind howling around me like wolves on the prowl. An inch of white powder covered the Jeep's windshield when I reached the hill's base. Dusting away the heavy flakes with my hand, I started the engine and drove to the dock.

Pine Lake

The craft parked in the slip was a boat like Armstrong's mansion was a house. It leaned more toward the yacht class.

Thornton waited for me on deck, a waft of steam flowing from the cup in his hand. I hurried alongside and jumped aboard.

With practiced ease, Thornton backed out and headed for open water. The mayor remained silent until we were in the middle of the lake. He shut down the engine and dropped anchor. With a wave of his hand, he motioned me to follow him below. The air inside enveloped us in a warm cocoon and eased the chill from my bones.

Thornton handed me a cup of coffee, and I found a seat at the bar.

I leaned against the leatherback stool. "What's this about?"

He took the seat across from me. "I'm aware of your situation with Harry London. I have something that will, shall we say, untangle you and your client from London's web." He paused for effect.

He had my attention.

"I have obtained videos from London's home security system. How the tapes came into my possession is immaterial. Let's just say I have friends in low places. The point is they show the abuse of his family."

A belated light switch flipped on in my head. I should have thought of that.

Thornton smirked. "The idiot placed cameras inside everywhere except the kitchen and bathrooms. It seems the good judge was so paranoid about his wife, he didn't stop to realize the tapes, in the wrong hands, could hang him."

I sipped my coffee. "Aren't you two friends?"

Thornton shrugged. "Acquaintances, hardly friends. Did you ever wonder how London became so influential in his short career in Hebron?"

"Actually, I didn't know London at all until recently."

Thornton leaned back and studied the cup in his hand. "London has more influence in local politics than anyone in Hebron, next to me. After his election to judge, he came into contact with Steve Clark. London punished Clark's enemies in his courtroom, and Clark paid him well. I tell you this so you know what you're up against."

He walked to the galley and refilled his cup. "The films came to me for a price, of course, but they're yours absolutely free."

He lifted the pot to see if I wanted more.

I shook my head. "Why would you give the tapes to me rather than turn them over to McKenna? She's the Assistant D.A." The question was rhetorical. I already knew the answer. He wanted something from me.

Thornton shrugged. "It wouldn't be good for McKenna's career for her to take possession. Questions would be asked."

"What do you want from me?"

He paused, stirring his coffee. "It's rather complicated. There is only one thing in my life I truly care about—McKenna."

As much as I disliked Robert Thornton, I could see he spoke the truth, and it galled him to ask me for a favor.

"McKenna married Alexander Clark. Did you know?"

"I heard about it." My heart tripped faster. It disturbed me more than I wanted to admit that she'd married the mafia boss's son.

"Alexander has pressed McKenna for inside information from the first day of their marriage. I believe that's the primary reason he married her—to find out what the D.A. knew about his dad's local operations. Things that could get McKenna disbarred and indicted if she caved. McKenna is basically honest, and she has resisted so far, but Alexander is making threats. Their union has been on the rocks for over a year."

Thornton set his cup on the bar. "Under normal circumstances this could be handled in the courts, but because of Steve Clark's connections, McKenna could wind up dead if she tries to divorce Alex. She knows too much." He got up from his stool and paced, his body weaved with the motion of the boat. "You probably think I made my bed, and you'd be right. And I would happily lie in it if I had only myself to consider."

"You're not asking me to murder Alexander...?"

"No, I know you better than that. That will be my job, and believe me, it's a job I look forward to. But I need a witness. Someone with a spotless reputation to tell the authorities he saw the *accident*." Thornton made the quote sign with his fingers. "That's the only way to keep Steve Clark from questioning the death of his son."

"My reputation is hardly spotless now. You do know I'm charged with accessory in kidnapping London's son?"

He nodded. "But with these tapes, you and his wife will be cleared. Alexander races boats, and I plan a boating mishap. You're our local war hero, Adams, and you'll get extra points once you take care of Harry London. No one would question your integrity. McKenna could live without fear from Steve Clark."

"That would make me an accessory to murder. Apparently, you don't know me at all. If I could help McKenna, I would do it, but not this way. I sympathize with your plight wholeheartedly, but I can't..."

Thornton's face flushed with red, a vein popped out on his temple. His cold gaze stared back at me, unblinking as those of a rattler poised to strike. He took a sip of coffee and looked at me over the steam from his cup. "It's a generous offer. You'd save three innocent people from monsters. Simple, really."

Our gazes locked, and I shook my head. "Sorry. You don't know how tempting the offer is, but the answer is no."

That deadly look washed down his face again. He shoved his cup to the table and then reached under the bar.

Cold fingers snaked down my spine. He had a gun under the counter.

He withdrew his hand. Empty. "Alexander Clark deserves to die for what he's put my daughter through. I'm sure I don't have to tell you that what happened here, stays here. If any part of this conversation becomes known, you'll be a dead man long before Steve Clark gets me. That's a promise."

I believed him. No reason not to.

I made a last-ditch plea. "I couldn't talk you into giving me the tapes because it's the right thing to do?"

Thornton's face hardened as cold as stone. Evil

resonated from pitch black eyes. Would he go for the gun again? It would be a long, cold swim back to the dock. Even more difficult wearing a bullet hole. The man was every bit as dangerous as Steve Clark, perhaps more so. Thornton hid behind a mask of respectability. I needed to add Thornton and the mafia to my list of enemies like a grizzly needed sleeping pills for a winter nap.

I shrugged acquiescence. "I didn't think so."

In silence, Thornton whirled and stomped up the stairwell to the deck, turned the boat around, and roared back to the dock.

It was a long, silent trip back.

I stepped ashore, and Thornton called out. "Remember what I said. And...the offer is still open if you change your mind."

I wanted those videos in the worst possible way. They would solve all of Rachel's problems and clear my name. But I wouldn't change my mind. The tapes would come at too high a price. There might be a chance I could find where Thornton hid them. Taking the disks from him wouldn't prick my conscience at all.

15

Bridger Mountain lodge

"I saw Ben Marshall at Fisherman's Wharf today." Goldie's voice quivered like a guitar string over the phone. "He sat across the room with a tough-looking man I didn't recognize."

She paused, inhaling a shaky breath that sounded in my ear. "A friend invited me to The Wharf for lunch. After the waiter seated us, I glanced over and almost fainted. I hope you don't mind that I called so late, and on a holiday. I've been too nervous to sleep since I saw him."

With great effort, I focused my sleep-dazed brain. In the semi-darkness, I glanced at the time on my cellphone. 1:23 am glowed in bright red numbers—officially now Christmas Eve. "That's why I left my card—in case something important came up. Are you certain the man you saw was Marshall? It's been a long time, Goldie. He would have changed a lot."

"It *was* Marshall. I'd know his face anywhere. He looked older, yes, but I'd stake my life on it."

I picked up on Goldie's fear. She had more reason to be concerned than she knew. "Did he see you?"

"I don't think so. He seemed engrossed in conversation with his dinner companion."

With the cell phone cupped under my chin, I slid my feet into my house slippers, and paced. This could be the break I'd prayed for. "I'll fly out today and check with you before heading on to San Quentin. The warden will be interested in this development. Can you stay the rest of the night with someone or go to a hotel?"

"Do you think that's necessary?"

"I'd rather err on the side of caution. Don't take time to pack."

"There's a girlfriend in the suburbs I can stay with, Judy Phelps. She'll take me in. I'll give you my cell number. You can call me tomorrow after your plane lands."

"Leave soon, Goldie. Let me know when you're safe, and make sure no one follows you."

"Noah, you're frightening me."

"I just want to make sure you're safe. OK?"

"I'll call when I reach Judy's." She gave me her cell number and disconnected.

I continued to pace until she called an hour later to say she'd arrived.

Too wired to sleep, I warmed up leftover coffee, and sipped it while I packed.

Dawn broke that morning, gray and overcast, as I drove to the Salt Lake airport. Forced to wait on standby, I grabbed the first available flight out. This time I had a window seat, but it still packed me shoulder-to-shoulder with my fellow traveler. Two hours later the *whump, whump* of wheels on the tarmac signaled we'd arrived on schedule.

Sunshine flooded through the terminal exit. I paused to let the warmth seep into my skin. Wyoming winters made me appreciate California weather.

I searched my pocket for the cell phone stored there before the flight started and punched the number Goldie gave me. "Hey, I just got in. You OK?"

She laughed. "Sure, never better. How about letting me act as your chauffeur today? My social calendar has been cleared in your honor."

It only took a minute for me to accept. I could keep tabs on her that way. I was still uneasy about her encounter with Marshall.

While waiting for Goldie, I placed a call to San Quentin. I'd taken a chance Tyler would be in today. On my previous visit, he hadn't worn a wedding band. No family pictures decorated his office. Our handshake told me all about John Tyler. The man was a maverick, a loner, and a workaholic. I was prepared to layover in case I'd guessed wrong.

The phone line buzzed, and then a mechanical voice gave me a list of options, which finally led to the reception desk. "Is Assistant Warden John Tyler in today? I realize it's a holiday, but if he's available, I'd like to speak to him." A long pause ensued. I waited on hold while lively mariachi music jumped in the background. The operator returned and told me he was in and made the connection. Within minutes, I had an appointment at three that afternoon. His voice sounded pleased to have company.

Twenty-five minutes later, Goldie eased her sleek, white Mercedes sports job to the curb in front of the Southwest terminal, flashed me a bright smile, and popped the trunk open. I tossed in my briefcase and slid into the seat beside her. In a white suit and golden tan, she looked like an ad for the local Chamber of Commerce.

We pulled into traffic and headed south. Warmth streamed through the sunroof as the classy automobile wound its way through the city's clogged arteries. The scenery along the San Rafael Highway passed in a lush, tropical blur.

❧

San Quentin State Prison

At the prison, the guard waved us through to the main office compound. Tyler's familiarity with Marshall and Jensen would save time. I explained my fake identity to Goldie en route. She only laughed and shook her head. "Sam Spade, huh?"

In short order, the trustee, Kevin, whose name Goldie elicited from him within minutes, led us back to Tyler's office.

Tyler's gaze locked on Goldie. He gave her an appreciative glance and then turned his attention to me. "Back so soon? How can I help you today?"

After introductions, Goldie related what she'd seen at Fisherman's Wharf.

Tyler listened intently as she told her story. "How well did you know Marshall, Goldie?"

"Too well," she said. "He was married to my friend, and although we didn't socialize, I saw more of him than I wanted to. We were neighbors for five years."

The warden shook his head. "Don't take this personally, but I don't see how it's possible for Marshall to be alive. We run a tight ship here, and the only dead man after that riot had fingerprints and dental records that belonged to Benjamin Marshall."

"With all due respect, John, I don't have an answer for that." She used his first name with the same familiarity he had used hers. "I can only tell you the man at Fisherman's Wharf was Ben Marshall. He's not the type of man I could easily confuse with someone else."

I raised my hand. "Just suppose, for a moment, that Goldie's right. The man was Marshall. Is there any way he could have pulled off a switch of identity with someone, Jensen perhaps?"

Tyler's lips curled into a half-smile. "That thought occurred to me. So I'm going to humor you folks and check this out. Not because I think you're right, but because I don't want there to be the slightest possibility that scumbag put one over on us. I'll go back over the old records. If anything jumps out at me, I'll let you know."

A promise to check it now was the best we could hope for. Tyler wasn't an ordinary everyday bureaucrat. I shook his hand and thanked him for his time.

❧❧

San Francisco, California

Goldie and I reached the "city by the bay" as the sun was setting, leaving layered shades of pink and gold on the horizon as it slipped into the sea. Somehow, it's hard to feel the Christmas spirit when the temperature is in the 70s. But it was nice to spend the day with Goldie. She was well read, politically astute, and easy on the eye. Good company.

I glanced over at her. "If you know a good restaurant where we can take advantage of this spectacular view, I'll buy your dinner."

"Deal, mister. I just happen to know a fantastic seafood place near here that overlooks the bay."

Twenty-minutes later, she whipped into a crowded parking lot. Tantalizing aromas wafted into the night air. Inside, the atmosphere and candlelight kept the mood mellow. Goldie ordered baked shark, and she frowned at me when I ordered a T-bone steak. I ignored her scowl.

She gazed out at the shimmering moonlight reflected on the water. "To look at me, would you believe I'm the daughter of a poor Texas sharecropper?"

I shook my head. "Nope, you look more like a product of an expensive finishing school."

Goldie's cheeks dimpled into a wistful smile. "That I owe to my husband, Abe. A small inheritance from my paternal grandmother provided my ticket off the farm. The first year at university, my roommate introduced me to her father, Abraham Marks."

She twisted the diamond wedding band on her finger. "I liked Abe right away, despite the twenty-year age difference. His wife had died just before Makala's fourth birthday. Abe and I dated long-distance while I attended college." Her eyes misted. "He was the kindest man I'd ever known. He introduced me to a life of art and culture I'd only imagined."

She brushed a stray lock of blonde hair from her forehead. "Over Makala's objections, we married after I graduated and I moved to California." She wiped away the frost on her tea glass with a manicured fingertip. "Your typical trophy wife, but he never treated me that way. After Abe died, I stayed here. It had become my home. I still miss him terribly."

The sad thing about May/December relationships was that no matter how loving, they usually left the younger spouse alone much too soon. I touched her hand. "I'm sorry. It must have been lonely for you after his death."

She swallowed hard. "Very lonely. I have friends, but it isn't the same. Now I regret we never had children." Her gaze lowered, and she fingered the cocktail napkin under her glass. "Tell me about you. You can't say you've never been tempted to get married."

The focus now on me, I leaned against the back of my chair. "I came close once, but it didn't work out. She realized what a bum I was and called it off."

Goldie's soft laugh floated across the table. "I don't believe that for a minute."

McKenna's face drifted into my mind unbidden. I pushed it back. "I'm not always as loveable as I seem."

I savored the last bite of the steak's charbroiled flavor, letting it linger on my tongue while I folded my napkin on the table. "Drive me back to your place. I want to check out your security system. If there's a problem, I can make temporary repairs until you get a locksmith. I'll grab a cab to the airport. For a while, I'd rather you not drive alone on the streets after dark."

Traffic inched like a herd of armadillos up the steep road to Goldie's townhome. We reached the gated entrance and Goldie's gasp made me turn to her. She slammed on the brakes, almost sending me through the windshield.

A burned-out stack of rubble occupied the space previously held by her home.

Wet concrete gleamed in the lights of a lone fire truck as two firefighters kept vigil near the blackened shell.

Goldie jumped from the car, gaze wildly searching the area. She crept forward, covering her mouth with both hands, face drained of color. Greasy black water covered her white sandaled feet. She stopped and stared at the wreckage—her home gone in less than twenty-four hours.

A cluster of neighbors milled outside the restricted area in open-mouth dismay. I angled across the pavement to where two firemen were storing their equipment away. Goldie walked beside me, her arms wrapped tight around her body, eyes wide and fathomless.

One of the men stopped us. "You can't come any closer; the area could still be dangerous."

I put my hands on Goldie's shoulders and pulled her forward. "This is Mrs. Marks; she owned one of the condos that burned."

The man turned to her. "We've been trying all day to locate you."

She couldn't or wouldn't speak, so I took the lead. "She spent last night with a friend and went out of town today. We just got back. What happened?"

"We think a gas leak in Ms. Marks's unit caused an explosion about four thirty this morning."

"But I had sprinklers in every room. The insurance company demanded it before they'd cover my art collection."

"Sprinklers won't stop an explosion, ma'am."

"Anyone injured?" I asked.

"Luckily, the woman in the other unit got out safely before the flames reached her apartment."

I gazed at Goldie, standing small and forlorn beside me. "We have reason to believe this may have been an attempted murder. Who do we need to speak to?"

The fireman pushed his hat back and cast a quizzical look at me. He motioned for us to wait. Jerking a cell phone from his pocket, he punched buttons and strode away. The call ended, and he came back to where we waited. "The fire marshal will meet you at the station. Do you know where it is?"

Goldie nodded.

Over the next hour, we explained our Ben Marshall theory and gave the investigator John Tyler's number at San Quentin. Goldie remained silent, only answering questions when asked. The interview ended, and we returned to her car.

Goldie grabbed my arm and placed her head against my good shoulder. "I donated all the stored artifacts to the museum after Abe died." She waved a hand at the rubble. "These were my favorites." She bit her lip and turned away. "I should have donated them all. Now they're gone. Money can't replace what I've lost."

I looked into her eyes. "Consider how lucky you are—you weren't here when the explosion happened. You missed the blast by a little over five hours." I put my fingers under her chin and made her look at me. "You would have been killed."

She moaned. "You don't understand. My collection is irreplaceable!"

"So is your life, Goldie." I pulled her in close for a long hug. "So is your life."

At the airport, we opted for the X-ray rather than the invasive pat down. I decided to walk Goldie to her gate before I went to my own gate.

With red-rimmed eyes and a small tremor in her hands, Goldie prepared to board a plane to her sister in Dallas. She presented a pathetic figure; wind-tossed locks disheveled—suit and shoes smudged with soot. Her sole possessions resided in the tiny overnight bag she'd taken to Judy's. The smell of smoke from the fire scene lingered in our hair and clothing. Our fellow travelers might object, but it couldn't be helped.

Soon her plane's jet engines whined into place, and a jetport unfurled and covered the exit hatch. Weary passengers disembarked and scattered into the terminal. There would be a mob of greeters to meet them at the luggage carousal. It was Christmas.

We found seats near the ticket counter as new attendants arrived and began a flurry of preparations for the next boarding.

I touched Goldie's arm. "Stay at your sister's until I tell you it's safe to come back. Marshall will have discovered by now that you weren't at home when the blast occurred. He'll start looking for you. Don't let anyone know where you're staying. Not Judy, not anyone. I can't protect you from Wyoming."

She nodded and leaned against my shoulder. "I thought you were trying to frighten me last night." She expelled a shaky breath with realization setting in. "You saved my life, Noah."

My hands on her shoulders, I turned her to face me. "You saved your life by heeding my warning. Don't forget that. Are you sure Marshall doesn't know about your sister or your past in Texas?"

She patted my hand and the corners of her mouth turned up in a feeble grin. "I never really had a personal relationship with Ben. Trust me, he doesn't know about Barbara."

The flight attendant announced her seat row over the intercom. Goldie tiptoed to kiss my cheek. My gaze followed her through the gate and until she vanished into the mouth of the jetport.

The pessimist in me made me wait until she was in the air. Through the large plate glass window, I stared as the aircraft soared into the black sky, and cold fingers of fear tickled down my spine.

The explosion hadn't been an accident or a coincidence. The odds against it were astronomical. Marshall had seen her and knew he had to prevent her from exposing him. He hadn't counted on her calling me. By telling John Tyler what she had seen, she sent forces into action that would put him back in prison.

Goldie had no idea how much danger she was in.

16

Bridger Mountains Lodge

After seeing Goldie safely on her way, I caught a red-eye to Utah. Once more on the ground, I drove to my frozen haven in the mountains. A little paranoid after Goldie's experience, I bolted the door, and checked all the locks on the windows. Everything was secure.

The place lacked the elegance of Jake's cabin, but God had provided. There were more than enough provisions for a six-month stay. By His grace, I wouldn't need it that long.

Hungry, I whipped up a late snack of sausage and waffles, and then crashed on the worn-out sofa in the game room with a monster headache. My C-drive bordered on overload. This wasn't how I'd envisioned spending Christmas.

Two aspirins later, I shuffled through an assortment of old DVD's, stuck one in the slot, and pushed play. Midway through the film, I shut it down, unable to concentrate with Goldie's peril still on my mind.

The next day, I called Lincoln Armstrong's private number. "Would it be possible to see you today? It's short notice, I know, but I have new information I'd like to share, and I prefer not to give it over the phone."

A short pause—pages shuffled in the background.

"I'm running behind because of the holidays, but I can squeeze in lunch. Can you meet me at Pine Lake Country Club? It's on the lake near my home, say eleven thirty?"

"Thanks. I'll see you there."

Sometimes it's easier to hide in plain sight than in dark corners. I'd grown a short beard, my usual close-cropped hair now sported a longer lumberjack look, and a pair of aviator sunglasses completed my makeover. In theory, no one would recognize me.

❧

Pine Lake Country Club

Two hours later, I pulled into valet parking under the portico at the country club entrance. The door captain's spine visibly straightened at the mention of Armstrong's name. "Ah, yes. Mr. Armstrong reserved a private dining room for lunch." He waved over a waiter and gave him the suite number.

When we reached the third door down the hallway, the waiter ushered me inside. Polished brass fixtures, mahogany paneling, and rich leather chairs grouped around the fireplace gave the room a cozy masculine air. A table set for two, dressed in linen finery, sat in the corner.

Armstrong rose from his seat when I entered, crossed the room, and shook my hand. "I took the liberty of ordering lobster for both of us. I hope you don't mind."

"Lobster is one of my favorite food groups."

Armstrong chuckled and settled back into his chair. He motioned me to sit. "I'm glad you called. Patience isn't my strongest virtue."

I took the seat across from him. "You've been more than tolerant. Now, I have what I think is very good news. Ben Marshall is alive. I have no physical proof of that, but I'm certain in my own mind. An old friend of Abigail's spotted him in San Francisco two days ago. Goldie, that's Abigail's friend, called Christmas Eve to tell me."

Armstrong leaned back in his chair. "You think it's possible Marshall's really alive?"

"Yes, I trust Goldie's instincts. She knew Marshall too well to make a mistake. I don't know yet how he manipulated prison records, but I believe he had the connections inside to pull it off. I'm convinced he's responsible for Abigail's disappearance. Now all we have to do is find him."

The cell phone in my jacket vibrated. I retrieved it and held it up. "Do you mind if I take this call? I've been expecting to hear from the warden at San Quentin, and this looks like it."

Armstrong shook his head, and I punched talk.

The warden's sandpaper voice sounded in my ear. "John Tyler here. Off the record, your friend was right. I verified the fingerprint in our system against the national files. Someone switched them on our end."

"How could he pull that off?"

"Again, just between the two of us, I figure he or a pal hacked into the prison's internal files from an office or the library and made the switch. Probably paid one of the staff or an inmate to change out the dental records."

"What's the next step?"

"We'll give the information to the authorities. They'll most likely put out an APB, and circulate his mug shot. See what turns up."

"Thanks for letting me know, John. This clears up a lot of questions. I'm confident Marshall is responsible for the explosion at Goldie's home night before last."

A pause. "What happened?"

"Nothing official yet. So far, investigators think the blast came from a leak in her furnace, but it's too convenient to suit me. They're still looking into it. The blaze destroyed two condos and a very valuable art collection."

Tyler growled. "That's the kind of reprobate Marshall is—anything to remove a threat."

I let him rant for a few minutes and then thanked him again. "I'll give the local officials a heads-up. They've had Mrs. Armstrong's case on ice for a few years."

When the call ended, Armstrong straightened in his chair. "That was the confirmation you needed?"

I nodded.

"Good. You've accomplished what I hired you to do. I hadn't dared hope for a resolution so soon." He shook his head and stared into the fire for a moment. "If it's agreeable with you, I'd like you to stay on this, at least until Marshall is behind bars."

"That may take some time, and the police will be doing most of the work—they have all the resources. And the authorities are still looking for me. That limits my mobility somewhat at present. I'm not trying to talk myself out of a job, just want you to know my limitations."

Powerful men aren't always good listeners. Not so with Lincoln Armstrong. He gave his full attention—heard and evaluated each word.

Armstrong pushed his chair back and walked to the hearth. He stood gazing into the flames. After a moment, he turned and faced me. "As you know, my experience with law enforcement leaves much to be desired. I'd like you to stay on the case."

"If that's what you want, I'll keep on it until this situation is resolved to your satisfaction."

He braced one elbow on the mantel and nodded. "Good. Then it's settled. You've gathered more information in a few weeks than the police did in three years." There was a chill in his gaze, a well of pain that ran deep into his soul. "I can't get my life back until I know what happened to Abby."

When the food arrived, the waiter placed a napkin on my lap, cracked the lobster, cut it into small bites, and did everything but feed me. While we ate, I spent the better part of lunch describing in detail the meeting with Goldie.

Obviously anxious to return to the office, Armstrong rose after the meal ended.

We exited the private room and stepped into the corridor.

A voice behind me called, "Noah, Noah Adams."

Visions of flashing blue lights and handcuffs seared my brain as I turned. There stood Jake Stein, with a huge smile on his face. My heart began to pump blood again. Jake glanced at my companion, visibly impressed. I hastily introduced the two men, and Armstrong excused himself. He hurried to the lobby and back to work.

Jake inclined his head toward Armstrong's disappearing form. "Why don't you ever bring me clients like that?"

"Because he keeps a battery of attorneys on staff."

Jake shrugged and looked up at me. "Where are you staying?" He wagged his hand. "Don't tell me where you moved to…I'm better off not knowing."

Jake followed me to valet parking. While we walked, I told Jake about my brush with the low-life in the alley.

"Any idea who set him on you?"

"I'm sure Harry London gave the marching orders. The thug's only interest was Cody's whereabouts."

Small lines formed at the corner of Jake's eyes. "Well, take care of yourself, kid. My life would be infinitely boring without you around."

"I'm touched by your concern. Any news on Rachel's situation?"

"Without the jailbreak charges, I could get everything she wants from Harry London. And if the federal boys find her, I'll have to go with what I've got and pray for a jury of battered women."

We reached the exit. "You coming or going?"

He stopped beside me, searched his pocket, and produced his valet ticket. "I'm headed home. Met some old partners here for lunch."

We handed our stubs to the attendant. While we waited for the cars to appear, I told him about Thornton's offer to give me the London security tapes.

Jake turned toward me in slow motion, mouth agape. "You've got to be kidding me."

I shook my head.

"Any way we could steal them?"

I contrived a shocked expression. "You, an officer of the court, are asking me to steal evidence? Besides, I haven't a clue where Thornton might've hidden them. Can't say I didn't think of that myself but dismissed it. If those disks disappeared, he'd know who snatched them. That kind of trouble I don't need."

Jake released a deep breath. "Yeah, it sounded too good to be true. That would make my job too easy. What I wouldn't give to have those puppies though. I could make a jury of terrorists weep."

His BMW and the Jeep appeared at the curb. Jake opened the driver's door of his Beemer and called to me. "Hey, you plan to keep my Jeep?"

I laughed. "Yeah. I kind of like it."

He rubbed his hands together and chuckled. "Good, I'll send you a bill."

৵৽

Hebron, Wyoming

For obvious reasons, I couldn't go to the police with the Marshall information. So I did the next best thing. That afternoon, I called Amos to meet me at a hangout for hunters outside of town.

Amos arrived ten minutes after me and settled into the seat across the table. The waitress placed mission jars filled with soft drinks on our table. Later she returned with chips and salsa. Waiters, with platters of sizzling fajitas and steaming enchiladas, passed our table and Amos's gaze followed the food. It was authentic Tex-Mex fare, and it was good eating.

"Order if you want to. I'm good with the appetizers." I dunked a chip in the salsa while he ordered. Then I told him about Ben Marshall being alive.

Amos's black eyes widened. "How'd you find that out?"

"Great detective work."

He hammered a fist against his chest.

I gave him a break. "Actually, the information

came when I ran into Goldie Marks." I explained how I'd met her and that she spotted Marshall in San Francisco.

Amos shook his head. "You're on the side of the angels, my friend." He hesitated. "Guess I shouldn't sell you short. You're the one who found the Marks woman. None of our guys ever checked Abigail Armstrong's past. They got hung up on the husband as her killer."

I shrugged. "Your guys went with the odds, and they were right. Just picked the wrong spouse. I don't care who gets the credit for discovering Ben Marshall's resurrection as long as we find the guy."

I slid John Tyler's number at San Quentin across the table. "Tyler will confirm everything in case your boss needs proof. If you speak to Tyler, he knows me as Sam Spade."

"You're kidding, right?"

"Nope."

Amos rolled his eyes and then shook his head. "I won't ask."

17

Bridger Mountain Lodge

I'd spent yesterday evening tightening hinges, unsticking windows and putting washers in faucets at the lodge. Paying for my keep. I needed the down time to unwind and work the kinks out of my mind. Manual labor cleared the cobwebs.

When the phone rang, I'd just taken the last bite of my fourth blueberry pancake. I reached across the red-checked oilcloth, grabbed my cell phone, and mumbled, "Hello."

A woman's voice asked, "Noah Adams?"

I swallowed the mouthful "Yes."

"Mr. Adams, my name is Barbara Nelson. I'm Goldie's sister. She told me you're a detective...I found your number in her phone book" She inhaled an audible breath. "Goldie returned to California yesterday to see her insurance agent." There was a pause. "She's been depressed over the loss of the antiques since she came home. I told her to handle it over the phone, but she refused...you can't reason with Goldie when she gets in one of her moods. I'm terrified something happened to her. I tried all day yesterday and this morning to reach her. She's not answering her phone. That's not like Goldie."

All the horrible possibilities ran through my mind. Why didn't she listen to my warning? Forcing a calm into my voice, I asked, "Did you try her friend, Judy?"

"She hasn't seen Goldie."

I took a last gulp of coffee. "I'll check it out. She probably just switched off her phone. I'll fly back to Frisco today." Even I didn't believe what I just said.

The line became silent for a moment. "Thank you. I'd go...but I wouldn't know where to begin. I really appreciate—"

"Don't worry. I'll call when I find her."

I hadn't planned to return to California so soon, but Goldie had placed herself in more danger than she could possibly imagine. And if I found her safe, I intended to send her a whopping bill for my services. I charge a higher fee for stupid. "Barbara, if you hear from Goldie in the meantime, call me right away." My anger at Goldie was tempered by my fear for what she might have wandered into.

I really should move to Salt Lake City. I'd spent more time in their airport than I had in Hebron.

Three hours later, I arrived at the terminal and caught the earliest flight out. My frequent flyer miles were going up faster than my blood pressure.

❧❦

San Francisco, California

In Frisco, I rented a car with the credit card Armstrong sent and found the nearest police station to Goldie's condominium. I had no reason to believe the California justice system had me on their radar, and the old Sam Spade ID would ensure I kept it that way.

Visitor parking contained only one empty spot. I slid the sedan into it and killed the motor. The building sat low and sleek, palm trees and red and yellow flowers hugged the structure's perimeter. Not the Taj

Mahal, but compared to Hebron's police headquarters, it was a giant step forward. Inside, the government-issue furniture appeared new, not like Hebron's rejects from a WWII clearance sale.

The desk sergeant gazed into his computer monitor. I cleared my throat. When he looked up, I handed him my business card and asked to speak to a detective. He pointed me to one of the colorful chairs against the wall.

Soon, a trim Latina ventured out. We exchanged introductions, and Rena Chavez led me back to her cubicle. Two small boys smiled at me from a silver frame on her desk. With only a trace of an accent, she offered me a seat.

I explained about the fire and told her Goldie's sister hadn't been able to contact Goldie. Chavez pulled a yellow legal pad from a drawer and took down the information.

I leaned forward. "I think she may be in serious trouble, Detective Chavez. I'm sure a man named Ben Marshall is responsible for the explosion that destroyed her townhouse on—"

Marshall's name made her eyes widen. She sat up straight in her chair and gave me her full attention. "You think Benjamin Marshall might be responsible for your friend's disappearance? What makes you think so?"

"I can't prove it, but Goldie is the person who identified Marshall, and her condo burned to the ground shortly thereafter. You can verify this with the fire marshal who filed the report." I gave her Goldie's description and the color, make, and model of her car.

Chavez stood and shook my hand. "Thanks for coming in. We'll put this information out on your friend. Where can I reach you?"

Her touch told me she was just what she seemed to be, an effective law enforcement officer and working mother. But suspicious, very suspicious.

"I came here straight from the airport. Haven't booked a hotel yet." I gave her my card, wrote my cell number on the back, and left to find accommodations for the night.

My stomach growled. It had been a while since the blueberry pancakes. I grabbed a bite at the coffee shop next to the hotel.

The chicken sandwich tasted like rubber. It was probably my anxiety, not the food. I couldn't sit by and do nothing while the police put Goldie in their queue behind a hundred other missing persons. Bureaucratic wheels turned too slow. I needed to find her *now*.

Leaving the unfinished sandwich on the table, I hurried across the parking lot to my car.

My mind ran through all the possibilities, and it occurred to me Goldie could have returned to the condo to try and salvage some of her treasures.

It was as good as any place to start.

I activated the auto's GPS and drove to the charred ruins of what was left of Goldie's home.

The security guard I'd met earlier was on duty at the gate. I described Goldie and her car. The guard leaned closer to the open window. "Yeah, Ms. Marks came by earlier today. But she left around one thirty. Said she might be back later."

"Did she mention where she was headed?"

The guard shook her head. "Sorry."

I asked for permission to look around, and the gate slid open. In the dim afternoon light, the property damage looked worse than it had at my last visit.

The strong smell of smoke and chemicals mixed with damp air burned my nostrils. The sky grew dark and waves of fog washed in from the sea, chilling the air. I sauntered around the deserted lot and hoped to find something that would suggest where Goldie had gone.

I kicked the mounds of ashes with the toe of my shoe without any idea of what I was looking for.

In a spot near two scorched bushes lay a red bird from her Christmas tree and a brass cherub doorknocker—untouched by the explosion. What were the odds?

Guilt gnawed my gut. Goldie got into this mess because of me. She hadn't known about Marshall's supposed death until I told her. That knowledge may have cost her life. Fear for her safety welled inside my chest and wouldn't let go. Goldie exuded an almost inextinguishable vibrancy. *Please, God, don't let that light go out.*

Where to turn next?

Back in the car, I drove down the hill toward the city. The gray mist thickened making the journey more hazardous. The mountain on one side, a steep drop off on the other. Mind preoccupied, I almost missed a hairpin turn that loomed unexpectedly through the fog, and I stomped the brakes.

Wrong thing to do on a slick highway. The tires skidded on the damp pavement and hurled the car into the mountain wall.

Annoyed at my stupidity, I jumped out and checked the right front fender. It rested resolutely against the wall of dirt, some of which dumped onto the car's hood. The fog and lack of light impeded my inspection, but the automobile appeared unharmed. I exhaled a deep breath and scurried back to the driver's side door, expecting a motorist to rear-end me any second from around the blind turn.

I flung open the drivers-side door when a double-line of black skid marks in the northbound lane caught my attention. The tire tracks ran onto the narrow shoulder.

Hair on the back of my neck prickled. I pulled the rental car around the curve and parked on the shoulder and then followed the tracks for almost a hundred yards. When the trail ended, trampled shrubs led to the cliff's edge. It didn't take a rocket scientist to see a vehicle had gone over the edge into the abyss below.

Coincidence? Or a nudge from God? I had to check it out. Heart pounding an erratic beat, I quick-stepped to the precipice and peered down the mountainside. Mist and darkness obscured the view. I returned to the car and searched for a flashlight. Inside the trunk lay a heavy-duty lamp.

I snatched it up and ran to the edge.

Hand shaking, I swept the beam through the murky shadows. Light reflected off metal about thirty feet below. I stuffed the flashlight into the waistband of my trousers and held onto brush as I made an urgent descent, scrambling for a foothold and a closer look. Whoever went over the cliff could be dead, or seriously injured.

The descent against the muddy wall sent my heart into my mouth. I envisioned my guardian angel placing a rush order for a pair of extra-large wings. I grabbed hold of a bush. The huge lump in my throat seemed to grow larger as I dangled in space until my feet finally touched down on a rocky ledge.

Then it came into view. There, almost covered in mud, limbs, and debris, sat a white Mercedes, the top crushed by the force of downhill motion. The roof almost flat against the headrests—the driver's side window smashed. Strapped in the seat, almost invisible, was Goldie Marks.

I leaned back against the outcropping, reached into my pocket, pulled out my cell, and prayed for bars. When the phone reflected a strong signal, I punched 9-1-1.

With help on the way, I jerked the car door open and the vehicle shifted away from me. It rested in a precarious position on a rock that kept it from tumbling to the canyon's rocky base. I held my breath as the car wavered like a teeter-totter then settled back into position on the boulder.

The crushed vehicle looked like an expensive tomb.

I pushed my hand inside the vehicle, pressed my fingertips to her throat and felt an almost indistinguishable thump. Weak, but she still clung to life.

The wail of sirens grew louder as emergency vehicles converged above my position, blue and white lights penetrated the fog casting an eerie glow on the scene.

A male voice called out. "Hey, you all right down there?"

"Yes, we're both alive, but my friend is trapped in the car. I believe her injuries are serious, and it looks like you'll have to cut her out of the wreckage."

"How much room do you have on that ledge and is it stable?" The same voice asked.

I gave the matter full consideration before I

replied. "Where I am is about four feet. The car is resting on a slightly larger spot. It's feels like solid rock so I assume its stable, but I don't have any idea how much weight it will bear."

"Hold on, buddy. I'm coming down."

A commotion drifted down from the crest above. Two firefighters descended to the ledge. They brought equipment down with them. When one guy attempted to attach a cable hook to the vehicle's rear-end, the automobile shifted forward, threatening to plunge into the abyss below.

The two men exchanged wide-eyed glances. The second man dashed to the backend and added his body weight while the other connected the cable. Next came the slow process of cutting away metal to remove Goldie from the wreckage without causing further injury.

My ledge became crowded, as two EMT's joined me. Within minutes, they'd placed Goldie onto a backboard, stabilized her neck with a collar, and positioned an oxygen mask over her nose and mouth. Cables invisible in the darkness, the board rose to the road above as if by magic.

With Goldie safe above, one of the EMT's turned her attention to me. "You hurt?"

I shook my head. "Just a few scratches."

A fireman strapped me into a harness and lifted my tired, damp body to the hilltop. Muddy and chilled, I followed the ambulance into the hospital's emergency parking.

Bay City Hospital, San Francisco

While I waited for news about Goldie, I made the dreaded call to Barbara. She answered on the second ring and listened silently while I explain where I was and why. Her voice quivered when she spoke. "I'll take the next flight out. Give me the name and address of the hospital again."

Detective Rena Chavez joined me later in the emergency room. She eyed the No Smoking sign and muttered under her breath. "It looks as though someone hit Ms. Marks' car from behind and shoved it over the cliff. The skid marks indicate she had the brakes on all the way before the car plunged over. How did you find her?"

"Her guardian angel," I said with all sincerity.

Two eyebrows formed one on Chavez's slim brow, her gaze questioning my sanity.

I exhaled, turned to her, and explained the steps that led me to Goldie. "A guardian angel is my answer. You can find your own."

Chavez looked down at her nicotine-stained fingers and picked at her cuticles. "For the record, we checked your rental car to see if the paint matched the dents on Ms. Marks's automobile."

"You figured I pushed her off the cliff? I found her, and I'm the one who told you she was missing."

Chavez shrugged. "Stranger things have happened."

Miffed, I turned my back on her and walked away. In her line of work, she was paid to be suspicious, but I was in no mood to deal with a non-believing, distrustful, nicotine addict who smelled like an ashtray.

తిళ్ళ

After more than a three hour wait, a tired doctor emerged, untying his green surgical mask. He pushed through the double doors and glanced around the waiting area, and then approached the nurses' station. The woman behind the desk pointed in our direction.

Chavez rose and made rapid strides across the tiled floor to meet him. I followed.

He leaned against the counter. "Are you relatives of Ms. Marks?"

Chavez flashed her badge. "No, I'm Detective Chavez, and this is Detective Spade. She doesn't have any family in the city."

The surgeon reached to shake hands. "The patient came through surgery fine, considering her injuries. After a short period, she'll be taken to intensive care. She had multiple internal injuries. We removed her spleen and repaired a laceration to her liver. She also has a fractured leg, two fractured ribs, and a concussion. She's a very lucky lady to be alive. After she's settled in her room, you can visit her for fifteen minutes every two hours, but she probably won't regain consciousness for a while."

He turned to the petite detective. "You need to hold your questions until later. It's important she rest as much as possible. She'll be in a lot of pain when she wakes."

When the doctor had gone, Chavez switched her attention to me. "I'm posting a guard outside her unit in ICU. You can't see Ms. Marks until she regains consciousness, and I've had a chance to speak to her."

I just stared at her, not believing she was serious about the possibility I was behind Goldie's accident.

While I waited for Barbara's arrival, I dashed down the street to my hotel and grabbed a shower and change of clothes to get rid of the filth I brought with me from the ledge. Tired and hungry, I went back to the hospital and catnapped in the waiting room.

❧

Barbara arrived around six o'clock the next morning, a younger, plumper version of her sister, shaken and full of questions I answered as best I could.

I spotted the half-full coffeemaker in the corner and poured two cups. It wasn't fresh, but it beat the heck out of vending machine sludge.

I glanced over at Barbara. "How do you take it?"

"A little cream and two sugars."

I handed her the cup. "This isn't gourmet, but maybe it will help."

She took a sip and grimaced.

Near her chair, a television droned on with some series rerun. Tears made tiny tracks down Barbara's cheeks. Tears that had nothing to do with the TV drama.

I took the chair next to her. "Have you found a hotel?"

She gave a weary shake of her head. "I came directly from the airport."

"I'm booked at the Palms Inn, about two blocks away. Why don't you get a room there? It's within walking distance, and we can clean up and nap in shifts. We'll last longer that way."

She nodded a tired acceptance. "Did you know Goldie paid for mine and our younger sister's education? Both college and grad school, the whole thing. That's the kind of person she is. Wanted us to have the same opportunities she had." Barbara laid her hand over mine. "Thank you for finding her. If she doesn't pull through..."

I placed an arm around her shoulders. "She's in good hands. I've been praying ever since I found her."

At the next visitation period, Chavez showed up and went directly to ICU. Fifteen minutes later, she stood in front of me. "OK, you can see her. I cleared it with the guard. Ms. Marks woke up long enough to tell me she didn't know the man who hit her car. I'll be back to get a formal statement when she's out of intensive care."

I nodded and watched her hurried departure to the elevator, betting she would light a cigarette before she reached the parking lot.

A short while later, the elevator dinged and Barbara emerged, somewhat refreshed after a nap at the hotel. We entered ICU together at the next visitation. Goldie's doctor stood at her bedside, her chart in hand.

Barbara cast him an anxious look. "How is she?"

He gave Barbara a sympathetic smile. "Her vital signs are stable. But don't expect any big changes for the next twenty-four hours. This will take time. She sustained a lot of injuries."

Barbara and I moved closer when the doctor left.

Both of Goldie's eyes were black, a large purple bruise marred her left cheek, and her right leg was in a cast up to her knee. Intravenous tubes ran from her arms while monitors emitted reassuring clicks and beeps. Even under pain meds, a soft moan escaped her lips from time to time.

Her condition reminded me how breakable we

humans are—life can be fragile, disappearing in a single breath.

That afternoon, Goldie came around during our visit. She didn't say much, mostly incoherent moans as she wandered in and out of a medication-induced haze, but she recognized us.

Goldie's recovery could take a while. I'd leave as soon as I knew she was out of the woods. Cody and Rachel were still in danger, and I couldn't put their problems on hold for long. Back in the waiting room, I called the ranch and Bill Hand answered.

"Still nothing from London?" I asked.

"No, I'm guessing he hasn't tried to trace Rachel's cell calls. Could also be he's playing cat and mouse to catch us off guard."

I told Bill about Goldie.

"Don't worry about things here. If London shows up, I can handle it unless he brings the police. Then the ball will be back in your court."

I asked to speak to Emma. "Hey Em, I haven't forgotten my promise to move Rachel and Cody. A friend here had a serious accident, but I'll take care of moving them as soon as I return. Shouldn't be more than a day or so."

"Take care of your friend. Bill and I had that talk. We're good. Rachel and Cody can stay here as long as needed."

I exhaled a deep breath. At least one part of my life was going right.

❧◈❧

The following day, a now conscious Goldie was moved from intensive care to a private room.

Barbara, Detective Chavez, and I entered her new accommodations together. Goldie flashed a weak smile and then winced in pain. Words tumbled from her mouth like water over Niagara. "I should have listened to you, Noah...I was so frightened. I remembered what you said about dying and finding out...I didn't think I'd ever get a chance to talk to you."

"Are you trying to rob me of my I-told-you-so moment?" I grinned down at her. "We'll have plenty of time to talk. Anytime you're ready. How do you feel?"

She touched her bandaged head. "I must look a fright." Pure Goldie to worry about her looks after what she'd been through.

"On the contrary, the hospital garb becomes you."

Chavez stepped to the bedside. "I'm Detective Chavez, Ms. Marks. I spoke to you yesterday, but you were pretty out of it. Do you feel like answering a few questions?"

She nodded.

I gave Goldie a stern look. "This time when they release you, go back to Texas with Barbara. Don't leave until I call you and say it's safe to come home. That's an order."

She nodded and lay back against the pillows. "I can't do anything else. I have a broken leg and a busted head—I'll be homebound forever."

Chavez kicked me out of the room while she questioned Goldie.

As I started to the door, Goldie called me back. "Can we talk...when the detective is finished? I'm afraid Ben might try again and..."

I gave her a quick nod and left the room.

A short while later, Chavez called me back in. She closed the door, leaned against it, and spoke to Goldie.

"Before I leave, did you get a good look at the man who pushed you off the road? Good enough to describe him to a police artist?"

Goldie gave a slight shiver. "Yes. I saw his face in my rearview mirror. It wasn't Ben, but I know he's behind it. Since I spotted him, my life has turned upside down. My home destroyed and I've been shoved off a mountain."

"I'll send an artist by sometime tomorrow," Chavez said.

Goldie pulled the cover up to her chin as though suddenly cold. "I'll do whatever it takes to find him."

"Good girl," Chavez said. "I've got to return to the office, but I'll be in touch." She motioned for me to follow her.

"Why does Goldie call you Noah?"

I gave a nervous laugh. "It's a pet name. She says I'm trying to save the world."

Chavez did the eyebrow thing again, turned, and headed for the elevators.

I returned to Goldie's room and moved close to her bedside. "Sure you're up to talking now? I've always got my finger on the trigger, so I'm ready when you are."

She forced a smile. "I'm ready."

Barbara leaned over and kissed her sister's cheek. "I'll see you later, sis."

I reached into my inside jacket pocket to retrieve a small black New Testament I kept for just such emergencies. Dragging a chair close, I took her hand, and then turned to Romans 6:23.

18

Hebron, Wyoming

I'd missed a lot of sleep during the two days spent in California. The trip from the airport to my Wyoming mountainside passed in a sleepy fog. Too tired to notice the cold, I started the snowmobile and shushed up the steep terrain. Inside the lodge, I cranked the heat to seventy degrees and fell into bed.

Fatigue couldn't hold back the nightmare triggered by the stressful events in California.

∂◦∾

A door slams down the hallway and jars me awake.

Craig is home.

Shouts begin, followed by a scream and the sharp crack of a revolver. I try to run to my mother, but my legs won't move. I struggle with the reality of what is happening. Fear spurs me into action, and I scramble out of bed.

Another door crashes.

Tommy cries out.

Another blast.

He's coming for me.

I use the only weapon I have—my invisibility.

Craig shouts, "Where are you, you little punk? I'm gonna…"

But I'm already past him down the hall, out the front door, and to the Raineys' home next door. Again flesh and blood, I plead for them to call an ambulance for my mother and Tommy.

Through the window of Mr. Rainey's home, I watch Craig stagger down the street. He waves the gun, curses, calling my name. Sirens fill the cold morning air.

The Rainey's try to restrain me, but I break loose and run to my mother's bedside. Her nightgown covered with blood—her heart pumps thick red liquid from the hole in her chest. I grab a throw pillow and place it over the wound. Somehow I must stop the bleeding. She reaches for my hand and shakes her head. "Tommy..."

I begin to cry, and she knows.

"Should have...listened...sorry." Her hand drops from my grasp.

I run to Tommy, but he too slipped away into death's cold grip.

Both dead—my fault.

I jarred awake at the jangle of the alarm, my pajamas damp with perspiration. I shook off the dream after a hot shower and cup of coffee. Dressed, I left to keep a doctor's appointment.

Just a precaution.

The noble healer X-rayed the shoulder. "You say you broke your collarbone a week or so ago?"

"Yeah, a possible fracture. That's what the EMT told me."

"I hate to disagree with a fellow professional, but there must have been a mistake. The bone shows no sign of a break or fracture, and broken bones don't heal that fast. However, there is something unusual in your bone structure. The density looks abnormal. I'd like to run a series of tests—."

"Sorry, Doc. I don't have time today. Maybe later."

He had a gleam in his eye I'd seen before. I'd

gotten the same response with every injury sustained since childhood. I'd been discharged from the Marines for a foot so badly fractured that medics said I would be crippled, only to be completely healed a month after leaving the service. The doc's gaze made me uncomfortable, and I left. I would not go back for those tests, couldn't risk what they might reveal.

A cold north wind blew large white flakes across the trail. At least it wasn't in my face. At the camp, I hurried inside, stoked a healthy fire in the hearth, and then went into the kitchen for a lunch of soup and sandwiches.

Later, hot cider in hand, I pulled a file from my briefcase and spread the papers on the coffee table. I searched through the police reports Armstrong had given me and reviewed again the statements taken from the country club guests and staff the night of the charity affair.

The list held no clues. None of the names looked familiar. Abby became upset shortly after she arrived that night. Ben Marshall must have a connection to the club. But in what capacity? A valet, a waiter, a guest? What?

Pine Hills Country Club wasn't too far from the retreat. I jerked on my coat and decided to interview the club personnel still employed there. If Marshall attended the event that night, and everything pointed in that direction, could he still be there?

Long shot, but possible.

My P.I. license got me inside. The earlier luncheon with Armstrong the day after Christmas helped. The guard remembered me and gave directions to the manager's office in the main lobby.

I handed my card to the receptionist. She took it,

dialed an extension number, and asked the manager if he would see me. Soon a door opened at the end of the hallway. A short man in a gray wool suit walked toward me. "Mr. Spade, I'm Wilson Arthur. How may I help you?"

"Do I call you Mr. Wilson or Mr. Arthur?"

"Just call me Wilson, that's my first name. People always get that backwards."

We walked down the corridor to his office. "Were you the general manager here three years ago?"

Wilson stopped in mid-stride and raised an eyebrow. "Ah, you've come about the Abigail Armstrong matter." A shadow passed over his face.

I nodded. "What was it like that night? Anything unusual happen that you can remember? New caterers, extra parking attendants, et cetera?"

"Yes to both questions. We held a charity function here, and the Chamber of Commerce had its awards banquet, as it does every year."

We reached the office. He opened the door, stepped aside for me to enter and pointed me to a chair by the window.

I took the proffered seat. "Did the police check out the extra help you used that evening?"

Wilson moved to his desk and leaned against the corner. "I assume so. They asked for a list of the regular staff, the temporary help, and caterers, as well as a list of all our members."

"Did you know Mrs. Armstrong?"

"Yes, quite well. She came here often for lunch. Her disappearance was a terrible, personal blow."

"Did you see her that night?"

He stood and walked to the large window overlooking a frozen fountain, framed by a backdrop of snow-covered cedars and white peaked mountains. Wilson turned back to me. "Yes, for a few minutes. Things were chaotic with the various functions in progress. Just before Abigail left, I met her walking toward me in the hallway—face white as a blank canvas. She looked ill. I called to her, but she appeared not to hear and returned to the ballroom. I should have followed her."

"Did you see anyone else in the passageway?"

Wilson nodded. "A man stood at the end of the hall, his back toward me. I didn't recognize him, but he was a large man with dark hair."

"When you say large, do you mean overweight, tall...?"

"Tall, about your height, definitely not fat, muscular was the sense I got, although I couldn't really tell."

"Did you get the impression he was a club member or one of the employees?"

"Definitely not one of the staff. He wore a black tuxedo."

"Thank you, Wilson. I appreciate that you made time for me in your schedule. Anything else you remember about that night?"

He shook his head and his mouth drew into a grim line. "Perhaps I should have done more to help her, asked questions. I've dealt with all the recriminations you feel when you lose a friend."

I asked a few more questions, to confirm what was in the reports and left. He hadn't told me anything I didn't already know, except the man in the hallway could have been Abigail's killer. Possibly, Ben Marshall.

Back at the Jeep, I drove to the mountain's base for

the ride home. Chill seeped through ankle-deep powder and slipped into the top of my boots as I trudged to the snowmobile. I hopped aboard leaving a trail a blind man could follow. The weather worsened and despite the extra layers of clothes I'd added, the twenty-minute trip felt like an eternity before the lodge peeked over the ridge.

After my short tour in Iraq, I didn't like to complain. A hundred and twenty in the shade gave me a real appreciation for long Wyoming winters, but I still hated the cold.

Once inside and warm, I took out the box of snapshots Goldie had given me, sorted through the collection, and scrutinized each one. I checked for dates and notations on the backs and then stacked them neatly back into the box.

It's a depressing business to look at photographs of a beautiful woman and child who died out of season. The keepsakes featured poses almost entirely of Joey. A sad-faced, little kid with a cute sprinkle of freckles. He appeared fragile and delicate, like his mother. There were a few shots of Abby and Joey at the zoo and at Disneyland. Even in what should have been happy occasions, the smiles never reached their eyes.

At the bottom of the pile, I found a silver frame with a portrait of the boy—smudges on the surface. In my mind's eye, I could see Abby weeping after the death of her son as she held the photo—the sorrow almost palpable.

A heartbreaking, but true fact—life has never been fair.

The musical sounds of the National Anthem shattered my reverie. Startled, I jumped to answer the call and the silver frame bounced from my lap and crashed against the hardwood floor. I ignored the busted glass and hurried across the room to grab my cell.

Amos's voice filled the line."I have good news."

I lumbered back to the bed and sat on the side. "Great, I can use it."

"The faxed photo of Marshall should be here today. The chief wants this case moved to the top of the pile. He's somewhat embarrassed about the way we handled the situation in the past." He chuckled. "This means we move you to the bottom."

"I guess it's too much to hope you locals would take me off the radar completely."

"One thing at a time. I only perform one miracle a day. The good news is, they haven't caught you yet. The bad news is, the FBI still wants you to lead them to Rachel and Cody."

I growled. "Did you call to cheer me up?"

He chuckled. "You OK up there? Need food or wood pellets?"

"I'm fine. If I'd been forced to bring supplies in on the runabout, it would have been tricky. But the pantry is stocked to the rafters. The lodge also has a Sno-Cat I've been tempted to use because it's enclosed. But it's also a hundred times slower than the snow jet. So far, I've managed to resist the urge."

After the conversation ended, I pushed the end call button and returned to clean up my mess. I searched the laundry room and found a broom and dustpan. Overhead lights twinkled on the broken glass like stars in the galaxy. I removed the photo and frame from the debris and placed them on the bed. I swept up the glass shards and dumped them into the trash bin.

When I picked up Joey's portrait, it appeared thicker than normal. A side view revealed another piece of cardboard stuck behind it. Over time, the photographs had sandwiched together and melded into one. A hurried search of the desk produced a letter opener, and I used it to gently separate the two. After the surgical removal, I gazed at a family portrait of Abigail, Joey, and Ben Marshall.

My skin felt clammy, and I almost tripped over my feet in haste to call Amos back. "I need you to meet me in Sally Benedetti's office. I've discovered something extraordinary."

His voice took on a puzzled tone. "Sure, but do you think that's wise? I just told you we still have your mug on the department's desperately-seeking list."

My confidence soared. "Not to worry, my friend. I don't think it'll be a problem."

He mumbled something about my sanity and hung up.

I called Sally.

After layering on my travel gear, I placed a hundred-dollar bill in an envelope and displayed it prominently on the kitchen table, with a note to replace the food I'd used. Pastor Miller would forgive me when I explained the circumstances.

Climbing aboard the snowmobile wasn't a problem this time. By the grace of God, this would be my final ride down that cold, forbidding mountain.

Before the meeting with Sally and Amos, I made a detour across town.

∂∞∾

At the crime lab, I hurried to Sally Benedetti's

office. She sat at her desk, a beautiful Irish lass with auburn hair, freckles, and sapphire blue eyes. I had told Amos Sally liked me, and she did, but not as much as she liked her handsome Italian husband. Sally had two kids in grade school and a Marine spouse stationed in Afghanistan.

We chatted until Amos hurried through the door, a breakfast sandwich in one hand and a cup of coffee in the other.

I glanced at Sally's computer screen. "Those Ben Marshall's fingerprints on the screen?"

She nodded. "Just like you asked."

Amos looked over my shoulder. "What are we looking for?"

I held up my hand. "Be patient. You won't believe what you're about to see."

I'd asked Sally to compare a partial set of prints I'd brought with me. The screen flashed and the other prints overlaid the first ones.

Sally gasped. "It's a fifteen-point match. Who would ever believe this?"

"Whose prints are those?" Amos asked.

With a broad smile, I explained. "Judge Harry London is Ben Marshall, murderer, escaped convict, Abigail Armstrong's first husband, and Rachel London's current one."

Amos's mouth dropped open. "Where'd you get London's prints, and who's the guy who died in San Quentin?"

"The second set of prints came from a coffee mug in London's office. As to the dead guy at Quentin, it couldn't have been anyone but Ralph Jensen. He and Marshall were the same size, and only one convict turned up missing after the riot. That's the only conclusion that makes sense."

Amos pulled up a chair and sat down with a thump. "You went into London's office? How'd you get the cup without being caught?"

I grinned. "You don't want to know."

He shook his head. "Well, I guess this clears you and may even let Rachel London off the hook."

I gave Amos the Marshall family picture.

Sally copied both sets of prints and handed them to him. She looked across at me. "Where is the real Harry London?"

That question had also occurred to me. "I don't know. But as soon as I get my hands on Marshall, I'm going to find out."

There was more to that statement than Sally and Amos would ever know.

I leaned against the wall of Sally's cubicle and couldn't keep the grin off my face. "Do you want to get the arrest warrant issued? That just might get you a promotion and a raise."

Amos stuffed the prints and photo into his inside coat pocket and his lips spread into a broad smile. "You bet I do. I only know about two judges and one D.A. who would sell their mother for the privilege."

I flipped my cell phone open and called Rachel.

After I explained the Marshall/London connection, the phone went silent for a moment.

"I—I can't believe it. Are you sure? Is it really over? I can take Cody home?"

"I'm sure, Rachel. The police are on the way to get a warrant issued for Ben at this very moment. He should be in custody within the hour. You don't have to worry about him anymore.

"The jailbreak charges against you still stand, but

I'll call Jake. Let's see what he can do before you return to Hebron."

I hung up, two calls still needed to be made. One to Jake and one to Lincoln Armstrong.

They were going to love this.

19

Hand Me Down Ranch

The ranch loomed clean and pristine when I arrived New Year's Day.

Emma had called and invited me for dinner. She wanted me to join them in getting the New Year off to a good start. My body and emotions were relaxed with the threat of Harold London off my back. I looked forward to a pleasant dinner with friends.

I could afford to take this last holiday off before beating the streets for new cases. Even though I was still officially on Lincoln Armstrong's payroll, it would only last until the police picked up Ben Marshall and put him away.

Cody's Christmas tree lights blinked from the living room window, soon to be dismantled and ornaments stored for another year. I had no warm fuzzies about holding on to the past year. It had been a real bummer. One I hoped not to repeat anytime soon.

Holidays alone had become a norm for me since my grandmother passed away. Today, I planned to enjoy this family gathering to the fullest.

Emma and Rachel passed out hot chocolate and rich bread pudding soon after I arrived. They planned a late dinner.

Bill challenged me to a game of chess, and we hunched over a chessboard most of the afternoon. Around 2:00 PM, Bill flashed an evil grin.

"Checkmate."

"You have no mercy."

He chuckled. "None, whatsoever. And if you don't finish your dessert soon, it's mine."

Cody eased behind me and perused the board. "You should've protected your queen."

I turned and ruffled his hair. "Where were you when I needed you?"

Cody grabbed my arm and dragged me into the living room. He'd displayed his Christmas gifts along the hearth for my inspection. He straddled a bright new saddle, his knees folded on the floor. His blue eyes sparkled with excitement. "Bill and Emma gave this to me. Neat, huh?"

"Very neat."

Bill entered the room and reached behind the Christmas tree. He brought out a colorful package and handed it to me.

"For me?" I was stunned.

He grinned and nodded.

Emma and Rachel entered and stood behind me. With careful movements, I unwrapped the parcel, unsure what to expect. When the paper lay on the floor at my feet, I discovered another box inside labeled, "Money Making Kit."

Everyone moved in close as I looked under the lid. When the cover fell to the floor, shouts of laughter filled the room.

On the box bottom lay a black Lone Ranger mask and a toy gun.

I gave Bill a grin. "Thanks. If I don't line up some new cases soon, I may have to use this."

At the dinner table Bill, Cody, and I salivated as Emma and Rachel brought in the meal. Tangy aromas of brisket and spicy yams made my stomach rumble. Corn bread and traditional black-eyed peas added to the feast.

Bill lowered his head, and we all joined hands." Heavenly Father, we thank You for the food You have so bountifully supplied today. We give thanks for the family and friends with us, and we thank You for the freedom to worship You. We ask that You bless the soldiers, at home and abroad, who daily put their lives on the line so others might know these freedoms we enjoy. And Father, thank You for Noah, who through your grace, made this New Year's Day one to remember. In Jesus's name. Amen."

That said it all.

The meal ended, and we returned to the den for coffee.

Rachel tapped her coffee cup with a spoon. "I have an announcement. As soon as the police have Harry, or should I say, Ben, in custody, I want to return to Cedar Hills Drive and put the house on the market." She turned to Emma. "If that's all right with you?"

Emma nodded. "You're welcome to stay here as long as you want."

Rachel heaved a deep breath. "I'm sure I'll have a delayed reaction to all the mystery surrounding the man I was married to, who turned out to be someone else, but right now all I can feel is joy—thankful that it's over." Her mouth curved slightly. Not a smile of happiness. More a cessation of pain and anxiety. "I haven't planned too far in advance yet. It depends on Jake—on how long it will take him to clear me of the jailbreak charges." She placed her hand on Emma's shoulder. "Words can never express how much I've come to care for you both and to appreciate what you've done for us..."

She hesitated and blinked back tears. "Looks like I'll have to buy a horse so Cody can put that new saddle to good use, although I'm not sure how that will fit into Crown Heights' restriction codes."

Cody stopped with a fork full of dessert halfway to his mouth. "Awesome."

❧

Hebron, Wyoming

On my way into the city the next morning, I took the turnoff to my grandparents' homestead, drove past the farm, and then to a church cemetery nearby. The gray sky mirrored my melancholy mood.

In the corner of the small graveyard stood five black marble headstones, side by side, covered with snow. I brushed away heavy flakes frozen to the smooth surface. The names of my father, mother, brother, and grandparents were etched into the black stone markers. I was the last of a long line of Adams's.

My mind raced back to that morning long ago, when Craig Reid shot and killed my mother and brother. My gifts had spared my life. Why the Lord saved my life that night, rather than my mother or Tommy, why he gave me the powers, I didn't know. Surely they were more deserving. The Lord knew my failings. How could I ever make up for their loss?

The guilt inside gnawed like a cancer that ate away at my soul.

I'd been the lone witness against Craig at his trial. Throughout the long ordeal, my most vivid memory was my grandmother's face smiling encouragement from the gallery.

After conviction, the state took ten years to put Craig to death. Every day he lived, my grief turned to rage, and the anger into bitterness that harden my heart. Somehow, his death, when it finally came, didn't end my hate, even though I desperately wanted to leave it behind.

A year after I came home from the service, my grandmother had died quietly in her sleep. The serenity of her death befitted the lady she was.

At my family's gravesite, my voice trembled—whether from cold or emotion, I wasn't sure. Perhaps both. "Thanks, Grandma, for standing by me through the fragile years, college, and the tour of duty in the Marines. I always think the emptiness of your death will pass, but it never has. Pray for me. That I will lose this heavy burden of hate for the man who took Mom and Tommy away from me." I traced her name with my finger on the headstone. "I wish you could have been with me today. I chalked up one for the good guys."

Back in my car, I drove home, to Bella, Brutus, and a late dinner with Mabel and Ted.

Later, feet propped up on the coffee table, I sipped hot cider Mabel had sent over with Ted. The television drama had ended, and I'd trudged across the frozen street to see Ted home.

After making sure Ted was inside safely, I returned to my place and to the basement. Home felt good. Bella lay at my side, and Brutus curled at my feet, as we watched the news. My mind fuzzy with fatigue, I only half listened to the newscast, until Bella raised her head and barked.

My feet hit the floor. The sixty-two inch TV displayed a photo of George and Tooie. I grabbed the remote and increased the volume.

A solemn field reporter stood in an office, surround by debris, police milling in the background. "—destroyed the office of local aviation entrepreneur, George Thomas.

"Fortunately, Mr. Thomas wasn't in the office when the vandal struck, but his dog wasn't so lucky. While Thomas locked down the hanger for the night, someone trashed his business. Mr. Thomas was unharmed, but the intruder killed his watchdog. We'll keep you informed as this story develops."

Twenty minutes later, I slid into the parking lot of the Hebron Municipal Airport. The camera crew had departed, but two police officers stood by. Silent. Stone-faced. They knew George. They knew Tooie.

George's muffled sobs filled the room as he cradled Tooie's head on his lap.

One of the cops was from my old days on the force. He shook my hand. "Hey, Noah. Glad things worked out for you in that Judge London mess." His gaze shifted to George, and he shook his head. "He's in pretty bad shape—didn't want to leave him alone."

I nodded my thanks to the officer, knelt beside George, and placed my hand on his shoulder. "I'm sorry, George."

His tear-stained face looked up at me, and anger flashed in his dark eyes. "Tooie never hurt anybody in his life. He...wouldn't bite...a biscuit." Sobs broke out anew.

I caught the eye of one of the officers. "There are a couple of blankets in the backseat of my Jeep. Would you bring them in for me?"

He nodded and left.

I pulled a chair over and coaxed George into it.

"We need to get Tooie home. Norma will be worried. Let me wrap Tooie in blankets and put him in my car. I'll drive you home."

George placed his head in both hands and nodded.

The officer returned with the blankets and laid them on the floor. "Anything else we can do? We've finished here."

I shook his hand. "Thanks, I'll take over. Any idea who's responsible?"

The officer shook his head. "George didn't see anybody, but he saw a dark blue or black sedan pull away as he reached the office. He didn't get the license number—worried about Tooie."

My head jerked up. "A blue sedan?"

The police officer studied my face. "Blue or black. You know who it was?"

I stared in the distance for a long moment and visualized the face of the thug that busted my shoulder. "Sounds like a guy I had a run in with a while back."

The cop pulled out his notepad. "You know his name?"

"No, but I could pick him out of a line-up."

The cops left and George looked up at me. "You know who did this, Noah?"

I brushed broken glass out of the chair beside him and sat down. "Sounds like the guy who busted my shoulder."

George shook his head, face gray, eyes red streaked. "Why would he come here, kill Tooie?"

A lump formed in my throat. "He must have followed me or found out we were friends. Perhaps he hoped you had information that would lead him to Rachel and Cody. He's a vicious thug. Gets his kicks hurting people."

A muscle twitched in George's jaw. "I'll show him vicious if I ever get my hands on him."

I picked up Tooie, placed him on one of the blankets and covered him with the other one. "He'd better pray you find him first."

Norma and the kids waited when George and I arrived. They were almost as distraught as George, so I hung around until after two o'clock while they cried and talked themselves into exhaustion.

⤫

Noah's home, Hebron, Wyoming

At almost ten o'clock the next morning I jerked awake, my brain still sleep-addled. In the kitchen, coffee in hand, a black mood hung over me that I couldn't push back. Both of my cases were solved, and Armstrong still paid my daily fee. At least until Marshall was behind bars. I should feel elated.

A special edition of the newspaper lay on my lap, I scanned the headlines:

LOCAL JUDGE HAROLD LONDON REVEALED AS ESCAPED CONVICT BENJAMIN MARSHALL

The front page featured pictures of London alongside Marshall's prison mug shot, their resemblance unmistakable. The story encapsulated Marshall's jailbreak along with speculation on the whereabouts of the real Harold London.

The telephone's shrill ring sent a subliminal warning. Thinking perhaps my dark frame of mind was playing tricks on me, I lifted the receiver with caution

"Cody's missing." It was Bill Hand.

I stood up, dumped the newspaper on the floor, and splashed a puddle of black liquid onto the counter top. "When? How?"

Bill's voice cracked. "We discovered him missing a little while ago. I moved back home since I considered Rachel and Cody were safe. Mom asked me to pick up a few things for her in town. I checked on Cody before I left. He was in the barn. I asked if he'd like to come along, but he wanted to stay with the foal." The line was silent for a moment. Bill cleared his throat. "When I returned, I couldn't find him—." His voice dropped, almost inaudible. "There were signs of a struggle in the snow outside the barn. Rachel's hysterical. She swears Harry took the boy."

A scalding mixture of guilt and helplessness curled like a tight fist inside my chest. My fault. I told Rachel they were safe. She let down her guard. And she was right. Harry London had taken the boy and could be anywhere. A stupid move on my part. I should've known it ain't over, 'til it's over. And it wouldn't have been over until Marshall was behind bars.

I ran my fingers through my hair and shook myself mentally. Couldn't allow my emotions to shut down now. I needed to be at the top of my game. "Rachel's right. Who else would take the boy? Have you notified the sheriff?"

"Not yet. Rachel's still wanted for jailbreak. I did ask Dr. McCall to give her something to calm her. What do you want me to do?"

Phone in hand, I headed upstairs to get dressed. "Take Rachel someplace safe and keep her out of sight until the authorities leave the ranch. I'll get in touch with Jake and with Amos Horne, a detective here in Hebron. We'll come down and Amos will deal with the sheriff."

I hung up and dialed Amos's number. "Why didn't you guys pick up Marshall?"

"I tried to reach you yesterday." Amos shouted into the phone. "When we arrived at the judge's office, he'd cleared out. Knew we were coming. Someone tipped him off. We put out an APB." He exhaled into the phone. "No leads so far. He could be anywhere."

My voice rose, even though I knew it wasn't Amos's fault. "I don't know where Marshall is now, but I can tell you where he's been. Cody's missing from the ranch."

"When and what ranch?"

"About an hour ago at Emma Hand's ranch near Green River, where he's been staying. Call the sheriff down there. Tell him what's happened."

"Is Rachel London there, too? The woman is wanted for jailbreak, Noah. I'd be jeopardizing my job." The line was silent for a moment, and then he heaved a deep breath. "But we now know she had reason."

"Rachel isn't there now, so you didn't know where she was, and you still don't. The boy was spending a week with Emma."

Amos signed into the phone. "I know the sheriff there. He may not tie her into the jailbreak since the kidnapping charges were dropped. How'd Marshall find them?"

"He must have traced Rachel's cell calls. I should have moved them a week ago. Can you get a chopper to fly us down, see if Marshall left any clues?

"No problem. The D.A. wants Marshall in the very worse way. Meet me at the airport helipad in thirty minutes."

Marshall hadn't grabbed his son out of love. He wanted to hurt Rachel. If he managed to take Cody out of the country, Rachel would never see him again, and the boy's life would become a living nightmare.

Hand Me Down Ranch

I peered out the helicopter window at the sparsely populated terrain below. White on white with patches of farmhouse roofs barely visible under a blanket of snow. The chopper noise kept conversation to a minimum.

The sun was out, making the landscape even brighter, but it wouldn't stay that way. Already snow clouds formed in the east.

The pilot set the bird down gently in the road about fifty yards from Emma's ranch. Amos ducked his head and jumped down first, and I followed. Wind gusts from the rotors kicked the fresh powder into a man-made blizzard, leaving us momentarily blinded until the blades eased to a stop.

The scene was a replay of every cop show I'd ever seen. The sheriff had arrived and strung yellow tape around Emma's barn. Uniformed men stood in groups with foam cups in hand, the hot liquid billowing steam.

Two men stepped forward.

Amos hurried to greet them. "Hey, Jason." Amos clasped the sheriff's hand and then shook hands with the deputy.

Amos waved a hand in my direction. "Jason, this is Noah Adams, a P.I. who's been working this case.

He's responsible for discovering Judge London's real identity. Noah, this is Sheriff Jason Billings."

He nodded and shook my hand. "Nothing much here to help find the boy. We found tire tracks that don't belong to any of the vehicles on the property, and fresh footprints outside the barn—a size thirteen man's shoe, the same size Ben Marshall wears. Not positive proof Marshall took the boy, but it squares with your suspicions. Two FBI agents are on their way from Cheyenne. We've set up road blocks, but we may be too late and we don't know what Marshall is driving."

It was a start. But too little, too late.

I gave Amos a wave and set off for the ranch house to find Bill.

He must have watched my approach. He opened the door, his face gray and somber.

"How's Rachel?"

"I took her to my place at the church. Emma's with her. She was asleep when I left, thank God. This is awful for Rachel and Cody, after all they been through."

I nodded and patted his back. I had no words of comfort to offer.

"Come in. I'll get you some coffee."

"Thanks, Bill, but I don't have time. We need to find Cody before Marshall gets so far ahead of us we can't catch him."

❧

Hebron, Wyoming

After the chopper returned to Hebron, I drove home. Events of the past few hours brought back waves of old memories and grief I didn't want to revisit. The deaths of my mother and brother, my inability to stop the carnage. The past was an old wound, unhealed. The slightest probe and it started to bleed. I dragged myself into the kitchen and called the only person I knew who might point me in the right direction.

"McKenna, can you talk?"

Slight hesitation. "Yes."

"Someone tipped London off. He's on the run and he's taken his son. I need your help."

"I knew he skipped. But how would I know where Harry London, sorry, Ben Marshall is?"

"I know you don't have personal knowledge, but your father might. Will you ask him?"

"You know I'd help—"

"McKenna, I believe Marshall plans to take his son out of the country. It's the only logical move for him with the FBI taking over the case."

A sharp intake of breath came through the phone. "I'll check with Dad. If he does know, I'll find out where. That's a promise. I'll call you back."

I couldn't. I wouldn't accept Cody was gone forever from Rachel's life. Not as long as I breathed. I failed miserably once. I paced and waited. Inactivity drove me mad.

Finally, the phone rang.

"Dad doesn't know where Marshall is. I told him about the boy. My father has his faults, but I believe him. He wouldn't hold back where a child's concerned. He suggested you try London's lake cottage."

"Where? Pine Lake?"

"Yes. He said he'd been there two or three times."

"Does he have directions to the place?"

McKenna read off detailed instruction to find the

cabin. I hoped Thornton leveled with his daughter. She had more faith in his scruples than I did.

"Noah, just FYI, this morning I received an anonymous package in the mail. It contained security tapes from Judge London's home. They were...brutal. We've dropped the jailbreak charges against Rachel London. She should never have been in jail to begin with."

Thornton must have decided they were no longer good for blackmail purposes, since London's real identity became known.

"McKenna, if you were close enough, I'd kiss you." The phone went silent. "Anyway, thanks for telling me and for the lead on Marshall."

There was an audible click, and she was gone.

McKenna's tip was the only place to start. I had no place else to go. The police probably hadn't discovered the cabin's existence, and I didn't have time to wait for them to mount up a posse. To take Cody to the lodge wouldn't be the smartest move Marshall could make, but his decisions hadn't shown stellar wisdom. He'd succeeded so far on lazy police work and dumb luck.

Try the cabin. I had nothing to lose.

I didn't enjoy the trip. Not surprising. I had ignored the media blizzard warning to stay indoors. Dressed in snow gear and boots I regretted returning Jake's Jeep so soon, even more so when my SUV slid across the street and bounced against the neighbor's curb. My four-wheel drive didn't handle in icy road conditions like the Jeep.

Snow fell in a curtain of white as I drove west. The weather worsened with each mile. Wiper blades struggled to push snow from the windshield and failed miserably.

Images of Cody filled my mind. His shyness when he first arrived at the ranch, his love for the animals, his growing self-confidence. Because of my stupidity, his life rested in his father's merciless hands.

Because of the weather, the drive took twice as long. Finally, in the distance, a shaped loomed into view of what I hoped was the cabin. My headlights penetrated the near white-out conditions to illuminate the outline of a log structure. Nothing moved. No lights, no smoke from the chimney. A wide expanse of fresh powder erased any footprints there might have been.

The only sound—that of my own labored breathing. Snow blew sideways as I mounted the steps and tried the door.

It was open.

That didn't square with what I knew about Marshall, the security camera freak. Wary, I eased inside the vestibule.

The stench of an unwashed body was my first signal of danger. I dodged to my right just as a fire poker missed my skull by millimeters.

20

Judge London's Cabin, Pine Lake

Reflexes and adrenalin kicked in at the same time. Every muscle in my body tightened. I grabbed the poker and twisted. A yelp of pain sounded behind me and I turned to face my assailant.

A shabby, dirty man knelt on the floor in front of me, right hand pressed against his chest. "You broke my wrist."

I took in great gulps of air as tensed muscles unwound, and then I glanced around. Papers and burnt matches lay on the fireplace and in front of the hearth. I had interrupted the old man trying to ignite logs in the fireplace.

I gazed down at him. "Let me look at your hand."

He shook his head and scooted away.

"Come on. Give it to me. I won't hurt you."

Currents of fear deepened the wrinkles in his weathered face, but he stayed put. "What do you want with my hand?"

"I want to see if it's broken. What's your name?"

His gaze roamed past me, not making eye contact. "People call me Bonehead. Just came in—trying to get out of the storm. Didn't intend to harm anything. You startled me—I wasn't leaving without a fight. I'd freeze out there."

I glared at him. "I can see where you got your nickname. That was a stupid move swinging the poker at me. I could have killed you." Holding his hand in mine, I pushed back the frozen fabric of his coat sleeve and moved each of his fingers.

The horrors of Vietnam, street life, hunger and extreme cold flowed through his fingers into mine, leaving me physically ill. I dropped my grip and moved away. "You don't appear to have any broken bones. Most likely, it's just a sprained wrist. Sit tight and I'll try to get some heat started."

In a closet near the entrance, I locate the circuit box, flipped on the master switch, and then turned on the lights. Recessed lamps cast a soft glow over the room. Encouraged, I located the thermostat and inched the heat bar up to seventy degrees. The welcome sound of ignited flames soon followed.

I hurried back to the hearth and started a fire. That and the central heating would warm the old man up quickly.

Bonehead tried to stand and stumbled.

I hurried to steady him. "Why didn't you turn on the furnace? That would have been quicker than building a fire."

He shrugged. "I hadn't been here long when you arrived. Didn't even look for a thermostat. Just wanted to get warm as fast as I could."

I strode toward the kitchen. "When the water warms up, I want you to take a shower. I'll see what I can find to eat."

He touched my arm and suspicion wrinkled his brow. "Why are you being so nice?"

I shrugged. "I've had to depend on other people's kindness a lot lately. I'm just returning the blessings."

Bonehead moved in close to the blaze in the hearth. Sparks crackled and floated in wispy waves up the chimney, filling the room with a woody fragrance. "I don't have any clean clothes, you know. Won't do any good to bathe without clean clothes."

"Perhaps I can find you something."

The old man hovered near the fire while I found the bedroom and swung the closet doors wide. Marshall had great taste. I pulled down a designer fleece-lined jogging suit and jacket and then grabbed clean skivvies and thermal underwear from a drawer. The items were too large, but I didn't think Bonehead would complain.

Back in the den, I handed the outfit to the old man. "The bathroom is down the hall. The water should be getting warm soon. This place has a tankless water heater."

"A what?"

"A tankless water heater. Great invention."

"I don't need a bath. I'll just get dirty again. "

"Trust me. You need a bath."

He mumbled and obediently shuffled down the hallway.

In the kitchen, I heated frozen pancakes and pre-cooked sausage and then made a pot of coffee. I left the food in the warming drawer while Bonehead showered.

Back in the den, I picked up the papers the old man had scattered on the floor.

For the next ten minutes, I sorted the documents into neat stacks. In one section, I found utility bills for an address in Rapid Bend, California. If Marshall paid the utilities, he probably owned the place. Not much to go on, but for the moment, it was the only lead available. Stuffing the invoice in my pocket, I returned to the kitchen, poured a cup of coffee, and went back to the den to wait for Bonehead.

Minutes later he emerged from the bathroom a different man, albeit somewhat swamped in his new attire. His gray hair hung long and wet above the jumpsuit collar.

I nodded an appreciative smile at the improvement. "Do you have another name I can call you besides Bonehead?" I knew the answer but wanted him to confide in me.

He finger-combed his beard and his watery blue eyes met mine. "Bonehead's been my name for more'n twenty years. It'll do, I guess, for the next twenty."

I shook my head. "No, it won't, Truman Marchant. Bonehead is not a name for a man created in the image of God."

His grip tightened on the edge of the sofa, and he lowered himself with shaky hands. "How'd you know my name?"

"It doesn't matter. But a decorated war hero shouldn't let anyone hang a moniker like Bonehead on him."

He raised his chin and tears pooled in his eyes. "Big deal. A hero from a war nobody wanted. You psychic?"

"Not exactly. You hungry?"

He nodded and his gaze wandered around the room. "This your place?"

I shook my head. "It just became the property of a very nice lady who, I hope, won't mind us using it until the worst of the storm passes. When I leave, I'll take you to my place. You can stay there. I'll trust you to take care of my home. If you make a mess or destroy anything, I'll hunt you down. That clear?" I settled my hand under his elbow. "Let's stop playing twenty questions and eat."

We stepped into the kitchen, and he attacked the food like a ravenous bear. Through a mouthful of pancakes, he said, "I've done things I'm not proud of," he swallowed. "Been trying to drown out the war for a long time. Never been able to do it. Doctors gave a fancy name to my condition, a war related stress syndrome of some kind. Couldn't handle stateside. Took to the streets like many of my comrades. Haven't been able to make my way back to where I was before the war. Thought sure the storm tonight would put an end to my problems."

I wasn't really worried about leaving the old vet in my home. The Lord knew I didn't have the answer to the homeless situation. He also knew no way would I put that poor soul out in this weather. Besides, the tiny homeless shelter in Hebron was filled to capacity this time of year.

The snow had lessened, but a white world surrounded us on the drive home, and Truman fell asleep soon after we started. In the silence, a gentle voice reminded me McKenna had not been my only source of hope. An unseen hand guided me to Ben Marshall's place, and led me to a clue to his possible destination. God answered in His own time, in His own way.

∂∽

Noah's Home, Hebron Wyoming
At home, I showed Truman around the house and to the guest room. The pups took to him right away. That was a good sign. Truman shuffled his way around, getting the feel of the place. He licked his lips,

and his fingers twitched. He wanted a drink, and I couldn't help him.

"Truman, sit."

The paper-thin creases around his eyes deepened, pain in his weak blue gaze. He rubbed his hands against his thighs, limped to a chair and plopped down hard.

I went to the kitchen, poured two cups of fresh coffee, and handed one to him. "I don't have any liquor. I'll give you some pain medicine to help you through the night. Tomorrow, I'll ask a friend to take you to the nearest detox center. That's the only way you can beat this thing—get your life back. Will you go?"

"Yeah, I know. I know. Just for the record, I've done that before." His shoulders raised and dropped in quiet desperation.

"How long ago?"

"Ten...twelve years."

"Tell me how you came to be in the mountains in the dead of winter." I knew most of it from my earlier touch, but I wanted to keep him talking to take his mind off his habit.

"You know where Evanston is?" he asked.

"Yeah, it's on Highway 80 a couple of miles from the Utah border."

He nodded. "Every spring a bunch of old hippies and tree-huggers go up there to commune with nature."

I grinned. "The locals call them Rainbow People."

"I've come with them a couple of years and stay in their camp. They give me food, liquor, and a little weed from time to time. It's a vacation of sorts. Gets me away from the smog in L.A."

I arched an eyebrow at him. "Evanston is a long way from that mountain cabin."

"Yeah, don't rush me. I'm coming to that."

I shut up and listened.

"The day the group headed back to California, I was drunk and they left without me. So I hung around Evanston, working a little here and there until it started to get cold. I hate cold weather. Then I made the stupid decision to see if I could hitch a ride to see my mother in Nebraska." Truman shivered and took a sip of coffee. "I caught a ride with a fellow who called himself Oscar something. He said he'd take me as far a Hebron. His cell phone kept ringing, and the last call came about two miles from the cabin. I know because I walked it. That last conversation riled Oscar. He pounded on the steering wheel and started swearing.

"When I asked him what was wrong, his face turned a shade of dark red I didn't like, and he said his job description had just changed. Then the sorry sod pulled a gun and made me get out of the car.

"I tried to explain I'd freeze to death out there in the middle of nowhere. He just waved the gun and told me it wasn't his problem, but if I could make it that far, there was a cabin that shouldn't be too far ahead. He turned the car around and drove back the way we came."

I rubbed the stubble on my chin. It was inconceivable someone would drive that far just to dump a homeless man in the mountains. "Truman, did he seem to be headed for that cabin? I didn't notice any other homes in the area when I drove in."

"Yeah, I gave that a lot of thought on my long walk. I think he set out for the cabin until that call. Then he changed his mind. I heard him ask the person on the phone if he still wanted the job done."

Could it have been one of Marshall's cronies headed to meet him there? Marshall could have changed his mind when he discovered the authorities were looking for him.

"What did the guy look like?"

"Typical hunter type. Wore a loud red plaid coat and a stupid red hat with earflaps. You know the kind hunters wear."

Truman, the fashion police.

"What was he driving?"

"A silver sedan." Truman ducked his head and stared at the floor. "I didn't pay a lot of attention. Oscar had a bottle of whiskey he shared with me."

"Your guardian angel was riding on your shoulder. Accepting rides from strangers in desolate country like this can get you killed."

"Now you tell me."

"Your mom's still alive?"

His head jerked up. "I...I think so."

"When was the last time you talked to her?"

"Christmas. Three or four years ago."

"So you're not sure. You have a phone number?"

"Y-Yeah."

That made me angry. "How can you not let your mother know you're alive and well? You ever consider how many nights she might worry about you? Go call her now. There's a phone upstairs if you want some privacy."

His face wrinkled like an accordion. He closed his eyes and took two short breaths. Finally, he nodded, turned, and trudged upstairs. In the quiet of my home, a soft cry of *Mama* drifted down the stairs followed by the quiet echo of sobs.

21

Noah's Home, Hebron, Wyoming

With Truman in bed, I warmed up a cup of Mabel's hot cider and took it to the den. Bella jumped up beside me on the sofa and nudged my hand, her signal she wanted some attention. I scratched her ear and then slid her head off my lap and grabbed the phone.

Detective Rena Chavez answered.

"Rena, this is Sam." I didn't have time to explain my false identity.

"Yeah. What do you need?" Her voice sounded strained—noncommittal.

How much had she found out about me? "I need to find a residence in Northern California that belonged to Harold London. I could try to track it down on the Internet, but time is an issue."

The phone line became silent for a moment. "I checked you out, *Sam*. I know your name isn't Sam Spade. The FBI warrant—"

"They dismissed that yesterday."

"I know, but I still can't help you. I won't jeopardize my job for a stranger who lied to me once already." A click and she was gone.

I drew in a deep breath. I liked Rena and wished I could make her understand why I lied. But I knew she wouldn't listen. So much for the fast way.

I called Amos and gave him the information I'd

tried to give Rena.

"Do you know what county the residence is in?"

"No, but I have the city name, a post office box, and a zip code. Amos—I also need to know if there's an airport close where a small plane could land. One more favor. Call the sheriff's office there and tell them to get to the place ASAP. I'm pretty sure Marshall's on his way there with Cody."

"Give me the zip code." In the background papers shuffled and someone hacked a cigarette cough. I expelled the breath I'd been holding and gave him the number.

"I'm on it. I'll call you right back."

Thirty minutes later, I had the physical location of the cabin and the name of the closest airport.

I called George and told him what I needed.

"That's at least an overnight trip. Let me clear it with Norma." He called a few minutes later." Meet me at my plane in fifteen minutes."

Everything settled, I began to get antsy. Had Marshall driven? Had he found someone to fly him to Rapid Bend? Wanted by the police, Marshall wouldn't take Cody on a commercial flight against his will. He would either charter a plane or drive. I was betting on driving since George had the only local charter service.

Upstairs, I shook Truman awake.

I placed my hand on his shoulder and held it there to ensure he gave me his full attention. "I have to leave. Something important has come up. There's plenty of food in the house. Don't let your friends show up here. My hospitality extends only to you."

He stared at me for a moment, taking in what I'd said. "My buddies are too smart to come this far north. No heat grates to sleep on in the mountains."

I asked him to look after the dogs and rushed to meet George. On the way to the airport I flipped open my cell phone. "Amos, sorry to bother you again. See if you can find out if a small plane left here for Rapid Bend, California. I think Marshall is headed to the place. If he's flying, I may already be too late. How soon can you check the outbound flights?"

"We may have it already. It's standard procedure to track all escape routes he might've taken. Let me see what we have. I'll call you back. FYI, we put out an Amber Alert."

My phone buzzed ten minutes later. "No flights have logged to that area from anywhere near here in the last forty-eight hours. You going up there?"

"Yeah. George and I leave within the hour. Thanks, Amos. You're the man."

He chuckled. "Yeah, I fight it, but it's bigger than I am."

I jumped into the SUV and headed to the airfield.

I prayed my hunch was right, and Marshall had decided to drive. Cody disappeared ten hours ago. I calculated it would take Marshall about fourteen to make the trip if he drove straight through. By the grace of God, we could get there about an hour before Marshall. The ETA would depend on headwinds, the weather conditions, and the distance to London's place from the airfield. But if I'd guessed wrong, I would have wasted a lot of precious time. If so, I could only pray the Amber Alert would turn up something.

I opened my cell and called George back. "George, does your kid still have the motorcycle?"

"Yes, why?"

"When we get to California, I may need transportation to Marshall's place. A small airport won't have a car rental agency. Can we take the bike on the plane?"

"I load small fishing boats sometimes, so it won't be a problem."

"I owe you one."

"You owe me more than one, pal."

I dialed Emma's number, and Bill answered. "Don't get your hopes up, but I think I know where Marshall may have taken Cody."

Bill whispered a soft, "Thank God."

"Exactly. I'm almost at the airport now. I'll leave it up to you how much you tell Rachel."

"Where is Cody?"

I explained my theory. "George and I will leave as soon as I reach the airport. Keep praying." I punched the off button and slung a wide arc of snow as I sped onto the airfield. George waited inside his truck. My SUV slid in beside the plane. We unloaded the bike from George's truck, tied it down in the back of the plane, and then climbed aboard. Gaze glued to the tarmac, George called the tower.

The radio squawked bad news. "I'd postpone this trip, George. We've got blizzard conditions headed east when you enter Utah. The bad weather's expected to last throughout the night, and you'll be meeting it head on."

George looked over at me. "I hope you're caught up on your prayer life. I'd hate to think we'd risked our lives on a wild hunch."

"If I'm behind, I'll catch up by the time we reach Rapid Bend."

The Uinta Mountains loomed high and bleak as we flew into the fierceness of the storm. Brutal winds tossed the plane like a ping-pong ball in a tournament.

Gripped by anxiety over Cody's desperate situation and the hazardous flight ahead, memories of my last combat mission surfaced.

Uncertain what I wanted to do with my life after college, I joined the Marines, newly commissioned as First Lieutenant. Political tensions in the Middle East escalated, and I found myself on the way to Kuwait. The third week there, my unit received orders to join a detachment inside Iraq territory.

In the predawn darkness, me and a crew of four jarheads, gathered on the tarmac to await our ride. Right on schedule, a CH53 Sea Stallion helicopter picked us up just as the desert sun caught fire in the eastern sky.

An hour later, deep inside the province, we started our descent somewhere near Tikrit. Easy going until alarms inside the cockpit went crazy. The pilot shouted and banked the chopper almost knocking me from my seat. I leaned forward and screamed in his ear, "What's wrong?"

He yelled, "A SCUD just locked on." His brow froze in a fierce scowl, and I knew the CH53 couldn't avoid the hit. The pilot tried to radio our position as he maneuvered the chopper closer to the ground. From my position in the cockpit, I watched in dry-mouth terror as the surface-to-air missile streaked toward us.

I shouted to the men in the rear of the craft. "Missile incoming!"

An immediate burst of activity erupted behind me as seat straps flew open and they prepared for the crash.

We were about twenty feet from the ground when the rocket struck and clipped off the 53's tail. No explosion, the tail just fell off. Miracle of miracles, the missile hadn't exploded. Out of the corner of my eye, I watched as it traveled a thousand yards to the right and buried its nose in a hill of sand.

A Scud dud from God.

Seconds before the missile made contact, I released my seatbelt and jumped from the aircraft behind the door gunner. Anticipating the impact, I bent my legs and rolled as I hit the sand dune below. A fire started at the rear of the helicopter just before it hit the sand. Wreckage rained around me and bounced like hailstones from the blackened sky.

I struck the ground hard. The impact pushed the air from my lungs. As I sucked oxygen back into my body, I realized none of the men were moving. The four Marines who'd jumped with me lay among the debris still and wounded.

A sear of pain in my right leg got my attention. The adrenalin rush after the crash postponed the pain and now shuddered up my spine like a living thing. I sat down in the sand, and gingerly felt the ankle. The bone was broken. I took a deep breath, gritted my teeth, pushed the bone back in place, and then laced the boot tighter to prevent swelling and to support my foot. In agony, I fashioned a makeshift splint from wreckage parts and secured it to the outside of the boot with my belt. Crude splint in place, I hobbled through the debris in search of the pilot.

Time froze and seconds inched forward like hours. I scanned the ground and realized the pilot must be trapped inside the chopper. Flames reached high into the sky from where the aircraft tail used to be. The fire hadn't reached the cockpit, but smoke hung thick and black—impossible to see inside.

I said a prayer, took a deep breath, and plunged

inside the darkened cockpit. Hot metal stung as my hands brushed against the hull. In the blackness, my fingers touched a shirt collar. I grabbed a tight hold, pulled the pilot from the seat, and backed out into daylight— lungs bursting for air.

The pilot showed no signs of respiration, but a faint pulse fluttered under my fingertips. I put my CPR training into practice. After the third series of air and pressure, he coughed up black smoke, struggling to breathe. His condition stabilized, I checked him for injuries. His right leg was broken and a bloody gash rested over his left eye. A one-man triage unit, I classified him as stable and moved on to the next injured Marine.

The first priority was to get them as far away from the wreckage as possible. No easy task, but the probability the aircraft might explode gave me extra incentive. Once they lay a safe distance from the wreckage, I checked their wounds. Repeated attempts to arouse them failed, which was probably a blessing. With an assortment of broken bones and burns, consciousness would bring a lot of pain.

Again, I searched the wreckage for medical supplies. Under a piece of the broken tail, I found two extra canteens, but the first aid kits hadn't made it.

I moved through the soldiers once more, checking vital signs. They carried bottled water in their pant cargo pockets, and I poured sips of water over parched lips and then stabilized the broken bones as best I could. The burns would have to wait.

The situation looked bleak even for a combat veteran, and I was still a rookie. All the radio equipment went down inside the 53. The helicopter and phones had GPS capabilities, but by this time, they had become metal soup. None of the men could walk out, and for certain, I couldn't carry them. Not to mention the nearby SCUD—a ticking time bomb. Rescue lay in the hope that U.S. troops would see the smoke from the wreckage.

Never imagine a situation can't get worse.

The roar of engines sounded long before the vehicles came into view over the rise. My hopes soared as I hid behind a sand dune and watched.

Someone *had* seen the smoke. I recognized the Republican Guard emblem on the trucks and groaned. Not what I'd prayed for. We had crashed behind the Iraqi battle lines, and all the fire power I had rested in my sidearm.

Article Two of the Code of Conduct ran through my mind. "I will never surrender of my own free will. If in command, I will never surrender my men while they still have the means to resist."

That was the sticking point. My men didn't have "the means to resist," but I was still conscious and had my pistol. I could commit suicide and follow the code to the letter or wait and pick a fight on my terms.

I waited. Time was on my side.

Within minutes, two Jeeps and four trucks surrounded the crash site.

After taking our weapons, the soldiers loaded my injured men into the back of a truck and shoved me in after them. An Iraqi colonel spotted the unexploded missile and yelled. Panic knows no language barrier. The column lurched forward leaving a massive cloud of sand in our wake. Three or four clicks later, we came to a halt—safely out of range.

A loud debate ensued outside my metal prison. I guessed the topic. The winds of war had shifted to our side, and the soldiers didn't know what to do with us.

Heat inside the metal vehicle soared to unbearable heights as the truck remained motionless. The soldiers confiscated our bottles and canteens. The men wouldn't last long without water and medical attention.

It was time to make my move. Invisible, I emerged outside on the sand.

The exterior proved a great deal cooler; at least it didn't burn my lungs when I breathed. I counted twelve soldiers, two involved in the ongoing debate while the others looked on. The water truck sat ten feet due east—the best place for an ambush.

Still invisible, I rushed to the water supply and waited.

Even with my bad leg, the first Iraqi never knew what hit him. I grabbed him from behind, rendered him unconscious, and then took his weapon. Within minutes, I had eight of our captors locked inside one of their trucks. When I confronted the last four, they surrendered without a fight. In hindsight, I think they felt safer with me than with their satanic leader.

Weapons confiscated, I locked three of the remaining troops in the cargo hold with their comrades. One of my injured men revived, held an M16 on the colonel, and ordered him to drive the vehicle to the nearest U.S. base camp. I followed behind in the truck with the injured Marines.

Dusk had fallen when we arrived at the American facility, and I gladly turned the enemy soldiers over to the military police. As they led the colonel away, he turned to me and asked, in perfect English, "How did you escape from the truck?"

I straightened and grinned at him. "New secret

weapon."

A little propaganda wouldn't hurt our cause.

Out of the fading light, medics surrounded me, the wounded soldiers, and the pilot. Early next morning, they shipped us to our base in Germany for more intensive care.

Weeks later, my grandmother looked on while the Secretary of the Navy pinned the Navy Cross on my uniform. He cited me for, "distinguished heroic and meritorious service achievement while serving in the Marine Corps in connection with military operations against an enemy of the United States."

The pilot, whose last-minute maneuvers saved our lives, was my friend George Thomas.

22

Rapid Bend, California

From the cockpit's front row seat, giant white fingers of wind and snow held back the plane, impeding our mission to rescue Cody. Panel lights in the cockpit cast a green glow onto George's dark skin, and his grim face added to my apprehension.

"How bad is it?"

He cut his gaze across the space between us. "You better pray the wing de-icers work."

I did what the man said.

Almost an hour behind schedule and emotionally whipped, we bumped down the frozen runway at the small Rapid Bend Airport. If my calculations were right, Marshall reached the lodge an hour before.

A well-lighted hanger beckoned, and George taxied toward the metal building. An attendant left the tiny terminal, hurried over, and hand-guided George to a parking spot. The clerk scurried back to the warmth of the office.

We scrambled out of the cockpit, never happier to feel terra firma beneath our feet. I slapped George on the back and he echoed a nervous chuckle over the storm's tempo.

Dim exterior lights blinked through the flakes, but the terminal and airfield appeared empty. One lone vehicle, barely visible in the faint glow, sat in front of the building adjacent to the hanger.

No police vehicles in sight.

Weather conditions on the ground looked worse than in the air. All things being equal, the possibility existed that the sheriff and Ben Marshall lagged behind us.

After unloading the bike, we joined the attendant inside the terminal.

He watched us move in close to the pellet store in the corner. "You guys must like to live dangerously to be out in this storm."

"Can't say I like it, but we had no choice." I said. "Any idea where Harold London's place is located?"

"I met London once, but he hasn't been around for a long time. Don't know exactly where he lives. Let me check around." After a few calls, the attendant scratched a rough map on the back of a computer printout while I peered over his shoulder. He handed me the crude directions, and I punched them into my jacket pocket and turned to George. "I'm going on ahead. Try to contact the sheriff and hurry him along. He may have set up roadblocks. Hopefully the local boys stopped Marshall on the way in, and I'll have taken a long, cold ride for no reason. You've got my cell number?"

"Yeah, good luck with that in this weather, and in these mountains." George followed me to the bike and patted my sleeve. "You be careful. Don't take stupid chances."

"Don't go soft on me. Be assured. I don't have a death wish."

George started toward the terminal—turned back as if to say something. If he spoke, the wind swallowed his words. He yanked the collar of his leather flight jacket close under his ears and went into the terminal.

Pulling the ski mask from my pocket, I tugged it over my face and kicked started the motorcycle. The bike roared like an unleashed animal as I left the shelter of the hanger and rode into the fierceness of the storm.

For the first mile, the motorbike wavered clumsily until I got the rhythm right. It took less time to realize I wasn't dressed for an excursion into the merciless elements trying to hold me back. Under most conditions, thermal clothing and my jacket would have been enough, but tonight they felt like shirtsleeves.

Vicious winds almost made me miss the lodge turnoff marked on the attendant's map. I swerved the bike hard left onto an ice-rutted gravel road that made my teeth tap dance. My best guess-timate put the cabin two miles off the main path.

I stopped a little more than a half mile in. The wind howled, and the bike felt as heavy as an eighteen-wheeler. Still, I managed to shove it out of sight into the roadside brush. Bent against an oncoming wind, I trudged up the path toward the lodge.

The moon had taken a holiday, and I longed for the pair of night glasses resting undisturbed in a closet at home. Hindsight was a wonderful thing.

I trudged the last quarter-mile in darkness—didn't want to use my invisibility until I reached the cabin. My mind calculated the odds that if I couldn't see the cabin through the snow and wind, Marshall couldn't see me.

Soon the outline of a building loomed ahead. Patches of light peeked through the shadowy silhouette. Out of the ocean of blackness behind me, car lights flickered, and the distinctive sound of a high-performance engine reached across the stillness over the wind's angry yowl.

The sheriff, or Marshall?

A quick dive onto the roadside ditch landed me in a deep snow-filled ravine. I sank like a rock in the deep drift. Head low, I brushed snow from my nose and mouth and realized the heavy bulge in my jacket had disappeared. My gun had slipped into the three-foot-deep powder surrounding me. I scrambled around in the wet cold and kicked myself mentally.

Stupid. Stupid.

A car whizzed by and clarified my dilemma.

It wasn't the authorities.

I didn't have time to search for the gun. Gusts whipped white powder down the gully as I charged up the road to the cabin.

My hunch had paid off.

Ben Marshall was behind the wheel. He parked his black Mercedes beside a snowmobile. With rapid movements, he jerked the back door open, reached inside and hefted Cody into his arms—asleep, or something more lethal?

I couldn't tell. Invisible, I followed them inside.

Marshall opened the door with one hand. Light and warmth gushed from inside. Had Marshall already arrived, then left? That didn't seem possible. He strode to the sofa and dumped the boy's limp body on the cushions. Cody's head bounced as it hit the throw pillow.

Still in stealth mode, I charged across the room and felt for a pulse. A steady thump answered my touch. Fuzzy images wended through the boy's mind, his kidnapping at the ranch, crying, his father yelling. A cup of hot cocoa his dad forced him to drink before they left Hebron. The boy's mind was clearing. He would wake soon.

My attention turned back to Marshall. He stomped down a wide hallway and shouted, "Andy."

It took only a second before a door opened and someone stepped into the corridor in front of Marshall. A man moved into the light. The thug who busted my shoulder. That explained the lights and heat.

Marshall returned to the living room, Andy in tow. "Everything ready?"

"Yeah. Couldn't get a flight out until tomorrow. Everything's grounded."

"That will do. I have a few things to finish up here tonight. Go bring in my luggage."

Andy glowered at him but moved obediently into the foyer. A blast of frigid air filled the room before he could close the door.

Using both hands, Marshall patted his jacket pockets, withdrew a folded piece of paper, and placed it on the lamp table by the sofa. Taking a seat beside Cody, Marshall shook the boy.

Cody's eyes opened and then closed.

Marshall shook him again. "Wake up, kid. We're going to call your mother."

Cody shook his head, disoriented. "Mom? Can I go home?"

"Yeah kid. You're going home."

My heart fell to my stomach and lay like a stone wheel. Marshall hadn't brought Cody all this way just to send him back to Rachel. The fact Marshall called Cody "kid" gripped my psyche with icy fingers. The man had disassociated himself from his son.

Steady handed, Marshall reached into a drawer on the end table, withdrew a gun, and settled back against the sofa. He grabbed Cody's arm and pulled him to a sitting position. Marshall lifted the receiver on the cordless phone and punched in a number. The smile on his face sent a tingle of apprehension through me as someone on the other end of the line picked up. "Rachel?"

A pause.

"This is Harry London. I need to speak to my wife."

Emma must have answered.

He handed the phone to Cody.

"Mom?" Another pause. "I don't know. A cabin somewhere—"

Marshall snatched the phone from Cody. "You know, Rachel, if you'd stayed home where you belonged, none of this would have happened. Just remember you're going to have to live with what you did for the rest of your life."

Marshall held the phone to his ear and placed the gun to Cody's temple.

Pulse quickening, a flash of insight hit me like a cattle prod against wet skin. Marshall's plan crystallized. I knew why he let Cody call Rachel.

I should have seen this coming.

Marshall had all the characteristics of a sociopath. A pervasive disregard for and violation of the rights of others. A male Medea seeking revenge against Rachel through Cody.

Once only a horror suggested in a Greek tragedy, the Medea Complex played out in nightly newscasts across the nation. A father who set his son on fire to punish his wife, a physician who killed his two daughters while his wife pleaded on the phone.

Cody screamed.

Sickened, raging mad, and visible, I rushed the

couch, and slammed my arm against Marshall's gun hand, just as the weapon fired. The bullet splintered into the wooden floor in front of Cody. Hysterical sobs burst through the phone where it lay on the rug.

"What ...?" Marshall jerked to his feet and whirled, looking for who or what had knocked away the revolver.

I stepped in front of him and landed a hard right to his jaw. The burning pain in my hand told me I made solid contact.

Momentum from the blow carried Marshall into the wall, but he bounced off the solid surface, and we both lunged for the gun. Marshall reached it first and swung the gun around. Breathing hard, he placed his hand on his jaw, wiggled it from side to side, and leveled the revolver at my chest. "Welcome to the party, Adams. I didn't dare hope you'd make it. My good fortune knows no bounds. I'm interested to hear how you found me, but you won't live long enough to explain how brilliant you were."

The outside door swung open. Andy rushed crossed the threshold, gun drawn, and edged in behind Marshall. "Where'd he come from?"

Marshall held the gun steady, his eyes never leaving mine. "I hoped you could tell me."

The need to buy a little time moved to the top of my list. "I figured this goon belonged to you. You hang with nice people, Marshall."

His gaze shifted toward the thug. "You mean Andy? Yes, he's mine. I'd forgotten you two met previously. He isn't always as competent as I would like, but he's very loyal."

"Maybe you should get a pit bull, they're prettier."

Andy roared and lurched at me, but when

Marshall held up his hand, Andy halted like a well-trained pet.

The judge bared his teeth in a smile, enjoying the moment. "I'm glad you showed up to keep me company while I take care of a little family business. It seems I also owe the discovery of my identity to you."

My jaw clenched. "If I have my way, the reunion will be short-lived."

His lips spread into a slow, sarcastic smile. "Don't be bitter, Adams. You've allowed me to clean up two messes in one night. By this time tomorrow, I'll be in Canada with a new identity and enough money to live comfortably for a very long time."

My blood boiled, like a savage animal straining for freedom. For the first time in my life, I knew I could kill another human being—commit willful, cold-blooded murder. "I'm warning you, Marshall, if you touch Cody—"

Marshall extended his left hand and gave me a hard shove. "What will you do?"

My fingers clasped his wrist and I pushed him away. Something almost electric passed between us. In that instant every foul crime Ben Marshall ever committed filled my mind. The stench of human depravity flowed over me like sewerage, and the pieces of Abigail Armstrong's disappearance fell into place.

I smiled, but it wasn't a pleasant smile. "I'll tell you what I'll do—make you sorry I ever came into your life." Brave words from a man who had no idea what his next move would be. I couldn't become invisible for another twenty minutes. Cody and I would both be dead by then.

The cocky curl on Marshall's lips straightened. His

chest rose and fell rapidly. He hadn't expected that reply and suddenly realized that somehow power shifted away from him—he surely saw it in my eyes.

The thug reacted like a dog sniffing the wind. His hand jerked up and he stepped forward.

Marshall shouted, "Wait. He's mine."

Cody screamed. "No. You can't."

In the tension of the moment, I'd forgotten about Cody. Marshall whirled and raised his hand. Then apparently remembered the scene outside Cody's bedroom and halted.

For a split second, the two men took their gaze off me. I took two steps forward, grabbed a two-handed grip on Andy's arm, and flipped him. He went down, emitting a loud *ahhhh* as he smacked into the hardwood floor.

I rushed him, hoping to wrestle away the gun. He saw me coming and rolled to the right knocking Marshall off his feet, just as he fired. My ankle suddenly felt like I brushed against a lit blowtorch, and wetness flowed into my shoe. No way could I reach Cody before his father regained his footing, but the impact from the collision with Andy sent Marshall's gun sailing into the air. It landed in front of a trophy case on the opposite wall.

Oblivious to the pain, I leaped toward Marshall's waist and missed, grabbing his leg on the way down.

"Run, Cody!" I yelled just as a booted foot sent a vicious kick and smashed into my face.

Blinding pain shot through my body, and blood, wet and salty, spurted from my nostrils and down my throat. Bright flashes of light danced behind my eyes— a kaleidoscope of colors. Instinctively, my hands covered my nose and I lost my grip on Marshall.

When my hold loosened, Marshall rushed to retrieve the weapon.

Cody beat him to it and aimed it at his father. The boy held the gun with both hands, tears streaming down his cheeks.

Marshall froze.

Andy now on his feet, stopped dead still, uncertain, his gun lay on the floor.

I rose to my feet despite unbelievable pain in my ankle. The salty taste of blood flowed from my nose down the back of my throat. "Cody, I'm coming. I want you to give me the gun. You don't really want to kill your father. It's a burden you'd have to live with always."

Cody's chin trembled. "I do—I have to—if I don't—he'll never leave us alone." Unexpected wisdom from a child. Cody's finger tightened on the trigger.

With faltering steps, I moved toward him. "I'll put him in jail where he'll never get out. Son, don't do this. It's murder."

The gun in Cody's hand belched smoke, and the acrid smell of gunpowder spread across the empty space.

23

Rapid Bend, California

The shot took off the bottom of Marshall's right earlobe. Recoil from the revolver knocked Cody backwards. He steadied himself and raised the gun again.

My gaze locked onto Andy as his arm slowly stooped, reaching for the gun at his feet. I roared like an angry bear and the noise distracted the thug long enough for me to leap forward and smash my forearm into the side of his head. The blow knocked the revolver from his grip, and it slid out of his reach.

My attention riveted on Andy.

I didn't see Marshall until he snatched up the cordless phone and hurled it at Cody just as the boy fired again. The shot soared past Marshall and thudded into the wall. The phone smashed into Cody's chest and sent him sprawling against the rough log interior, gasping for air.

Marshall snatched the gun from Cody's limp fingers. He turned the weapon toward me. No way to reach him before he fired. My mind numbed. What would happen to Cody if I went down?

"Get up, Cody. Run."

But Cody was too dazed to move. He slumped back against the rough logs, helpless.

Marshall looked down at the gun in his hand, and then up at me. Blood from his ear trickled down his neck, and he wiped at it, smearing the red stain onto his collar. His eyes seethed with rage as he pulled back on the trigger.

A whispered prayer slipped from my lips. "Lord, please protect Cody."

I wavered upright on one foot, waiting for death. My only regret, I had failed to protect Cody, leaving him at the mercy of his deranged father.

Noise from the front door distracted Marshall and gave me the split second I needed to dive for the thug's revolver. Two shots banged against my eardrums, but only one from the gun in my hand. I felt no pain. In fact, I felt no new ache at all.

Marshall never got off a shot. His eyes lost their focus as two dark circles spread over his shirt pocket. One from the gun in my hand, one from the entryway.

Like a disjointed scene from a morph-commercial, I turned to the entrance.

Inside the foyer stood George and a uniformed policeman, his gun pointed at Marshall's now lifeless form. Absorbed in my struggle to survive, the troops' arrival hadn't registered until they'd distracted Marshall.

George glanced over at Andy. "This the guy who killed Tooie?"

My hand over my bleeding nose, I nodded.

Before anyone could stop him, George rushed forward, grabbed Andy, and sent a left jab to his stomach that lifted him off the floor. George clutched the thug's collar, raised him up and sent another blow to his chin like the Golden Gloves champion George had once been. The thug groaned and gasped for breath. George muttered through gritted teeth, "This one's for Tooie, you low-life scum." The blow knocked

Andy across the room. He slid down the wall and bounced to a sitting position. Before George could inflict further damaged on Andy's unconscious form, a deputy rushed forward. Pushing George back, the officer handcuffed Andy.

I dropped the gun and hobbled to Cody's side. He lay where he'd fallen after the phone's impact, his face pale, his body trembling. I jerked a wool throw from the back of the sofa and wrapped it tightly around the boy. On unsteady feet, I lifted him onto my arms and felt him quiver. I whispered, "It's over, Cody. It's over."

Another deputy rushed forward to take Cody from me. I shook my head, and the officer backed away. With one hand, I signaled George to give me the phone that lay on the floor, the line still open. Rachel's voice sobbed Cody's name over and over.

I pressed the phone to my ear. "Rachel, its Noah. Cody's all right. He's fine. I'll bring him home to you as soon as we finish up here."

Bill's anxious voice came on the extension. "Is it true? Cody's OK?"

"He'll be fine. He took a blow to the chest, but he seems OK. He's suffering from shock. I'll have him checked out before we fly home. Probably sometime tomorrow."

"How are you?" Bill asked. "Your voice sounds strange."

I took a gulp of air through my mouth. "I'm fine. Just having a little nose trouble at the moment. Marshall's dead. I'll tell you all about it when we get home. Right now, Cody needs my attention."

EMT's arrived. They checked Cody for broken ribs before loading him onto the stretcher. The female emergency tech covered the boy in warm blankets. Another of the medics took charge of me and stopped the bleeding from my injuries. He determined the nose was broken, but the bullet passed through my foot, apparently missing the ankle bone.

A deputy held an umbrella over Cody's face to keep away the snow as they loaded him into the ambulance. The EMT asked me to wait until the next emergency unit arrived.

I shook my head. "I'm going with the boy."

One of the EMT held up his hand. "I'm sorry. You can't ride in the back. You can sit up front with the driver if you like."

I stared into his eyes. "This boy was almost killed by his own father. His mother is in Wyoming. I *will* ride with him. Right now he needs someone he knows close by."

The sheriff nodded at the medical technician, and I climbed in beside the stretcher, settled onto the bench, and took Cody's hand. "How do you feel, champ?"

He turned his head toward me. "O-K. I want my mom."

I squeezed his hand. "Sure thing. Just as soon as a doctor takes a look at you, we'll be out of here."

"My dad...is he...?"

I nodded.

The sheriff stuck his head inside. "We need to talk."

Every limb on my body suddenly felt weighted. "I know you have a lot of questions, but I need to go with Cody. I can't let him do this alone. I'll be glad to answer any questions you have at the hospital."

The sheriff tugged his hat over his brow and nodded as deputies transported Andy to a sheriff's cruiser. "We have to take Marshall's friend into custody, but I'll catch you later. I need your statement on what happened here tonight."

George peeked around the door, worry lines on his forehead. "How are you doing? You look awful."

I nodded. "I'm getting there."

❧❧

Rapid Bend, California

It was past midnight when we reached the hospital. It took the remainder of the night and into the morning for the medics to fix my nose and foot, and to stabilize Cody. The sheriff made his promised appearance, and I gave him the detailed story, chapter and verse.

At eleven o'clock the next morning, the hospital released us, and George picked up his two wounded passengers in a taxi to take us back to the municipal airport. On the trip out, Cody looked up at me. "I'm hungry."

George rubbed his hand across his overnight stubble. "Me, too."

I tapped the driver on the shoulder. "Any place close where we can catch breakfast?"

He nodded. "There's a waffle shop about a block away on the right."

Cody and George signaled their approval.

"That'll do just fine." I said.

We arrived at the airport, fed, bandaged, and ready to go home. George stored the bike at the airport hanger until he could return.

Cody settled into the plane's back seat, his head against a pillow I borrowed from the hospital.

"Thanks, Noah. I was awfully scared."

From the seat beside George in the cockpit, I turned to face him. "Don't thank me, champ. Thank God. He guided me to you."

He didn't reply, just turned and gazed out the window.

"Something wrong with thanking God?"

He turned an earnest blue gaze at me. "How could God give me a Dad like...?"

I twisted to one side and inhaled a deep breath. "Cody, l have no idea how God picks the parent lottery. I drew a bad stepfather, every bit as bad as your father. For a long time I asked that same question."

"Did God answer?"

"Yeah, sort of. God never promised life would be easy. But He did promise He would never leave or forsake us. That was my answer. Lean on Him when things go wrong."

"How do you do that?"

"My grandmother told me a story once, when I was brooding over the loss of my family. She related a passage from the life of a Christian woman named Corrie ten Boom during World War II. Corrie lived in Holland and helped Jewish people escape from the Germans after they invaded Holland. Do you know what the Nazi's did to the Jewish people in the countries they took over?"

Cody nodded. "I saw a movie about it."

"Well, because Corrie ten Boom and her sister Betsy hid Jewish people in their home until they could flee to another country, the Ten Booms were arrested and sent to a concentration camp. A terrible place. The prison camp didn't allow Bibles, but by some miracle,

Corrie and Betsy sneaked one past the guards.

"Once inside, they were thrown into a dreadful room infested with fleas. Fleas were everywhere, covering their bodies, clothing, hair, and beds. Corrie asked that same question. How could a merciful God let them fall into the hands of those cruel people, and put them in that awful place? After all, they had helped many of His people escape to freedom."

The boy propped up on one elbow, giving me his full attention. "Did God give her an answer?"

"Not right away. The night they arrived at the concentration camp, Betsy actually prayed and thanked God for the fleas. Corrie didn't understand how her sister could do that. While being tormented by the vermin, the sisters moved freely among the other women prisoners with their Bible. They led many of those women to Jesus. Most of those women died in the gas chambers.

Even Betsy died from lack of food and medicine. Before Betsy passed away, she and Corrie learned why they enjoyed so much freedom to preach God's message.

"After Corrie was released from prison she wrote a book. In that novel, she recounted all the miracles God performed while she and her sister lived in captivity. You see, because of the fleas, the German guards would not enter that room, and because they didn't come in, many, many women were saved. The fleas were a blessing, not a punishment. Can you understand what I'm saying?"

Cody shook his head. "I-I-I'm not sure."

"It is through pain and suffering that we grow closer to God. When we trust Him in all things, He can use us for His plan. Because I knew what you and your mom were going through from my own experience, I determined to help you and others like you, so you wouldn't be hurt anymore. Understand?"

Cody focused on my face, absorbing what I'd said. After a moment, he nodded.

When I turned back around in my seat, George's gaze found mine. He raised his thumb.

My eyes drooped from pain medication as I slipped the cell phone from my pocket and fumbled with the numbers on the lighted screen.

George took the phone from my hand. "Give me that before you hurt yourself. I'll call Rachel."

My head rested against the seat of its own volition. "Tell her we're coming home."

When George finished he placed the phone into my jacket pocket. A grin spread across his rugged face. "Boy, Marshall sure rearranged your mug. You won't have to worry about being a trophy husband any time soon."

Despite the pain in my face, I laughed.

24

Hebron, Wyoming

My body found new places to ache on the flight back to Hebron, but a cleared runway smoothed out the bumps when we touched down. Snowplows on overtime.

I shaded my eyes against mid-afternoon sun that bounced off white banks along the tarmac. Ahead in the hanger's shadows, a small crowd gathered as we taxied to a stop. Rachel, Bill, Emma, Amos, and Jake stood hunched against the cold, collars pulled close around anxious faces.

George killed the engine, and a sobbing Rachel jerked the aircraft door open.

Cody fell into his mother's arms. "Don't squeeze so tight, Mom. My chest's a little sore."

Rachel gulped a deep breath. "Sorry. I'm just so..."

She held him close, her gaze searching his face as though unable to comprehend he was here, alive, and by her side.

Cody snuggled closer and wrapped his arm around her waist, the haunted, frightened look in his eyes—gone.

George swallowed, making his Adam's apple bob. He turned and waved us forward. "Come on into the office. It's warmer, and Norma has coffee and donuts waiting."

Inside, refreshments in hand, the group listened

silently as I told our story, my face and limp a testament to how close we came to losing our lives.

When I finished, Amos slapped my shoulder. "So, Marshall is dead and the thug is in custody."

I laughed. "That's as concise a summary as could possibly be made."

An hour later, after I'd retold our adventure from every angle, downed three donuts and two mugs of coffee, they let me go home.

❧

The darkening sky and unlighted windows gave the old condo a forlorn atmosphere. Where was Truman? Had he pulled up stakes and left the dogs alone? Perhaps he left a note.

I slipped the key into the lock and it clicked open. Warm air greeted me. Perhaps Truman wasn't too far away since he left the heat on. I tossed my coat on a chair and flipped the light switch.

Before I reached the kitchen, a soft knock sounded at the front door. I turned and retraced my steps.

Mabel greeted me with a broad smile. "Hey, stranger. It's great to have you home. Maybe now Ted will stop moping around. By the way, your friend Truman is at my place. He and Ted are watching a game."

She handed me a Styrofoam box. "Leftovers from the restaurant. I figured you wouldn't want to cook."

I lifted the lid. A large charbroiled T-bone and baked potato spoke to my taste buds. "Leftovers, huh?"

"Didn't anyone ever teach you not to question your elders?"

"Thanks, Mabel. You're a sweetheart. How's my buddy doing?"

"Driving me absolutely insane, missing you and the dogs. Truman has helped." She chuckled. "I hate to tell you this, but you come in a distant third place to the dogs."

"The story of my life. Got time for coffee?"

"Sure. I'm going back to work, but I have a few minutes to spare."

We entered the kitchen, and I flipped on the light switch.

Put on the coffee," Mabel said. "I'll get the mugs."

I made the brew and retold the story of Cody's rescue while I ate.

After I finished the steak, Mabel left for work, and I went upstairs. My eyelids were weights, but I needed a shower before settling into a warm bed. In the bedroom, I kicked off my shoes in the dark and stumbled toward the bathroom. A flash of color in my peripheral vision made me turn.

A big man in a plaid shirt and red hat sat on my bed, a gun pointed at my gut.

The hit man who'd dumped Truman in the blizzard.

He attached a silencer to the revolver and tightened it down. "You're a hard man to catch up with."

"I didn't know you were looking or I would've left my itinerary."

He chuckled but his eyes weren't laughing. "Smart guy. I like taking down smart guys."

"You here while my friend Mabel was downstairs?" Visions of this jerk hurting Mabel made my legs weak.

"Yeah. I figured she wouldn't stay long. Didn't

want a massacre. Creates too much media attention. I'll leave behind a few narcotics. So it looks like a drug deal gone bad. Beside, London only contracted one hit."

"You should probably know your boss is dead. If you haven't been paid, you may have a problem collecting."

"I make it a policy to get the money up front."

"You could just keep the cash and go on your way. I won't tell."

"Can't do that. I have a reputation to uphold. I always get my man—or woman, as the case may be."

Wrong. I had not lived through the trials of the past twenty-four hours just to be killed in my own bedroom.

"Your work ethic is commendable. Your mother would be proud."

He stood and hitched up his baggy trousers with one hand. "Let's get this over with. I've wasted too much time on you already, and as they say, time is money."

I waited to see if he had any more clichés. Apparently not.

A deep growl I recognized sounded outside my bedroom window. Attila, the satanic mutt next door.

The gunman's gaze shifted to the window for a microsecond. When he looked back, I wasn't there. At least, he couldn't see me. His mouth fell open, but he didn't shoot, giving me enough time to get out of firing range. Early on, I discovered the force field wasn't bulletproof.

"Adams? Where...?"

"Lose something?" I touched his shoulder and jumped back.

His arms flailed in the air, and he spun in circles, his gaze frantically searching the room.

"Oscar, don't worry about Adams. He's not important."

"W-who are you?"

"The Angel of Death and you have a lot of accounting to do." I had his attention.

He pulled a handkerchief from his hip pocket and mopped his brow. "H-How do you know...?"

"I know all about you, Oscar. Your name, how many people you've killed, when and where the bodies are buried. I know about the hit on the judge in Phoenix, the state senator's wife in Nashville. I know them all, Oscar."

"N-Now what?"

"I'm going to give you a break you never gave your victims. Pick up the phone and call the Hebron Police Department. Ask for Detective Amos Horne. Give him your confession. Tell him everything. I'll wait until you finish."

"And if I don't?"

"Then it ends here and now. You meet your Maker. There are things worse than death. Dying would be the easy part. You ready for that?"

"They'll give me the needle. What did you do with Adams?"

"Don't worry about Adams. I'll take care of him. He won't know a thing. This is just between you and me. Do it now, Oscar. If you don't, there won't be a second chance to make things right. Your call." Confessing to the police wouldn't make things right with God, but it was a chance for redemption.

Oscar hesitated, hands quivering. "I-I-I- can't."

"Do it, Oscar."

He licked his lips and then reached for the phone.

When he'd finished, I emerged from the bathroom with my Glock in my hand.

"Where'd you come from?" Oscar shook his head. "Never mind."

I handcuffed Oscar to the stairs and we waited for Hebron's finest to arrive.

The hit man looked at me. "You believe in this life-ever-after stuff?"

"Absolutely."

"You know what happened upstairs?"

I shook my head. "We were talking, next thing I knew I was in the bathroom. What did happen? What made you call the police?"

"You wouldn't believe me if I told you."

Ten minutes later, Amos knocked on the front door, a couple of police officers in tow. Cops led the subdued hit man away, still shaking his head.

Amos took a seat at the bar in the kitchen. I filled a mug of coffee and shoved it to him. He took a sip and looked over the cup's rim. "That guy's on the ten most wanted list. How'd you get him to confess?"

"It was his idea. Guilty conscience I suppose."

Amos shrugged. "He kept mumbling something about the angel of death."

৵৽৾

Hebron, Wyoming

Next day, I drove to Lincoln Armstrong's place to hand in my final report. He received the summary and read it slowly. "I don't know how to thank you, Noah."

Although it lacked the details of her death, my précis told him where to find his wife's body. In an ironic twist, Ben Marshall buried Abigail at the cabin where I ran into Truman.

During the struggles with Marshall the day he died, my touch revealed he ran into Abigail at the country club the night he received the Hebron Civic Man-of-the-Year award. Fearing she would expose his new identity, he arranged a meeting four days later and killed her.

Armstrong read slowly, and then peered silently into the fire, his long sought goal accomplished. His name was now cleared, all doubts erased. The location of Abby's body was in the report, her murderer found, and now Ben Marshall faced the ultimate Judge. Armstrong could bring her home. Burial would be the final closure that allowed him to grieve and go on with his life. A right denied him for too long.

25

Hebron, Wyoming

A few weeks later, Armstrong invited me to the funeral service. "I've moved Joey's body from California. I'm burying him beside Abigail. She would have wanted that."

George and I had picked up Goldie Marks in Salt Lake in his new plane. She hobbled down the steps to the tarmac and onto George's plane. In Hebron, we drove in silence to the Armstrong estate.

The double ceremony was simple and touching, with only six people in attendance: Armstrong, Goldie, Pastor Bob Miller, Amos, George, and me. Armstrong kept his promise. The burial place he selected lay by the lake she loved, with a marble headstone beside the redwood bench.

We stood braced against a chilled breeze as two caskets sat on elevator straps over the empty graves. Pastor Miller ended with a simple line from the Beatitudes, "Blessed are the meek, for they shall inherit the earth."

Tears rolled down Armstrong's face as the bodies lowered. The grave marker listed Abigail and Joey's names, date of birth, and death. The simple inscription read, "Mother and Son, Peace at Last."

Our small band returned to Armstrong's home for the wake. Underneath the sadness of the occasion lay a feeling of satisfaction—our quest complete.

It occurred to me as I watched Armstrong and Goldie interact that something might develop there. That would be a good thing. They were two lonely people who needed someone to fill their lives.

Before I left, Armstrong pulled me into the library. "I told you I didn't know how to thank you. Maybe this will help."

He handed me an envelope. It contained my final check from the Armstrong Empire—including a hefty bonus, followed by the offer of a permanent job.

"I'd like to offer you a job in my new security firm. It will offer protection to dignitaries going into danger zones like Afghanistan and Iraq." He nodded. "I want to hire only the best of the best. Ex-SEALS, Green Berets, Rangers, etcetera. I would like you to head up the division for me. Recruit the best, run the show. I could make it worth your while. I'm calling it *Armstrong*."

I chuckled. "I bet you had to give that a lot of thought. Your offer is very flattering and sincerely appreciated. But I can't accept, Lincoln. I'm doing the work I love—and I have a wonderful Boss."

He wagged his head slowly from side to side and smiled. "A man who can't be bought. I like that. I'm sorry to hear it, but I do understand."

"You wouldn't have an opening in your new division for a Vietnam War hero, would you?"

He hesitated. "You have someone in mind?"

"Yeah, a guy who could use a job, right now. His name is Truman Merchant. Probably not the man to head up your division but perhaps you could find something that fits his particular skills."

Armstrong reached to shake my hand. "Send him

to see me. I'll give him an interview. It's the least I can do for a hero."

26

The London home, Hebron, Wyoming

The next day I returned to Cedar Hills Drive.

I eased up to the intercom phone and lifted the receiver. Moments later the gates slid open. From the outside, the house looked much the same, except for the landscaping. Snow had melted and new plants showed signs of spring, a time of new beginnings.

In the circular drive, I stopped at the front entrance and gave the horn a short blast. The neighbors would love that.

Squinting at the morning brightness, Rachel stood in the entryway. Her smile outshone the sun. "I'm so glad you came." She reached and gave me a lingering hug.

"I wouldn't have missed it." I maneuvered past her into the foyer.

The interior, at least what I could see, rooted me in my tracks. It popped with color, entirely redecorated—earlier drab walls replaced with candy-apple red and matching tints in throw pillows and painting. "Wow!"

She waved her arms wide. "Do you like it?"

"What's not to like? It looks amazing."

A loud squeal echoed from the upstairs landing and a bolt of energy shot down the flight of stairs and leaped from the bottom step into my arms.

I caught Cody and swung him to the floor. "Hey, kid, you have to give me a warning before you do that.

I'm an old man."

Cody scoffed. "You're not old."

"Being around you makes me feel ancient."

He bounded out the door and yelled over his shoulder. "Come see my tree house! OK?"

I waved. "Sure thing. Be out in a minute."

Rachel stepped close and touched my arm. "Before the others arrive, I want to say something. I can never—"

I held up my hand. "No need to say anything. You may have noticed it wasn't a one-man show. I only did what anyone would have, and I had lots of help from my friends."

She placed her fingertips to my lips. "Just let me say this, Noah Adams. You not only rescued Cody and me from Harry's...I mean Marshall's abuse, you risked your life to save my son. I can never repay that. Not ever"

My face grew warm. "You could start by getting me a cup of coffee."

She released me and led the way into the kitchen. "You're hopeless. Totally hopeless. I'm having a party for the over-the-hill-gang responsible for my liberation, Jake, Amos, George and Norma. Bill and Emma are already here. Jake made all the phone calls."

"Over the hill? I beg your pardon."

She laughed. "If the shoe fits—"

I took a stool at the island. "I expect something better from you than clichés. Where's Bill?"

Rachel pointed to the backyard and chuckled. "I put him in charge of the steaks. He says he's a master chef on the grill."

"How're things going with you and Cody?"

She drew vegetables from the refrigerator and

pulled out a cutting board. "We're good. Cody's back in his old school, and I've decided to enroll in law school for the fall."

I raised an eyebrow and whistled. "Law school? That's a big decision."

"And one I didn't make lightly. Financially, I'm good for a long time, but I can't sit around and do nothing. I want to help women in my situation, to repay the blessings I've received. I got the idea from Jake. After the home security tapes appeared in the D.A.'s office, the authorities dropped the jailbreak charges. Watching Jake inspired me. He's quite a man, your Mr. Stein."

"One in a million."

Rachel glanced around the room. "There were a lot of bad memories here, but we're past that now. Redecorating helped erase all presence of Harry London, and I took a baseball bat to the security cameras. If we decide to sell this place in the future—perhaps find a ranch somewhere—we can do that. Cody loved ranch life. But for now, I think we need time to heal before we make a permanent move." She laid the knife on the cutting board. "What happened to the real Harold London? Do you know?"

I took a sip of coffee. I couldn't tell her my touch of Marshall during the episode at the cabin revealed the whole story. So I improvised. "I've pieced together most of it. When Ben escaped, he headed north and came to London's lake cabin, the place where Marshall took Cody. He killed London and buried his body on the grounds.

"Apparently while at the lodge, Marshall discovered the similarities in their age and background. He simply took London's identity. The real London was partner in a law firm in New England and had no family. Since Marshall practiced law in San Francisco, he had no trouble taking the Wyoming Bar exam under London's name. He simply became Harold London."

Rachel shook her head. "Poor man."

"Marshall hired a detective to dig up all the information on his victim. The reports were at the cabin. London left his law firm in New England after a nervous breakdown. He was recuperating at the cabin when Marshall shot him. With that information it became easy for Marshall to step into the man's shoes."

The intercom phone rang. Rachel lifted the receiver and said with a smile in her voice, "Glad you're here. Come on up. Noah arrived a few minutes ago." She released the gate and turned to me. "That's the rest of the party."

As soon as they were in the foyer, Cody rushed in and grabbed Amos's hand. "Come see my tree house. It's big enough for all of us."

Amos waved at me, and laughing, followed Cody outside.

George and Norma greeted me with handshakes and hugs. George's eyes inspected my face. "Norma, do you still think he's prettier than I am, with that nose?"

With her back to George, she turned to me and winked. "Yeah, I must say I do. The scar across his nose gives him a rugged, sexy look."

Tugging his baseball cap down, George said. "I'll be outside if you need me."

Jake strolled over and surveyed my slightly misshapen beak. "Should have known I'd find you in the kitchen. Why is it that every time I see you, you have a broken bone?"

I smiled into his kind eyes. "Hazardous duty. As to being in the kitchen, Rachel has taken me under her wing since you've stopped feeding me."

He turned to Rachel. "Better give me some grilling utensils so I can help. You have no idea how much food this boy can put away." Rachel tied a frilly apron around his waist, handed him metal tongs and sent him out back. I looked at Rachel and shook my head. "Jake will be in charge of the steaks before Bill knows what hit him."

I put both elbows on the island and leaned toward Rachel. "Any other plans for the future?"

She glanced through the window at Bill as he backed away from the grill and Jake moved in. Her mouth turned up in a gentle smile. "Nothing firm, but there are definite possibilities. Bill was my rock during that horrible hour while I thought Harry shot Cody." She shivered. "I don't even want to think about it."

Norma moved to help Rachel, and I joined Amos outside. The weather was still crisp, but the sun's rays soaked into my skin. The sun couldn't compare to the warmth that filled my soul. I had learned to forgive myself.

We stood and watched as a young boy joined Cody under the big oak that held his tree house. Within minutes, Cody laughed and followed his friend up the ladder into his private abode.

God bless the resilience of children.

As I watched Cody and his friend, two small faces floated through my mind—mental pictures of Joey's sad-eyed photograph and Tommy's love for baseball, their violent deaths, all came to the forefront. Children who died too soon—great promise lost in early, senseless violence. Remorse overcame me, so poignant it manifested itself as a sharp pain in my chest.

I punched my hands into my jacket pockets and gazed at a tiny blade of grass trying to get a jump on spring. Perhaps, in some small way, the death of Ben Marshall balanced the scales of justice.

I dedicated Cody's rescue to Tommy and Joey.

There was no way to save all the abused children.

But by God's grace, I would save all I could.

Made in the USA
Monee, IL
10 March 2020